MAR -- 2013

True Love at
Silver Creek Ranch

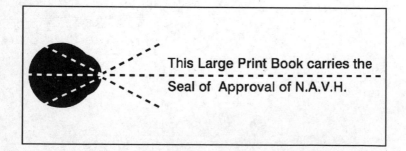

This Large Print Book carries the
Seal of Approval of N.A.V.H.

A VALENTINE VALLEY NOVEL

True Love at Silver Creek Ranch

Emma Cane

THORNDIKE PRESS
A part of Gale, Cengage Learning

GALE
CENGAGE Learning®

Detroit • New York • San Francisco • New Haven, Conn • Waterville, Maine • London

GALE
CENGAGE Learning·

Copyright © 2013 by Gayle Kloecker Callen.
Thorndike Press, a part of Gale, Cengage Learning.

Thorndike Press® Large Print Romance.
The text of this Large Print edition is unabridged.
Other aspects of the book may vary from the original edition.
Set in 16 pt. Plantin.

LIBRARY OF CONGRESS CIP DATA ON FILE.
CATALOGUING IN PUBLICATION FOR THIS BOOK
IS AVAILABLE FROM THE LIBRARY OF CONGRESS

ISBN-13: 978-1-4104-5581-9 (hardcover)
ISBN-10: 1-4104-5581-5 (hardcover)

Published in 2013 by arrangement with Avon Books, an imprint of HarperCollins Publishers.

Printed in the United States of America
1 2 3 4 5 6 7 17 16 15 14 13

To Angie Marasco Callen, who has brought such joy into my son's life — and ours. Thank you for joining our family and making him so happy.

ACKNOWLEDGMENTS

My thanks to Jim and Angie Callen; Lieutenant Colonel Don "Gordo" Gordon, USMC; Molly Herwood; Maggie Shayne; Melissa Swenton; Captain James Weiser, USN; and Christine Wenger. They were all gracious enough to answer my research questions. Any mistakes are certainly my own. And as always, to the Packeteers and the Purples. Brainstorming would be boring and lonely without you.

CHAPTER ONE

Her chestnut quarter horse, Sugar, was the first to notice something wrong, startling Brooke Thalberg from her troubled thoughts. The November wind high in the Colorado Rockies, just outside Valentine Valley, was unseasonably brutal, whipping snow off the peaks of the Elk Mountains like lumbering giants exhaling icy puffs of breath. Sugar raised her head, sniffing that wind, ears twitching, leaving Brooke unsettled, uneasy, as she rode the pastures of the Silver Creek Ranch. She was checking the fence line so that the cattle didn't find their way through and wander toward someone else's land.

It was usually peaceful work, but today she was looking down the long road of her future and feeling that something was . . . wrong. And she hated to feel that way because she'd been blessed with so much.

Sugar lifted her head and shook her mane,

neighing, her body tensing. Whatever she sensed wasn't going away. Brooke lifted her own head —

And smelled smoke.

A shot of fear made her vault upright in the stirrups. She scanned her family's land, focusing on the house first, framed between clusters of evergreens and aspens. But its two-story log walls seemed as sturdy as always, a faint haze of smoke rising from the stone chimney. The newer barn and sheds nearest the house seemed fine, and gradually she widened her search until she saw the old horse barn, farthest from the house — smoke billowing through the open double doors.

She kicked Sugar into a gallop, leaning forward over the horse's twitching ears, the breath frozen in her throat. *Oh, God, the horses.* Frantically, she saw that several trotted nervously around the corral as if they, too, knew something was wrong. She tried to count them, but it was as if her brain had seized with the terror of what she was seeing.

Sugar's hooves thundered beneath her, faster than even in her barrel-racing days, the ground a blur. The smoke pouring out of the open door grew darker and more menacing, twisting Brooke's fear ever higher.

At last she reached the barn and threw herself off Sugar's back, stumbling momentarily in the dirt before she found her balance. The smoke made her lungs spasm in a cough, but even that didn't make her second-guess what she had to do. She pulled her neck scarf up over the lower half of her face and ran inside, keeping to a crouch. Immediately, the world became darker as the smoke swirled around her. Her shallow breathing was hot and stifled beneath the scarf. If she let herself panic, she could become disoriented, lost, so she kept a firm grip on her emotions. She'd yet to see flames, but she could hear several horses, their neighs more like screams that tore at her heart.

"I'm coming!" she cried, flailing toward the stalls.

She ran into something hard and was only saved from falling to the ground by hands that clasped the front of her coat.

A man pulled her toward him, a stranger, tall and broad-shouldered, his face beneath his cowboy hat obscured by a scarf just like hers was. She could only see a glimpse of his narrowed, glittering eyes, focused intently on her. Who was he? Had he set the

11

fire? she wondered with outrage.

"Are you all right?" He shouted to be heard above the growing roar of the fire and the frightened cries of the horses. "How many horses are there?"

For a moment, her mouth moved, and nothing came out. She saw the tack-room door hanging ajar, its interior full of fire that crackled and writhed. The sight momentarily stunned and mesmerized her, then she suddenly snapped into a sharp awareness. She couldn't worry about who this man was or what he was doing there. He'd offered to help, and that was all that mattered. Mentally, she counted the horses she'd seen out in the corral. "Should be two inside — no three!"

"I'll take that side" — he pointed through the smoke toward the west side of the barn — "and you start here."

She nodded and turned her back, beginning to fling open each stall door. At the fourth door, she was met by hooves pawing through the air. She cried out, diving sideways as they slammed into the wall right beside her. Before Dusty could rear again, she grabbed a blanket hung near the door, flung it over his head, and grabbed ahold of his halter. For a moment he fought her, but she wouldn't give up.

"Please, Dusty, be a good boy. Come on!"

At last he seemed to dance toward her, and she felt a momentary triumph. She started to run, leading him toward the double doors open to the corral. As they reached fresh air, she pulled the blanket off Dusty's head and he charged to the far end, where the other horses huddled nervously.

Brooke turned around to head back into the barn, only to see the stranger leading two terrified horses outside. *Thank God,* she prayed silently. But could she have counted wrong? How could she take the chance? She tried to race past him back into the barn, but he caught her arm and wouldn't let go.

"You said three horses!" he shouted from beneath the scarf.

A groan seemed to emanate from the barn timbers, turning both their heads. Smoke wafted out in great streams to the sky, but the fire still seemed contained in the tack room.

"I can't be sure until I check each stall!" She tried to yank her elbow away, but his grip was strong. A blast of heat wafted out, engulfing her, making her sweat even more beneath her layers of winter clothing. She felt almost light-headed.

He loomed over her, and now she could see the sandy waves of hair plastered above his ears, and his narrowed eyes, brown as the sides of the barn but so intent on her.

"I checked all six on the west side. I didn't hear anything more coming from the east after you'd gone."

"I can't take that chance. I only got through four stalls on my side." She stared at the herd of horses clustered uneasily at the far end of the corral. Nate's horse, Apollo — was he there? She'd never forgive herself if anything happened to him. And then she saw the dappled gray gelding, and relief shuddered down her spine.

The man didn't answer her, and she turned to see him disappear into the barn, the smoke swirling out and around him as if to draw him deep inside. A stab of fear shocked her — why was he risking himself for her? Her eyes stung as she reached the entrance, but he was there again, stumbling into her, the upper half of his face dirtied by the soot, his eyes streaming.

"It's empty!" he called.

She could have staggered with relief that her beloved horses were all right — that this brave man hadn't been injured.

But relief was only momentary as she began to think about the structure itself, built by her family well over a hundred years

14

before. She hugged herself against the sadness.

As if reading her mind, he said, "You can't do anything now. And I hear sirens."

The fire engine from Valentine Valley roared down the dirt road that wound its way through the ranch. The horses were going to be even more frightened, so she ran to the end of the corral and opened the gate so they could escape into the next pasture.

When she returned to the stranger's side, they were pushed out of the way by the trained professionals. Most were volunteers, like Sally Gillroy from the mayor's office, who liked to gossip, and Hal Abrams, the owner of the hardware store where her dad and Nate met fellow ranchers for coffee. She recognized all these men and women, but it was strange to see their grim faces rather than easygoing smiles.

"Are you all right?" Hal demanded, his glasses reflecting the flames that had begun to shoot out both doors.

Brooke nodded, still hugging herself, feeling the presence of the stranger at her back. She almost took comfort from it, and that was strange.

"Horses all saved?"

She nodded again, and was surprised to feel a wave of pride and even excitement.

15

Knowing she'd risked herself made her feel more alive and aware than she'd felt in a long time. Everything in life could be so transitory, and she'd just been accepting things that happened to her rather than making choices. She couldn't live that way anymore. She had to find something that made her feel this alive, that gave her more purpose and focus.

And it scared the hell out of her.

"You're in the way," Hal said. "Go on up to the house and clean up. We'll wet down any nearby buildings to keep them safe. But the barn is a goner." He turned his shrewd eyes on the stranger. "Is that blood?"

Brooke spun around and saw that the stranger had lowered his scarf. In another situation, she might have been amused at the dark upper half of his face and the white lower half, but she saw blood oozing from a cut across his cheek.

"I'm fine." The stranger used his gloved hand to swipe at his cheek and made everything worse.

"Come on," Brooke said wearily, refusing to glance one last time at her family's barn although she could hear the crackle and roar of the fire. "The bunkhouse is close. We'll wash up there and see to your face."

And she could look into his eyes and see

if he was the sort who set fires for fun. He didn't seem it, for he didn't look back at the fire either, only trudged behind her.

The bunkhouse was an old log cabin, another of the original buildings from the nineteenth-century silver-boom days, when cattle from the Silver Creek Ranch had fed thousands of miners coming down from their claims to spend their riches in Valentine Valley. Brooke's father had updated the interior of the cabin to house the occasional temporary workers they needed during branding or haying season. There were a couple sets of bunk beds along the walls, an old couch before the stone hearth, a battered table and chairs, kitchen cabinets and basic appliances at the far end of the open room, and two doors that led into a single bedroom and bathroom.

The walls were filled with unframed photos of the various hands they'd employed to work the ranch over the years. Some of those photos, tacked up haphazardly and curling at the edges, were old black-and-whites going almost as far back as photography did.

Brooke shivered with a chill even as she removed her coat. The heat was only high enough to keep the pipes from freezing, and she went to raise the thermostat. When she turned around, the stranger had removed his hat and was shrugging out of his Carhartt jacket, revealing matted-down hair and a soot-stained face. He was wearing a long-sleeve red flannel shirt and jeans over cowboy boots.

To keep from staring at him, she pointed to the second door. "Go on and wash up in the bathroom. I'll find a first-aid kit."

He silently nodded and moved past her, limping slightly, shutting the door behind him. He might be hurt worse than he was saying, she thought with a wince. As she opened cabinet doors, she realized the kit was probably in the bathroom. Sighing even as she rolled up her sleeves, she let the water run in the kitchen sink until it was hot, then soaped up her black hands and started on her face. If her hair hadn't been in a long braid down her back, she'd have dunked her whole head under. She'd have to wait for a shower. Grabbing paper towels, she patted her skin dry.

A few minutes later, the stranger came out of the bathroom, his hair sticking up in short, damp curls, the first-aid kit in his hand. His face was clean now, and she could see that the two-inch cut was still bleeding.

"You probably need stitches," she said, even as the first inkling of recognition began to tease her. "You don't want a scar."

He met her gaze and held it, and she saw the faintest spark of amusement, as if he knew something she didn't.

"Don't worry about it, Brooke."

She hadn't told him her name. "So I do know you."

"It's been a long time," he said, eyeing her as openly as she was doing to him.

He was taller than her, well muscled beneath the flannel shirt that he'd pushed up to his elbows.

And then his name suddenly echoed like a shot in her mind. "Adam Desantis," she breathed. "It's been over ten years since you went off to join the Marines."

He gave a short nod.

No wonder he looked to be in such great physical shape. Feeling awkward, she forced her gaze back to his face. He'd been good-looking in high school — and knew it — but now his face was rugged and masculine, a man grown.

She got flashes of memory then — Adam as the cool wide receiver all the high-school girls wanted, with his posse of arrogant sidekicks. He'd been able to rule the school, doing whatever he wanted — because his parents hadn't cared, she reminded herself. And then she had another memory of the

19

sixth-grade science fair, where all the parents had helped their kids with experiments, except for his. His display had been crude and unfinished, and his mother had drunkenly told him so in front of every kid within hearing range. Whenever Brooke thought badly of his antics in high school, *that* was the memory that crept back up, making her feel ill with pity and sorrow.

"Your grandma talks about you all the time," she finally said. Mrs. Palmer spoke of him with glowing pride as he rose through the ranks to staff sergeant, a rarity at his age.

"Hope she doesn't bore everybody," he answered, showing sincerity rather than just tossing off something he didn't mean. "I hear she lives with your grandma. The Widows' Boardinghouse?"

"The name was their idea. They're kind of famous now, but those are stories for another day. Come here and let me look at your cheek." He moved toward her slowly, as if she were a horse needing to be calmed, which amused her.

"I can take care of it," he said.

"Sit down."

"I said —"

"Sit down!" She pulled out a kitchen chair and pointed. "I can't reach your face. I'm tall, but not that tall."

"Yes, ma'am," he answered gruffly.

She pressed her lips together to keep from smiling.

He eased into the chair just a touch slowly, but somehow she knew he didn't want any more questions about his health. Adam Desantis, she told herself again, shaking her head. He wasn't a stranger — and he wouldn't have started the fire, regardless of the trouble he'd once gotten into. She told herself to relax, but her body still tensed with an awareness that surprised her. She was just curious about him, that was all. She cleared her throat and tried to speak lightly. "I imagine you're used to taking orders."

"Not for the last six months. I left after my enlistment was up."

Tearing open an antiseptic towelette, she leaned toward him, feeling almost nervous. Nervous? she thought in surprise. She worked what most would call a man's job and dealt with men all day. What was her problem? She got a whiff of smoke from his clothes, but his face was scrubbed clean of it. She tilted his head, her fingers touching his whisker-rough square chin, marked with a deep cleft in the center. His eyes studied her, and she was so close she could see

21

golden flecks deep inside the brown. She stared into them, and he stared back, and in that moment, she felt a rush of heat and embarrassment all rolled together. Hoping he hadn't noticed, she began to dab at his wound, feeling him tense with the sting of the antiseptic.

Damn it all, what was wrong with her? She hadn't been attracted to him in high school — he'd been an idiot, as far as she was concerned. She'd been focused on her family ranch and barrel racing and was not the kind of girl who would lavish all her attention on a boy, as he seemed to require. Brooke always felt that she had her own life to live and didn't need a boyfriend as some kind of status symbol.

But ten years later, Adam returned as an ex-Marine who saved her horses, a man with a square-cut face, faint lines fanning out from his eyes as if he'd squinted under desert suns, and she was turning into a schoolgirl all over again.

Adam stared into Brooke Thalberg's face as she bent over him, not bothering to hide his powerful curiosity. He remembered her, of course — who wouldn't? She was as tall as many guys and probably as strong, too, from all the hard work on her family ranch.

A brave woman, he admitted, remembering her fearlessness running into the fire, her concern for the horses more than herself. Now her hazel eyes stared at his face intently, their mix of browns and greens vivid and changeable. She turned away to search the med kit, and his gaze lingered on her slim back, covered in a checked Western shirt that was tucked into her belt. Her long braid tumbled down her back, almost to the sway of her jeans-clad hips. It's not like he hadn't seen a woman before. And this woman had been a pest through his childhood, too smart for her own good — seeing into his troubled life the things he'd tried to keep hidden — too confident in her own talent. She had a family who believed in her, and that gave a kid a special kind of confidence. He hadn't had that sort of family, so he recognized it when he saw it.

He wondered if she'd changed at all — he certainly had. After discovering his own confidence, he'd built a place and a name for himself in the Marines. His overconfidence had destroyed that, leaving him in a fog of uncertainty that had been hovering around him for half a year now.

Kind of like being in a barn fire, he guessed, feeling your way around, wondering if you were ever going to get out again. He still didn't know.

After using butterfly bandages to keep the wound closed, Brooke taped a small square of gauze to his face, then straightened, hands on her hips, to judge her handiwork. "You might need stitches if you want to avoid a scar."

He shrugged. "Got enough of those. One more won't hurt."

He rose slowly to his feet, feeling the stiffness in his leg that never quite went away. The docs had got most of the shrapnel out, but not quite all of it. The exertion of the fire had irritated the old wound, but that would ease with time. He was used to it by now, and the reminder that he was alive was more than he deserved, when there were so many men beneath the ground.

After closing the kit, Brooke turned back to face him, tilting her head to look up. They stared at each other a moment, too close, almost too intimate alone there. Drops of water still sparkled in her dark lashes, and her skin was fresh-scrubbed and free of makeup. She looked prettier than he remembered, a woman instead of the skinny girl.

Adam was surprised at the sensations her nearness inspired in him, this awareness of her as a woman, when back in high school she'd barely registered as that to him. He'd dated party girls and cheerleaders — including her best friend, Monica Shaw — not cowgirls. Now she held herself so tall and easily, with a confidence born of hard work and years of testing her body to the limits.

She cleared her throat, and her gaze dropped from his eyes to his mouth, then his shirtfront. "You have a limp," she said. "Did one of the horses kick you?"

"Had the limp on and off for a while. Nothing new."

She nodded, then stepped past him to return the med kit to the bathroom. When she came back out, she was wearing a fixed, polite smile, which, to his surprise, amused him. Not much amused him anymore.

"I'm glad you're not hurt bad," she said. "You did me — us — a big favor, and I can't thank you enough for helping rescue the horses. How'd you see the fire?"

"I was at the boardinghouse and saw the smoke out the window." If the trees hadn't been winter-bare, he might not have seen it at all, which made him think uneasily of Brooke, battling the fire alone. "Where are your brothers? They might have come in handy if I hadn't seen the fire. I assume they still work on the ranch?"

She nodded. "They're at the hospital with my dad, visiting my mom. Did you remem-

25

ber she has MS?"

He shook his head. "I never knew."

"She never talked about it much, so I'm not surprised. Most of the time, she only needs a cane, but she's battling a flare-up that's weakened her legs. The guys took their turn at the hospital today, while I rode fence. Guess I found more than I bargained for." She eyed him with speculation. "So you're back to visit your grandma."

She put her hands in her back pockets and rocked once on her heels, as if she didn't know what to do with herself. That stretched her shirt across her breasts, and he had to force himself to keep his gaze on her face.

"Grandma's letters were off," he admitted. "She seemed almost scattered."

Brooke focused on him with a frown. "Scattered? *Your* grandma?"

"My instincts were right. I got here, and she was a lot more frail, and she's using a cane now."

"A cane? That's new. And I see her often, so maybe I just didn't notice she'd slowly been . . ." She trailed off.

"Declining?" He almost grumbled the words. Grandma Palmer was in her seventies, but some part of him thought she never changed. She'd been the one woman who could briefly get him away from his parents

26

to sleep on sheets that didn't smell of smoke, to eat meals that didn't come from a drive-thru. He was never hungry at Grandma Palmer's, whether for food or for love. There weren't holidays or birthdays unless Grandma had them. All he'd been to his teenage parents was an unwanted kid, the result of a broken condom, and they blamed him for making so little of their lives. He saw that now, but at the time? He'd been relieved to enlist in the Marines and start his life over.

Now he and Grandma Palmer only had each other. His parents had died after falling asleep in bed with cigarettes a few years back, and he hadn't experienced anywhere near the grief he now felt in worrying about her. He might have only seen her once or twice a year, but he'd written faithfully, and so had she. The packages she'd sent had been filled with his favorite books and food, enough to share with his buddies. He felt a spasm of pain at the memories. Some of those buddies were dead now. Good memories mingled with the bad, and he could still see Paul Ivanick cheerfully holding back Adam's care package until he promised to share Grandma Palmer's cookies.

Paul was dead now.

When Adam was discharged, it took everything in him not to run to his grandma like a little boy. But no one could make things right, not for him, or for the men who had died. The men, his Marine brothers, who were dead because of him. He didn't want to imagine what his grandma would think about him if she knew the truth.

"Those old women still seem strong," Brooke insisted. "Mrs. Ludlow may use a walker, and your grandma now a cane, but they have enough . . . well, gumption, to use their word, for ten women."

He shrugged. "All I know is what I see."

And then they stood there, two strangers who'd grown up in the same small town but never really knew each other.

"So what have you been up to?" Brooke asked, rocking on her heels again.

He crossed his arms over his chest. "Nothing much."

In a small town like Valentine Valley, everyone thought they deserved to know their neighbor's business. Brooke wouldn't think any different — hell, he remembered how she used to butt into his in high school, when they weren't even friends. She'd been curious about his studies, a do-gooder who thought she could change the world.

She hadn't seen the world and its cruelties, hadn't left the safety of this town, or her family, as far as he knew. *He'd* seen the world — too much of it. There was nothing he could tell her — nothing he wanted to remember.

"Oo-kay then," she said, drawing out the word.

He wondered if she felt as aware of the simmering tension between them and as uneasy as he did. He wouldn't let himself feel like this, uncertain whether he even deserved a normal life.

"What am I thinking?" she suddenly burst out, digging her hand into her pocket and coming out with a cell phone. "I haven't even called my dad."

She turned her back and stared out the window, where the firemen were hosing down the smoldering ruins of her family barn. For just a moment, Adam remembered coming to the Silver Creek Ranch as a kid when his dad would do the occasional odd jobs for the Thalbergs. He'd seen the close, teasing relationships between Brooke and her brothers, the way their parents guided and nurtured them with love. Their life had seemed so different, so foreign to him.

And now Brooke would never be able to understand the life he'd been leading. So he turned and quietly walked out the door.

CHAPTER TWO

Brooke stood beside the ruins of the old barn, arms crossed, her chin tucked down inside the wool lining of her coat. The firemen were gone, and she was alone, staring at the remains, which hissed and steamed, even as ice flowed down cooling wood beams like frozen waterfalls. A few blackened timbers rose out of the debris, fingers pointing up at the blue sky. Incongruous against one another, really, she thought, feeling almost distant with disbelief.

And then the parade of pickups came barreling down the road on the other side of the pasture. Black Angus cattle raised their heads to look, then dropped them again, searching for grass tufts free of snow. Their grunts and lowing were the sound track of Brooke's life, always playing in the background. She could see Josh and her dad in one truck, Nate and his fiancée, Emily Murphy, in the other. Brooke smiled, relieved that Emily had come along, too. Something about her just . . . settled Nate. Nate had always been a genial workaholic, driven about the ranch, especially the business end of it, a man who helped everyone even when they thought they didn't need it. That tendency had kept him away from long-term commitments until he met Emily. "Helping" her had become loving her, and though both Nate and Emily had resisted, they'd each decided that love was worth taking a risk.

Brooke envied them. Valentine Valley had worked its magic, bringing the two of them together although they'd fought it worse than a calf at branding time. Despite living in Valentine her whole life, there'd been no romantic magic for Brooke, not yet anyway.

Nate and Emily jumped out of their pickup first, followed by Scout, Nate's herding dog with black-and-white patches across his coat. When they saw the barn, they reached for each other's hand, their faces full of dismay. Scout gave a little whine and gingerly went forward to investigate the scent.

Nate was tall, with their mom's black hair and his biological dad's green eyes. Doug Thalberg had adopted him when he was only five years old after falling in love with

31

his divorced mom, Sandy. Emily was much shorter than Nate, strawberry blond hair back in the ponytail she favored when she worked at Sugar and Spice, the bakery she owned.

Emily didn't spend much time staring at the ruins — she ran to Brooke and hugged her, then pulled back and gripped Brooke's upper arms. "Are you okay?" she asked, her gaze roaming her face as if searching for signs of injury. "Your clothes are covered in soot."

Brooke looked down at herself. "I'm okay." She wasn't sure if the sudden realization that she could have died was making her weepy, but she gazed on Emily like the sister she'd never had, so grateful to have her in her life, to have her care.

Then her dad gave her a bear hug that almost crushed her rib cage.

"Oh, Brooke," he whispered, the sound rough.

For the first time, she felt a sting of tears. But she was okay, she reminded herself, and so were the horses . . . because Adam had helped her. "I'm fine, Dad. I'm so sorry about the barn."

He broke the hug and cleared his throat, not bothering to hide the dampness in his eyes as he scanned her face. "The barn?

What do I care about the barn as long as you're all right?"

Beneath his Stetson, Doug Thalberg's hair was the same plain brown as hers and Josh's, but his was graying, along with the full mustache above his lip. His eyes, usually twinkling as if he knew life's hidden amusements, now studied her soberly. "I called Hal after talkin' to you. He says you ran into the barn yourself and saved the horses. That was too dangerous, Cookie."

Brooke felt a flush of warmth at her dad's use of his childhood nickname for her. "Any of you'd a done the same thing," she countered.

"Always said you were brave," Josh said, his grin lopsided.

As usual, he was unshaven and sleepy-eyed, as if he'd just rolled out of bed. For some reason that escaped Brooke, women seemed to like that look.

She shrugged, suddenly feeling a bit too warm at the praise, although the winter wind continued to tug at her braid, and a few strands of hair danced in front of her eyes. To her surprise, Josh threw his arms around her for a quick squeeze, then passed her off to Nate, who almost lifted her off the ground.

"Okay, okay, I'm fine," she said, hearing

the quiver in her voice and hoping no one else noticed.

Keeping an arm around her, Nate looked back at the ruins, as if by staring he could make things better. "We hear you had help. A stranger driving by?"

"Not a stranger. Adam Desantis."

Nate's eyes widened. Brooke expected Nate to start in on Adam's past and felt strangely defensive on Adam's behalf. Nate had never approved of Adam's antics or arrogance. But to her surprise, Nate tugged on her braid, gave a relieved grin, then let her go.

"I'll have to thank him personally for keeping my little sister safe."

She blinked at him, even as she rolled her eyes. "Maybe I kept *him* safe." But she couldn't help glancing at Emily with amazed respect, knowing the other woman was responsible for the gentling of Brooke's big brother.

"I didn't know Adam was in town," Doug said. "But his arrival was certainly lucky for us."

"He saw the smoke from the boarding-house when he was visiting his grandma." She still felt a little surprised at the memory of getting off the phone with her dad, only to find that Adam had gone. She had seen his old battered pickup truck driving off toward the boardinghouse and felt both regret and interest.

"Whose grandson is he?" Emily asked with interest.

"Mrs. Palmer," Brooke said.

"Ah." Emily nodded. "Does Adam resemble her?"

Josh chuckled before Brooke could say a word, and even she had to smile at the thought of a male version of Mrs. Palmer. She had a thick Western drawl, a big, blond wig, a penchant for clothing with outrageous prints and colors, and a nose for everyone else's business. The latter she had in common with her widowed friends.

Then they all sobered as they turned back to the smoldering ruin.

Brooke sighed. "Hal said he doesn't think the fire was deliberately set."

"According to his preliminary report," her father corrected. "There's been some vandalism in town recently."

"Graffiti on the town gazebo hardly equates to starting fires," Brooke said, knowing she sounded like she was defending whichever teenagers were involved.

"And let's not forget that we did have a case of arson last year," Nate pointed out.

Brooke met Emily's curious eyes. "He's

35

right. Cody Brissette was eighteen when he started a fire at the park along Silver Creek, and ended up burning down a pavilion. He claimed it was an accident, that they'd only been trying to get warm, but it didn't matter. A kayaker was injured when he tried to retrieve his equipment from the blaze. The kid's still in jail."

Emily winced.

"He's a man, not a kid," Josh said mildly. "He had to accept the consequences."

"So he couldn't have started this fire," Brooke said. "This is an old barn. Maybe the wiring went bad."

"If only we'd been here," Nate said with a sigh, turning back to the pile of blackened, steaming timber.

"And what would you have done?" Brooke asked patiently. "I was riding fence, and by the time I saw it, it was too late."

"I know," Nate said.

He always thought he was Superman, so she didn't take it personally. She'd ridden beside her brothers from the time she was ten years old, doing everything that needed to be done on a ranch, from guiding cattle to pasture to changing tires. She'd long since proven herself a man's equal.

Doug draped an arm around her shoulders and squeezed. "I'm just glad you're okay," he whispered gruffly.

She leaned her head against his shoulder, and they all went back to silently studying the wreckage.

"What did you tell Mom?" Brooke asked her dad, suddenly worried about how this trauma could affect her mom's recovery.

"About the fire?" He hesitated. "I tried to minimize your involvement, but I'm afraid she figured me out. I think she's okay, but —"

"I'll go visit her, put her at ease."

"A good idea," Doug said with relief.

Nate glanced at Josh. "I never did like to use this barn much once we built the new one — too far away from the main house."

Josh rubbed his chin. "Mighty cold walk in the winter."

Brooke rolled her eyes, knowing there'd be a lot of discussions later. She glanced at Emily. "You want to come to the hospital?"

Emily grinned. "Can we stop at the Widows' Boardinghouse? Your grandma will be worried, too."

When Emily had first come to town last spring, she'd had no place to go, and Nate had taken her there, where the widows had made a fuss over her and insisted she stay until her building was habitable. The building had been vandalized by the last tenants, and Emily — with Nate's help — had made the repairs herself. Instead of selling and going back to San Francisco, she'd stayed to open her own bakery, a dream she hadn't known she had.

Brooke thought Emily's idea to visit the widows a good one, and she tried to tell herself it wasn't because Adam Desantis was staying there.

The two women went back to the main house, so Brooke could shower, then drove Brooke's Jeep to the boardinghouse on the edge of the property overlooking Silver Creek. The house was a white, three-story Victorian, with pretty gingerbread trim and wraparound porches where you could always find a perfect view of the mountains. A sign out front said WIDOWS' BOARDING-HOUSE as if they took in guests. Not paying guests, but they certainly sheltered the occasional lost person who needed a home. As if Emily was thinking the same thing, the two women shared a grin.

"I still miss it here," Emily said, as they drove around behind and parked near the back porch.

"Really?" Brooke asked in disbelief. "You have your own apartment, no one to report your every movement to."

Emily smiled. "I felt cared for."

Together, they crossed the porch and entered the kitchen. Brooke never failed to smile when she saw all the cow decorations, from the horns on the wall where she now hung her coat, to the cow and bull salt and pepper shakers, to the pastoral scenes of grazing cows during all four seasons that lined the walls.

The three widows were gathered in the breakfast nook, papers spread across the table, but they all looked up with various exclamations of surprise and relief when they saw their visitors. Adam wasn't among them, and Brooke felt a little disappointed, although she told herself it was natural to be curious about him.

The widows tried to unobtrusively gather together their papers, as if they had something to hide. Brooke exchanged a glance with Emily, who pressed her lips together to conceal a knowing smile. Brooke wondered what new project the widows were working on for the Valentine Valley Preservation Fund. They were the most active ladies on the committee, from handling the grant applications to dealing with possible investors. But they always kept their projects private until they were ready to reveal them. And then sometimes all hell broke loose.

Grandma Thalberg rushed forward first,

her hair unnaturally red and curly above a face skillfully highlighted with makeup. She wore crisp jeans and a turtleneck, with a corduroy vest for added warmth. Her eyes filled with tears. "Brooke!" she cried, throwing her arms around her granddaughter. "Oh, you brave, brave girl!"

Hugging her back, Brooke found herself sniffing at the powerful emotions that surged between them. Her grandma spent more time at the ranch than not, the home she'd once ruled over with Grandpa Thalberg. Brooke remembered countless hours on her knees weeding the garden at her side, hearing the stories of the ranch from the silver-boom days, tales that had been passed down through the generations.

Brooke looked over her shoulder at the other two ladies. Mrs. Ludlow resembled someone's perfect vision of a grandma, with her cloud of white hair, pressed slacks and blouse, and her smooth use of a walker. Then Brooke saw Mrs. Palmer, and she remembered Adam's concern. Mrs. Palmer's blond wig was still perched atop her head like a crown. Her face was devoid of her usual makeup, making the lines of age starkly visible, though she was wearing a bright red-and-green polka-dotted dress as a token of the approaching holiday season.

She had a cane over her arm, but at least she didn't use it as she rose smoothly from her chair.

"Oh, Brooke, I was so worried about you!" Grandma Thalberg said, managing to give Emily a quick hug before continuing her scrutiny of Brooke.

"When Adam saw smoke," Mrs. Palmer said excitedly, "he just ran off before I could ask anythin'."

She didn't *sound* any different, Brooke thought with relief, and her stride was brisk as she approached.

"Everyone is okay." Brooke towered over the three old women and Emily, and felt like a mother duck trying to reassure her ducklings.

"I could hardly stop to explain."

Brooke heard the deep male voice, and her breath gave a little hitch of surprise. Adam was standing in the doorway that led to the first-floor bedroom suite the widows used for guests. He was wearing only a t-shirt and jeans over boots, and his short, sandy hair was damp and wavy. The bandage was a white patch on his tanned cheek. His shoulders seemed to touch both edges of the doorframe, then he leaned against one side and crossed his arms. His somber eyes regarded the newcomers, and she felt flustered. That, she thought, was an alien word to her — "intrigued" was far better.

Emily gave the sweetest smile and walked toward him, hand outstretched. "Adam, I'm Emily Murphy, Nate's fiancée."

"Adam Desantis. A pleasure to meet you, ma'am," he said, as they shook hands.

Then his gaze slid past her to Brooke, unreadable, but enough to make her nervous. And she was never nervous.

Emily glanced over her shoulder at Brooke, eyes wide with innocence. "Brooke said you were very brave, going into a burning building."

Brooke forced herself not to roll her eyes.

"It must be all that Marine training," Emily added, when he said nothing.

He gave her a small smile. Brooke tried not to study him, but it was difficult. He seemed so . . . different. She remembered a young man who would jump into every conversation to make himself a part of it. For a boy whose grades weren't all that great, he'd always raised his hand in class even if he didn't know the answer. He liked to be in the spotlight. He had opinions, and a belief in himself that was a bit overinflated . . . more than a bit. Now there was a calmness about him, a watchfulness, that hinted at deep thoughts he didn't mean to

42

share. He glanced at her more than once, and she couldn't look away.

And there was his body, of course, the finely sculpted arms and chest of a soldier beneath the tight olive t-shirt, the narrow hips, the thighs that jeans had to stretch across. Brooke felt a little flushed at all the scrutiny she couldn't seem to stop.

"If only I'd read the cards this mornin'," Mrs. Palmer berated herself, "I would have known somethin' was goin' to happen."

She was leaning on the cane now, when she hadn't seemed to need it a moment ago, and her voice had a faint quiver to it. Brooke tried to catch Grandma Thalberg's eye to give her a bemused look but couldn't.

" 'Read the cards'?" Adam echoed with confusion.

"Tarot cards," Mrs. Palmer said, reaching out to Adam as if her walk across the kitchen had tired her.

Brooke frowned as she watched Adam lead his grandma back to the kitchen table. "What don't I know about Mrs. Palmer's health?" she whispered to her grandma.

Grandma Thalberg just waved a hand as she whispered back, "We're all getting old, dear. You can't expect our strength to stay the same. Renee's fine."

Fine? Well, she'd seemed fine at first, but

she didn't now. Brooke felt a little pang of worry at the thought of Grandma Thalberg too old to weed the vegetable garden or serve dinner to all the neighbors who came to help at branding time. Adam must have felt the same, by the way he hurried back to Valentine from . . . where?

"Tarot cards," Adam was saying, doubt laced through his deep voice as he sat down opposite his grandma.

His limp had disappeared, and Brooke was relieved he hadn't been seriously hurt.

"I didn't practice the art when you were small," Mrs. Palmer told Adam. "I learned it much later. I like seein' the patterns that tie the present to the future. I can offer guidance and possibilities for someone who needs them — without soundin' like I'm buttin' in."

"I must admit I was skeptical," Mrs. Ludlow said, shaking her head, "especially when she convinced Mrs. Wilcox, who works part-time for Monica, that her head-strong daughter might be with child but everything would work out fine. And don't you know, the boy proposed the next day, right on the Rose Garden bridge."

Adam continued to frown, and Brooke chuckled, though she could have told him not to try to see logic in what the widows did. Surely Mrs. Palmer had written to him of their continued exploits. They'd certainly done a few wild things when he was a boy. But he was already gone when they'd given cap guns to all the kids attending the grand opening of the toy store, only to set off the smoke detectors.

Adam began, "Grandma, you know —"

"Can you stay for dinner, girls?" Mrs. Ludlow smoothly interrupted. She gestured to Grandma Thalberg. "Rosemary is going to make her famous chicken salad. And we still have cookies from the Sugar and Spice left over from the school bake sale."

Emily grinned, then her expression clouded as she looked at Mrs. Palmer. "I know you're on the schedule at the bakery tomorrow, Mrs. Palmer. I'd be happy to cover for you if you're not feeling well."

"You work?" Adam said to his grandma in surprise. "You didn't mention that on the phone. You don't need to do that."

"It's only been the last few months, and I enjoy it," Mrs. Palmer insisted. "We all work part-time for Emily, along with several of our friends. That way none of us works too much. So don't worry about me, dear. If I'm feeling poorly, Connie and I will exchange shifts."

Mrs. Ludlow nodded regally. "Of course

we will."

Adam didn't look convinced, and Brooke didn't want to hear the negotiation.

"We can't stay for dinner, Grandma, but thank you," Brooke said. "We're on our way to see my mom."

"I'm sure she needs to see for herself that you're okay," Grandma Thalberg said. "You go on, and we'll expect you both another time."

"Of course," Brooke said, reaching for her coat. "Thanks."

"Can I speak with you for a moment?" Adam interrupted.

Emily bit her lip and let her big blue eyes go all innocent. It was a handy talent, Brooke thought with fond exasperation.

"I'll wait here with the ladies," Emily said. "You two go ahead and talk in the parlor."

If Adam thought "parlor" an old-fashioned word for the living room, he didn't say so. Brooke led him through the formal dining room — too close to the kitchen — feeling all prickly with the knowledge that he was looking at her. She didn't know what the heck her problem was. She stopped in the parlor, where the widows' crafts decorated everything, from crocheted afghans on the back of the couch to needlepoint pictures of ranch landscapes on the wall. Turning to face Adam, she saw him looking around with bemusement.

"I keep thinking this place is old," he said, "but then I look beneath the Little-House-on-the-Prairie décor and see all the remodeling."

"*Little House on the Prairie*?" she echoed, amused. "That was barely in repeats when we were kids."

"Grandma insisted I watch with her," he said without embarrassment.

Brooke had to admire his attitude. She saw his gaze focus on an antique tin candle mold.

"She absorbed more of it than I thought," he said. "She wanted mementoes of the show, and I told her about eBay, but didn't think she could manage a computer since she never wrote me an e-mail."

Brooke gestured behind her to the old dinosaur of a computer, with its big cube monitor. "They have that, so you never know. As for the house, my brother Nate is responsible for the other improvements. He remodeled the place before they moved in, gutted the kitchen, put in all new windows, anything you can think of."

"Surprised he has the time."

She shrugged. "He made the time. We all love our grandmas."

"Now do you see what I meant about mine?"

She sobered. "I do. She does seem . . . off. I asked my grandma, who only answered that everyone gets older."

"Not an answer," he practically growled.

Brooke could sense his frustration, but he didn't pace, didn't betray it with movement. He was always so still. It was not a normal characteristic of the men she knew, and she found it oddly attractive.

"I'm not going anywhere until she's doing better," he continued. "I'll talk to her doctor, whatever it takes."

Brooke felt both interest and uneasiness at the thought of his staying. She wasn't sure she liked the way he made her feel, a jumpiness she hadn't experienced with the few guys she'd dated over the years. Heck, she was usually as easygoing as her brothers.

Or maybe she was honestly attracted to the man Adam Desantis had become.

"You're staying here at the boarding-house?" she asked although she knew the answer.

"Yeah." A frown deepened the lines of his brow as he gave another glance around, then sighed.

Brooke smiled. "The décor not masculine

enough for you?"

His gaze came back to her and didn't let her go. "Something like that. And what's this about tarot cards?"

Brooke put up both hands. "*That,* you're going to have to discuss with her. Now I've really got to go, Adam. See you later."

She turned back toward the kitchen, wondering if he was checking her out from behind. But she didn't glance at him again, and by the time she'd donned her boots and coat, and reached her car, she was feeling almost disappointed not to know.

"Now *that* was interesting," Emily said with amusement as she buckled her seat belt.

Though Brooke suspected she was referring to Adam, she gave a whistle as she backed out of the driveway. "Poor Mrs. Palmer. I had no idea."

Emily's smile faded a bit. "She started using the cane just this week. I tried to make her sit and frost cupcakes, but she says she likes being out with customers. The other two widows are taking it in stride. Hopefully that means it's nothing too serious."

"Adam thinks it is. That's why he dragged me into the parlor."

"That's why?" Emily batted her lashes at her. "I don't know if you're right about that.

49

Seems to me Adam just wanted to be alone with you."

Brooke felt a touch of guilty pleasure mixed in with her suspicion. But she kept her eyes on the dirt road as it became asphalt right before entering Valentine Valley. "I've never been the type he was interested in."

"As your dad said, war can change a man. Maybe he's figured out that Valentine is where he belongs, and he's ready to find a wife and make babies."

Brooke coughed as if she were choking. "Where the hell did *that* come from?"

"Should I take the wheel so you don't kill us?" Emily laughed merrily until she wiped tears from her eyes. "The expression on your face . . ."

"Look, I'm glad if Adam straightened himself out. According to Mrs. Palmer, he did well in the Marines. But I don't think people's personalities change all that much. He was full of himself in high school until he was caught joyriding in a stolen car."

Emily winced. "Well, we all make mistakes . . ."

"The judge was good to him, a first offender and underage, so they assigned him to the supervision of the football coach. And yes, by focusing on football, he found

50

something he was good at. But he was still so arrogant. He had no use for me, and I had no use for him." *But I could think of a few uses for him now . . .*

"I understand," Emily said solemnly, even though her eyes twinkled. "Maybe he's not thinking that now."

"Let's not go crazy," Brooke said, but she felt a little thrill of pleasure. *Stop it,* she told herself.

They reached the light where Main Street ended at Highway 82, and she turned onto the highway toward Aspen. They drove the twenty minutes in silence. Snow blew across the road occasionally, but it was clear for the most part. As they reached the exclusive town, she loved seeing the mountains crowded with skiers and snowboarders, stretching up toward the blue sky. On the left were tiers of mansions built into the foothills and sprawled across the valley, their windows reflecting the sun.

At the hospital, Brooke led the way into her mom's room, then held a finger to her lips for Emily's benefit. Sandy's eyes were closed, a book across her lap. The room was a flower garden, vases brimming with roses, daisies, and multihued carnations, all nestled in Baby's Breath or greenery. Brooke recognized Monica Shaw's handiwork in

51

more than one display. "Get Well" cards lined the windowsill.

Brooke hesitated a moment, telling herself her mom looked no different, that she was petite and always appeared small in a hospital bed. She had Nate's deep black hair, helped a bit with coloring now, and it framed her face in an attractive way. Even in the hospital, Sandy made sure she looked pleasant, her face accented with makeup, her nightgowns pretty and feminine. She liked to wander the halls in her wheelchair, visiting cancer patients or sick kids. More than once, Brooke had accompanied her on these visits, and was always so in awe at her ability to brighten someone's day. But then, her mom had always done that for Brooke, meeting her bus after school with a home-made snack, playing games or doing crafts on a rainy Saturday, listening to Brooke's dating woes — heck, she even did that now. Her throat closed up a bit at the thought that someday her mom wouldn't bounce back so easily.

Emily put a hand on her shoulder, her face sympathetic. Brooke reminded herself of her good fortune; Emily had lost her stepdad when she was young, and her mom — whom she hadn't been close to — died a few years ago. Sandy had practically adopted

Emily since the engagement. Sandy approved of everything Emily had done to change her life for the better —

Then why was Brooke so afraid to make changes in her own life? Her brother Josh was renovating the loft of the barn into his own apartment, above his workshop, where his late hours tooling leather wouldn't bother the family. He was making a change. And then there was Emily, who'd transformed herself and discovered the truth of her family history. Brooke hadn't been able to stop thinking about that accomplishment. Her mind had worried at it, unable to see what was bothering her. But confronting the barn fire seemed to clarify all her emotions, the restlessness she'd been feeling since Emily's arrival. Brooke needed a change in her life, something different, but she was afraid that admitting it to her family — to her mom — would make them think she didn't love them or didn't want the same ranching life they had. And she did want those things! But she wanted . . . something else, too. If only she knew what it was.

Time, she told herself. She'd give herself the time to figure out what had changed for her, what she needed to make her happy. And it wasn't about needing any kind of a relationship with a man. Dating wouldn't solve her problems and would only complicate things, so she wasn't going there.

Brooke chased her confused thoughts away and approached the hospital bed.

Sandy blinked open her brown eyes on a yawn, then smiled. "Brooke! I'm so glad you came."

She gave her mom a kiss on the cheek and sat on the edge of the bed. After squeezing Sandy's hand, Emily pulled up a chair.

Brooke realized her mom was blinking back tears. "Hey, I'm okay," she quickly reassured her, then leaned down to give her a gentle hug. "Dad must have told you I didn't even get a scratch."

"Oh, don't mind me," Sandy said when she sat back, waving her hand and blinking furiously before scrutinizing her. "I don't think your bravery at the burning barn even singed a lock of hair."

Brooke blushed. "I wasn't brave. I was scared to death. But all I could think of were those poor horses."

"And you saved them all?"

Brooke nodded and gave her a brief description of the fire.

Emily chimed in, "Don't forget the help of Adam Desantis."

Sandy's eyes went wide, then she studied

her daughter. "I heard a stranger helped you, but not his name. I remember Adam." Her expression grew sympathetic. "He's visiting Renee?"

Brooke nodded, then decided not to ask her mom about Mrs. Palmer's health, remembering how the old woman had used her cane only after Adam entered the room, and how Grandma Thalberg had brushed off her concerns. Brooke would keep an eye on the widows.

"Have the doctors said how much longer you'll be in here?" she asked, almost wincing at how false and bright her voice sounded. She was trying to convince herself that her mother would be fine.

"A day or two. I admit I'm feeling anxious to be gone. I don't like being away from the ranch. Your father depends on me."

"Of course he does — he's a man," Brooke teased.

Her mother's smile was halfhearted, and Brooke's uneasiness increased.

"You know I'll make sure everything goes okay back home," she said earnestly.

"I know you will, sweetie."

Brooke told herself the doubt in her mom's voice was about her concern for the ranch and her frustration about not being there. Then why did Brooke suspect it was something else?

CHAPTER THREE

On the way back to Valentine, Brooke's throat was so tight she couldn't talk about her mother. She was glad when Emily received a text from Monica asking them to meet her for dinner at the Halftime Sports Bar. When they reached town, they drove down Main Street, lined with clapboard storefronts, all brightly colored, one to three floors in height. Interspersed were the occasional stone buildings like the Royal Opera or the Hotel Colorado, each of which took up most of a block. The Halftime was nestled between the deli and the Open Book. Neon beer signs winked in the two windows that bracketed the front door, and inside, sports memorabilia covered darkly paneled walls. Flat screen TVs gave perfect viewing to every table in the place. The bar was overflowing with the after-work crowd, most of whom raised a hand or called a greeting when Brooke and Emily entered.

"Brooke!" Monica called from a table near the back.

They bypassed the hostess, and Brooke grinned at her best friend since childhood. Monica Shaw was a slim, black woman with curls that just brushed her shoulders. She had the high cheekbones and exotic eyes of a model, if not the towering height. In truth, she was a small-town girl, now the owner of Monica's Flowers and Gifts. She'd never wanted to move to the big city, like her twin sister, a reporter for CNN. That had caused some family problems, but they'd had a good talk and cry, and now Monica was excited about her spring trip to visit Melissa. Her store was right next to Sugar and Spice, so it was Monica who'd first befriended Emily and helped convince her to stay in town. Nate owed Monica for his good fortune — as Monica was always quick to remind him.

"I heard the news!" Monica said, shoving her plate of nachos into the center of the table.

"News?" Brooke's thoughts immediately went to the recent arrival of Adam. She dipped a nacho and groaned with happiness as she devoured it. She'd forgotten to eat lunch in the middle of that crazy day.

"The barn fire?" Monica answered, her

face full of disbelief. She glanced at Emily. "Are you sure she didn't get hit on the head?"

Emily only shrugged as she concentrated on the nachos.

"Sorry," Brooke said sheepishly. "I've explained it so many times today, I thought I'd already told you!" She had herself better under control now, and wouldn't worry her friends by falling apart. She could treat this lightly, as if she risked her life every day. Well, okay, sometimes she did, where the occasional runaway bull was concerned.

After they ordered beer and salad and chicken wings, she gave a brief account to Monica — and then to several of the guys from the bar, who went back and told their friends.

"Surely everyone knows by now," Brooke said with a groan. "But I can't blame them. Every rancher worries all the time during the dry season that a windstorm will send a fire our way. Thank God it's almost winter, or this could have been worse."

Their waitress, Linda, a mom with school-age kids who often biked with Nate and his friends, looked Brooke over as she set a bottle of beer before each of them. "I won't make you repeat the story, as I'm sure the guys'll be talking about it at the bar. But

I'm glad you're okay."

Brooke smiled. "Thanks, Linda. Believe me, I'm glad, too."

"She had help," Emily said. "Do you remember Adam Desantis?" she asked both Linda and Monica.

Linda blinked in surprise. "He was a few years behind me at school, but yeah, who could forget?"

Emily grinned. "Now that I've met him, I can see why he's so memorable."

Monica turned on Brooke with speculation. "He's back from the Marines?"

"Visiting his grandma like a good boy," Brooke said.

As she walked away, Linda called over her shoulder, " 'A good boy' isn't how I remember him."

The three women laughed. Brooke watched as Linda started a conversation at one end of the bar, then each head turned, relaying the news of Adam's return like falling dominoes.

"I remember him, too," Monica said, leaning back in her chair with a little sigh.

"Of course she does," Brooke said conspiratorially to Emily, even as she snatched the last nacho. "She dated him."

Emily gasped and leaned toward Monica. "Really?"

Monica waved her hand delicately. "It only lasted a few weeks. He was a football player, and I was a cheerleader. It's amazing how those stereotypes just keep happening, generation after generation." When their laughter faded, she asked, "So has he changed?"

"Wait, wait, I need to know more about the actual dating," Emily said.

"He was a good kisser," Monica admitted, "but I wasn't interested in going farther, not right away. So we broke up."

"Told you he was a jerk," Brooke said. "Poor Monica would call me for sympathy. We shared a lot of ice cream those few weeks."

"He could be funny, too," Monica pointed out.

"You're defending a guy who broke up with you because you wouldn't put out?" Brooke still felt defensive on her behalf.

"Oh, please, he was a hormonal kid. So has he changed?" Monica repeated patiently.

Brooke hesitated, trying to ignore how very curious Adam made her. "He seems kind of a quiet guy now. I never thought I'd say that about him."

"He might have seen some bad things," Emily said.

They all sobered. Brooke couldn't help

61

thinking how very young he'd been to go off to war. Just eighteen. She could only imagine how Mrs. Palmer must have felt, and he her only grandchild. Many men never came back. She'd known one of those, someone who'd gone to Colorado State with Nate. Though she'd only met him once or twice, it had been a blow to know he'd died such a terrible death. And the poor man's family . . . She'd been so glad to hear that Valentine Valley had begun a program to help returning veterans. She didn't know much about it, but she'd mention it to Mrs. Palmer when she got the chance. Of course, the widows probably knew all about it.

Thank God Mrs. Palmer hadn't lost Adam. He was the only blood family she had left. Her older brother was dead, and she'd only had one daughter. But she liked to say that the widows were the sisters she'd never had. Brooke's gaze traveled from Monica to Emily, and she realized she knew exactly what Mrs. Palmer meant. She didn't know how she'd function without her girl-friends.

"At least Adam's back, and he's safe," Monica said, breaking their somber moment of reflection.

Brooke smiled at Linda, who set down individual salads for each woman, and a huge plate of wings in the center of the table.

"I'll be back with another round of drinks," Linda called.

Monica wiggled her eyebrows at Brooke. "I'm sure Adam grew up to be fine-lookin'."

Brooke and Emily glanced at each other, then broke into grins.

"Okay, yes, he's fine-looking," Brooke said, lifting both hands in a placating manner.

"More than fine-looking," Emily breathed, leaning over the table and lowering her voice. "Downright sexy."

Brooke cleared her throat pointedly, even as she felt overly warm at the thought.

"Well, of course, not as sexy as Nate," Emily smoothly added.

Brooke winced. "I don't want to hear that about my brother. Speaking of the two of you" — she rounded on her future sister-in-law — "do we have a wedding date?"

Emily actually blushed. "No," she whispered.

Monica and Brooke groaned.

Brooke took the first bite of her salad, chewed, and swallowed. "I thought you and Nate were in discussion about that."

"If Nate had his way, the date would be next week," Emily said glumly, using her fork to toy with a piece of lettuce.

"Well, we know that's not going to happen." Monica reached to touch Emily's hand. "I know you both want a pretty wedding you'll remember forever, but you could be planning it now. What's going on, Em?"

"It's Stephanie," Emily said with a heavy sigh.

"Your sister?" Brooke asked, uncomprehending.

"My half sister." Emily's voice took on a touch of bitterness. "Or so she keeps reminding me."

When Emily had come to town earlier that year, she'd discovered that the father she'd thought of as her own, the one who'd died when she was seven, had in fact been her stepfather, and that her biological dad was right in town, oblivious that he had another daughter. Brooke and Monica had both encouraged Emily to face the truth, and through some investigating, Emily had discovered that her father was Joe Sweet, part of the family who owned the elegant Sweetheart Inn, as well as an extensive ranch. Though shocked, Joe had been delighted to add another daughter to the brood that already included three sons in their twenties and a sixteen-year-old daughter, Stephanie. Brooke knew that the young men were fine with Emily, and understood their dad's teenage love affair. Steph hadn't taken it well upon discovering that she wasn't Daddy's only little girl, and that Daddy hadn't been perfect. To Joe's frustration, she hadn't blamed *him* — she'd focused her anger on Emily.

"Wait, wait," Brooke said. "You asked her to be a bridesmaid. I saw her face — she was thrilled!"

"I thought so, too." Emily's voice trembled. "I thought it was something we could share while getting to know each other. But it's not working out that way. Suddenly, my wedding and I are the focus of every Sunday-dinner discussion."

Monica winced. "That might be a problem."

"I play it down, or steer the conversation away," Emily insisted, shredding her napkin on the table.

"She's gotta grow up sometime," Brooke said. "You can't keep delaying your wedding. Everyone wants to see me in a fancy dress! Because, of course, I clean up well," she added, hoping to lift her friend's spirits.

Emily smiled sadly. "You sound like your brother — although not about the dress." Her smile strengthened. "But we only just became engaged last month. I think we have time. And now that the . . . newness of my arrival is wearing off, perhaps Steph can begin to move past it."

"Or perhaps she'll think she's gotten her way," Brooke pointed out, feeling affronted on Emily's behalf.

"Ooh, now who's the pessimist here?" Monica picked up her first chicken wing. "I think Emily's right. There's time. It's not like they have to be celibate until the wedding night."

Brooke practically snorted into her beer, sending the other two into fits of laughter.

"Couldn't you have waited until I swallowed?" she demanded, wiping at her lips with the back of her hand.

Emily finally stopped giggling enough to say, "Look, my youngest brother Daniel is closest to her, but he's away at college. When he comes back for Thanksgiving, we're going to put our heads together and come up with a plan."

"Works for me," Monica said, starting on the next chicken wing.

"And I was thinking about finding another way to get involved in Steph's life," Emily said hesitantly. "She's a member of the teen group that meets at the community center. Maybe they need volunteers . . ."

"No," Brooke said with compassion. "You

don't want Steph to think you're pushing into her life without her permission. I think she'll see right through that."

Emily's shoulders slumped. "Really? But I've got to find *some* way to get her talking to me."

"You will," Monica insisted. "Give it more time."

They ate their way through most of the chicken wings, then sat back with satisfaction.

"I have interesting news," Brooke said.

"*More* interesting news?" Monica fanned herself. "How will I bear the excitement?"

Brooke grinned, then glanced at Emily. "Remember Leather and Lace?"

"Of course, the naughty lingerie store that was interested in buying my building. I felt like I let them down when I decided to open Sugar and Spice."

"You didn't let them down too much. They haven't given up on making Valentine Valley the home of their third store. They're looking into purchasing another building, and will be visiting soon. The owner's written to the preservation-fund committee about a grant to renovate a run-down building on Grace Street, behind Hal's Hardware."

"That's right across the street from Wild

Thing," Monica said with a grin. "It'll fit right in with the nightclub crowd."

"Hey, I've seen their store in San Francisco," Emily said. "It's a classy, upscale place."

"Nothing naughty?" Brooke asked, feigning disappointment.

Emily smiled. "Well, I didn't say that."

Monica turned her suspicious gaze on Brooke. "And since when do you need naughty lingerie? Is there something you're not telling us?"

Brooke had a momentary flash of Adam and how she'd felt when they'd been standing close. "Nothing going on here," she insisted.

"Girlfriend, join the club," Monica said. "Maybe the Valentine mojo only works for *some* people."

They clinked the last two chicken wings together as Emily smiled and shrugged.

Before the explosion, Adam had dreaded the idea of leaving the Marines for a civilian existence. He thought life would be vanilla without all the constant alertness and threat of danger.

But he'd changed his mind, having had enough of danger and the consequences of one wrong move. But that didn't mean he wanted vanilla, either. For the first time, he understood what that truly meant. Oh, he got in long runs every day like a good Marine, even through the snow. But he had absolutely nothing else to do. He was starting to go stir-crazy, and the memories of his dead friends were getting too close to the surface. Since his discharge, he'd been able to battle those memories into the furthest corners of his mind through physically demanding work. It had been good to think of nothing but the job, then be so exhausted that he could sometimes keep even the nightmares away.

But he didn't have that anymore, and he was starting to think of his buddies, of Eric, who used to be afraid of heights but was so proud of the jump wings he'd won at Army Airborne School, of Zach, a young dad who'd collected rocks for his son. And then there was Paul, the cookie thief, a greenie with an attitude and ego that had taken a blistering in boot camp. It had been Adam's job to show the young man that his training had prepared him for anything the mountains of Afghanistan could dish out. As their sergeant, it had been Adam's job to keep them all safe, and he'd failed.

And still he pushed the memories away. Two days had passed since the fire, and when the wind was right, he could still smell the residue. When he wasn't talking to his grandma, he did odd jobs around the boardinghouse — fixing a drip in an upstairs bathroom; hanging a framed photo for Mrs. Thalberg; nailing a spindle back in place on the porch railing that Mrs. Ludlow's walker had slammed into. The widow sedately assured him she hadn't been hurt, but the skunk she'd been scaring away ran fast.

So far none of the jobs required a trip to a hardware store, but Grandma had more on her list, and soon he'd be forced to go into town. He wasn't exactly looking forward to it. Most people would remember him and would ask all about his service with the Marines, his part in the war. To acquaintances, he was good at deflecting, but with people who believed they knew him and deserved every answer? He wasn't sure what he was going to say.

Grandma Palmer had made it easy. He'd said he didn't want to talk about Afghanistan, and she'd never asked again. She was giving him time, he knew, assuming he'd eventually open up. She didn't know what had happened, and it was best that way. No point in anyone else suffering. He deserved to take it all on himself. His grandma didn't need to know about such sorrow. Together, they used to make annual trips to the cemetery to honor their deceased relatives, especially her husband, his grandpa. She'd told him stories that even she chuckled over, but as a boy who was used to gauging his parents' moods, he'd seen the old sadness in her eyes. He was kind of surprised she hadn't suggested the cemetery yet, considering his own parents were there now. Not that he cared to visit them.

He'd found himself outside a lot over the past two days, whenever he needed to get away from sweetly chattering voices. The snow-covered mountains still loomed as majestically as ever, but they were familiar, *his* mountains, unlike the mountains of Afghanistan, rugged and barren in places, permeated with danger.

And then there was the Silver Creek Ranch. All he had to do to see it was stand on the back porch. The boardinghouse was part of the ranch property, so after a line of evergreens and aspens, he could see Thalberg cattle leisurely milling across snowy pastures, or huddling together for warmth when the late-autumn wind swept across the Roaring Fork Valley from Glenwood Springs to Aspen. He saw the occasional rider, too, but because of the distance, it

71

was hard to know whether it was Brooke or not.

He found himself thinking about her too much, which surprised him. Since leaving the Marines, he hadn't given much thought to women at all. Certainly he'd met them on the Gulf, where he'd been a longshoreman unloading cargo south of New Orleans. But it was as if he didn't know what to do with one anymore. That had panicked him a couple months ago, so he had a one-night stand. All the parts worked, and he made sure she had a good time; he was just uninterested in more, so he didn't try to date. He knew, during those months, it wouldn't have been fair to burden a woman with his problems. His life had been work, TV, and the occasional evening out drinking with the men from the shipyard. And books, of course. He enjoyed a good mystery. Grandma offered to take him to the Open Book when he was ready.

Instead of beer-drinking buddies with sports conversation to help him forget, he had tea-drinking ladies and their committee discussions about preserving the town. He wasn't very interested — Valentine had never really felt like home. Grandma would have loved to discuss that, too, but he shut down any conversation about his parents.

They'd been self-centered and negligent; they weren't worth thinking about.

But in idle moments, his thoughts returned to Brooke. She hadn't been on his radar in high school, and, truth be told, he hadn't thought about her in years. But ever since she'd raced with him into a burning building to save her horses, she'd lingered in his mind. Maybe his mind was trying to tell him he needed a woman, because hell, he'd gotten a hard-on the moment she'd put her hands on his face to clean his cut. She'd been leaning over him, and although she was dressed as a cowgirl, he'd been able to see the edge of her lacy blue bra, and he hadn't stopped looking. So if thoughts of her plagued him, it was only what he deserved.

But he really needed something more to do. And when his grandma spread out her tarot cards in front of him late that afternoon, he decided it was time to head into town. He could have walked it — Valentine was only about eight blocks wide and long. But he felt a little more invisible in his pickup.

The preservation-fund committee must have been doing good work because everything looked so polished and clean. Though there was a little more than a week until

73

Thanksgiving, Christmas decorations lined Main Street — banners hung from the light poles, red and green ribbons tied everywhere. Businesses had already turned on the twinkling lights in their windows as dusk approached, fake candles in the apartment windows above. Each evergreen had been transformed into a Christmas tree, with gleaming decorations peeking from beneath a dusting of snow. Adam knew it must help their tourism business. The area was packed with skiers looking for sightseeing and shopping opportunities when they weren't on the slopes, and Valentine Valley was only a half hour's drive from Aspen. But this wasn't the part of town he'd come from.

He kept driving past the "historic downtown," past the old homes and the bed-and-breakfasts until he reached the trailer park on the outskirts of town, near the highway. Rusted single-wides were mixed in with newer models, and some had Christmas lights, too, but it all felt . . . forced, as if they were pretending everything was fine this holiday. And maybe for them it was.

He reached the spot where his parents' trailer had been, and there was nothing there, as if it were haunted. He imagined that beneath the layer of snow, the earth was still scorched. A gang of kids threw a football around nearby, slipping in the snow, laughing. Adam smiled because that used to be him. Other kids in Valentine were snowboarding today, but these probably couldn't afford to. It had been difficult to be a kid in the Rockies who didn't snowboard, another thing to set you apart.

But life was what you made of it, and Adam had used his childhood to motivate him to change himself. These kids would, too. And in some ways, Adam had been lucky. He'd had a horse to love and take care of. His father rode it when he was hired on as a temporary hand at the nearby ranches — including the Silver Creek. Adam's job had been to look after old Star, feed him, exercise him. Being responsible for something other than himself had been satisfying though he hadn't realized it at the time. His dad must have sold the animal, he mused. Surely, it had a better home now.

He wasn't ready to go back to the boardinghouse and his grandmother's patient glances, so he stopped in to Tony's Tavern for a beer. The tavern was close to the highway, and there was usually a motorcycle or two. Inside, the décor was full of neon signs between mounted deer heads. The bar ran the length of the front room, flat screen TVs showed college basketball, and the dartboard had a line of men waiting to use it. In back, he glimpsed a pool table under a spotlight.

The bartender glanced up as Adam hung his coat on a hook by the door, then slowly grinned. "Adam Desantis," he said, and it wasn't a question.

Adam smiled and strode to the bar, where they shook hands across the top. "Tony De Luca."

Tony had shaggy brown hair that still seemed long to Adam after the high and tight haircuts of jarheads. But Tony's expression was open and friendly, and Adam knew there would be no judgment here, no expected answers to questions he didn't want. Tony was a few years older than him, but they'd known of each other. And talking to someone else would help him forget other bars in foreign countries, and the ghosts of other men.

Adam ordered a beer and took a seat at the bar. "Still playing hockey?"

"I'm on a few teams. I've even got my boy playing."

"Wow, a family man."

Tony shrugged his burly shoulders beneath the flannel shirt. "Not so good at the family part, but my son and I are a team."

He set a bottle down in front of Adam,

who took a welcome sip.

"Divorced?" Adam asked.

Tony nodded. "You?"

"Out of the Marines now. No family — except my grandma."

"Glad to see you've come back. Valentine always welcomes its heroes. A group of vets meets here regularly for a darts league."

Adam's smile faded. He was putting the past behind him and had no wish to relive someone's idea of the "glory days." "I'm nobody's hero, Tony. I just did my job."

Tony nodded and turned to ring up another customer. When he came back, he asked, "Are you sticking around town for long?"

It wasn't the first time Adam had been asked. "I don't know. Depends on how my grandma is doing. And don't tell me you need a guy for your team. You know I didn't play."

"I know. Just wondering if you were looking for something to do."

"You have no idea," he said dryly.

"Having fun at the boardinghouse?"

"Word gets around."

"Hey, you gotta expect that. Heard you were involved in some excitement at the Silver Creek Ranch."

"Then you heard it was nothing much.

Horses are safe."

"And Brooke." Tony watched him closely as he dried a beer mug.

"She's safe, too." Adam took a swig of beer, meaning that in more than one way.

There was a sudden bark of laughter from the back room, and inside, he felt the flinch he always got at loud noises. His weakness really pissed him off.

Before Tony's innocent questions could go further — how had he forgotten how nosy everyone was in a small town? — he said, "I'll check out the game in back."

Adam could feel Tony watching him as he headed for the back room, but at least it was friendly interest. As he moved down the length of the bar, others gave him curious looks. A couple guys were close to his own age, and if given a moment, he might have recognized them, but he kept moving.

The bikers in their leather vests and jeans had taken over the pool table, and Adam worked his way into the lineup and won a few games. He was a master at the concentration required to line up a good shot, after all his years with the rifle as his constant companion. As a civilian, he didn't carry a gun, only a pocketknife. It bothered him that he still thought of ways he would defend himself if necessary, but after all those years at war, it was hard to abandon the mind-set. But the bikers were good sports and didn't mind being defeated.

There were women in the bar, too, and as he left, more than one gave him a "Welcome home, soldier" glance, but he couldn't muster up the interest. As he got in his pickup, it dawned on him that that was the story of his life lately, no interest in anything. It was time to get on with it, to accept his ghosts, to find a better reason for life than just existing.

CHAPTER FOUR

Late the next afternoon, Adam had his head under the kitchen sink, reinstalling the garbage disposal after the sink had clogged, when he saw his grandma's legs as she walked slowly toward him with the aid of her cane. She was wearing a dress, striped in bright orange, and he knew she hadn't been wearing that earlier. He would have remembered it. Ducking his head out from beneath the kitchen sink, he squinted up at her. She wore a matching orange bow in her blond wig.

"Going out for dinner?" he asked.

She smiled gently. "And so are you. The Thalbergs are celebratin' Sandy's discharge from the hospital, and they also want to thank you for helpin' Brooke rescue the horses."

Adam frowned. "Brooke already thanked me."

"Her parents didn't." She raised a hand

that faintly trembled. "And I didn't tell you because I knew you'd holler. Rosemary's already gone, and I need a ride. So shower and let's go."

"I wouldn't holler," he insisted as he rose to his feet. "And I'm bothered you think I wouldn't take you to the Thalbergs."

"Oh, I knew you'd take me," she said, smiling. "But I needed you to stay." Her hand was still quivering where she rested it on the cane.

"Of course I'll stay, Grandma. Anything you'd like."

"My, you're so accommodatin'." She batted her wrinkled eyelids at him.

It was hard to smother a grin. "I'll shower quick."

At the Silver Creek Ranch, Adam parked his truck outside the front door. As he helped his grandma up the stairs, the door opened, spilling a shaft of yellow light through the gently falling snow.

A man strode out onto the porch, and Adam recognized Doug Thalberg.

Mr. Thalberg reached out a hand. "Adam, good to see you."

Adam took his hand in a firm grip. "Mr. Thalberg, sir, thank you for the invitation."

"We're not all that formal," Mr. Thalberg said, stepping aside to usher them in. "Your

81

grandma is practically family, and that makes you the same."

Which made Adam uncomfortable, but he had nothing to say. He glanced toward where he knew the ruins of the barn were.

"The burned smell still makes the cattle uneasy," Mr. Thalberg said. "I'll never get used to the change myself. I've spent my life lookin' at that barn. But not much we can do to clean it up until winter is over."

Adam escorted his grandma inside, noticing the massive stone hearth that must have been part of the original ranch before they'd expanded the house. Bookcases were built along each side, a modern touch. The furniture was dark, the rugs and pillow in greens and reds. It seemed like a man's room but one a woman would be comfortable in.

And through an open doorway, he saw Brooke bending over to pull a pan out of the oven. And immediately, his mind was focused on the curve of her hips in her dark pants and the way her blue sweater clung. He made himself look away.

Mrs. Thalberg wheeled her way toward him, and when she reached up, he took her hand. "Thank you for the invitation, ma'am."

"Oh, please, Adam, the pleasure is all

ours," she said, her smile bright but a little tired at the edges.

"You didn't have to go to so much trouble for me."

"It was mostly for my mom," Nate Thalberg said, smiling as he reached to shake Adam's hand.

"Good."

"But we're grateful to you, too."

Adam nodded, even as he felt Nate studying him. That was smart. Never assume you knew what anyone was thinking — or how they'd changed over the years.

Josh came forward next and held out his hand. "Good to see you again, Adam."

Josh was a couple years younger than Nate, and when he wasn't snowboarding, he'd stuck to the cowboy sports of bronc busting and steer wrestling. It hadn't brought them together much, so by Josh's grin, he figured the youngest Thalberg had a pretty open opinion of him.

Mr. Thalberg clapped him on the back. "We felt it only right to thank you proper for your help the other day."

"That's good of you, sir. I'm sorry about your barn."

He shrugged. "Insurance will help. I'm just grateful no one was hurt. Not sure you should have risked yourself like that."

Brooke came into the room, setting a selection of cheese, crackers, and fruit on the coffee table.

Adam gestured toward her with his chin. "As if she weren't going to do it herself?"

Brooke frowned, Josh grinned, and Nate rolled his eyes.

"How about if we stuff ourselves with cheese and not talk about this anymore?" Brooke asked.

Adam couldn't agree more. He helped his grandma to sit in a rocker near the fireplace, where she'd be warm. She wasn't exactly skinny, thank goodness. The elder Mrs. Thalberg came out of the kitchen and joined them. But he couldn't help glancing again at Brooke near her mom, her face glowing, earrings dangling, the hair around her face bobby-pinned back. She was all made up for the evening, looking very different from the jeans-clad cowgirl of the other day.

He started to fix his grandma a small plate of appetizers when she took it out of his hands.

"Go talk to the young people, Adam," she said, shaking her head. "Rosemary and I will keep each other company."

He fixed a plate for himself and went to the bookshelves, turning his head to scan them. He couldn't miss how the younger Mrs. Thalberg nudged Brooke toward him. He felt an anticipation he hadn't felt in a long time. Her legs looked long and lean, and her breasts bounced gently as she moved toward him.

"Glad you could come," she said, handing him a cold bottle of beer.

He accepted it, surprised to feel the touch of her fingers. "Thanks for the invitation."

Brooke kept to herself that she hadn't even known about it until an hour ago. Her mom had acted all excited, like it was a big surprise, and maybe it had been. Grandma Thalberg and Mrs. Palmer must have cooked something up together, she thought, trying to hide a smile. That's what grandmas did when their offspring were unattached.

"How's your mom?" Adam asked.

Brooke glanced at her, able to tell that she was tired already. "It was hard to keep her out of the kitchen today even though the celebration was for her. She needs a lot more rest."

"When was she diagnosed?"

"She's known since Nate was a toddler. Her first husband left her when he found out."

Adam frowned, his eyes taking on the coldness of winter. "Scum."

"Yeah. I can't even imagine dealing with that kind of betrayal. But it had a good outcome. She met my dad, and they fell in love. Dad adopted Nate, and they had me, then Josh. I can't complain about that."

"I guess you can't," he said, his expression pleasant but not quite smiling. "Will she be in a wheelchair for long?"

"The symptoms come and go. She usually uses a cane, and I'm hoping she can get back to that again." Her voice trailed off, and she couldn't help glancing at her mom again. Taking a deep breath, she changed the subject. "I hear you got out of the boardinghouse at last."

When he focused on her, dark brown eyes intent, she felt again that rush of nervous anticipation. He was wearing jeans and a forest green crewneck sweater that looked really good on him. He'd left the wound on his cheek bare, its long, thin scab healing well.

He smiled faintly. "I'd forgotten how fast news travels around here."

She shrugged. "People talk about newcomers. It's even more interesting when someone they know comes home after a long time. So many people leave for the bigger towns and cities."

"If so, you'd never know it. Valentine looks

good, spruced up."

"A lot of that has to do with our grandmothers. They like to preserve historic buildings and keep out bad businesses — and by that I mean chain stores, nothing else."

He arched a brow.

"They're worried about some big department store coming in and forcing La Belle Femme or the Mystic Connection to close."

"I'm not sure I know what those stores are."

"A clothing store and a new age store. Your grandma is a major customer of the latter. Haven't you seen her room yet?"

"I replaced a cracked windowpane. She has so many crystals hanging in the sun, it's only a matter of time before another breeze blows them around."

"She's very motivated to keep those little businesses open — for the tourists, of course," she added innocently. "Surely you've seen the widows working over their papers."

"Heard them late into the night, too. The Valentine Valley Preservation Fund committee," he said, as if reciting something he'd had to memorize.

Brooke grinned, and his smile widened. She realized she hadn't seen that on his face, and that was probably a good thing, considering how flushed it made her. "There are other committee members, of course, but the widows do most of the work. My grandma handles the paperwork, the behind-the-scenes stuff about the grants themselves. Mrs. Ludlow is the legal eagle, sitting in on town-council meetings, press conferences, the investors' corporate board meetings."

"If you're wondering, Mrs. Ludlow is visiting her grandchildren tonight." He took a sip of his beer.

"I *was* wondering, thanks."

Adam glanced at Mrs. Palmer, who was chatting with Grandma Thalberg. "And my grandma? What's her role on the committee?"

Brooke eyed the old woman, hiding her interest in what Mrs. Palmer was up to regarding her grandson. "She's the public face, helping at grand openings, the one who deals with the businesses applying for grants. That's usually fun, but when she has to deliver bad news . . . well, she knows how to handle that, too."

Adam nodded. "She's always been good with people. Seems like a sedate hobby for elderly ladies."

Brooke's mouth dropped open. "Sedate? I

can't believe you're applying that adjective to our grandmas. Maybe Mrs. Ludlow, but that's about it."

"What don't I know?"

"Surely you remember when they chained themselves to the old house that had been a mining-town brothel?"

She saw the memory dawn in his eyes.

He shook his head. "How could I have forgotten?"

"Maybe you've been a bit busy these last few years," she said, her voice softening with compassion.

He ignored that. "Women's history," he said, snapping his fingers. "Now I remember. The story of Chinese immigrant prostitutes. They're not still doing that stuff."

Smiling, she tilted her head as she turned to walk away. "You go on thinking that, soldier."

He caught her arm, and she stopped in surprise, feeling the strength of him. Their eyes met, held, and he let her go.

"You can't leave me hanging," he insisted, then added, "About the widows."

Brooke glanced around the living room. Nate and Josh were talking to their dad, beers in their hands. Sandy had joined the widows near the appetizers and was accepting a glass of wine from her mother-in-law.

No one seemed to be paying any attention to them even though Adam had touched her. It was just on her arm, but she felt it reverberate right up her spine. It had been a while since she'd felt that with a man. The shared awareness made it feel like they were alone in the room.

"Tell me more about the widows' antics."

She sighed as if she were put out, but it was no hardship to keep talking to him. "You do know she dresses up like a pioneer woman on the Fourth of July."

His eyes lightened, even if he didn't grin. It made Brooke feel good to elicit some kind of amusement from him. She had a sense he didn't see life's humor much anymore.

"There's an old silver mine in the mountains up above us," she continued, "and they got it into their heads that we needed a mining museum, like they have in Leadville or Creede. On the first warm spring day, they held a picnic up there, with lemonade stands and cookies and stuff for sale, all to lure investors. Did I mention the first warm day of spring? Seems the snakes that now live in the mine decided to come out after the winter. In a group."

Adam chuckled. "No one was bitten, I hope."

"Nope, lots of running around, and the

state eventually declared it environmentally protected. Shall I tell you about the séance to drive away the ghosts in one of the B&Bs?"

He held up both hands. "Nope, spare me. The tarot cards are wacky enough. She keeps trying to give me a reading. To show me how it's done, she read them about you."

Brooke blinked up at him in surprise. "Me? Do I want to know my future?"

He paused, and their eyes met and held, until she forced a laugh.

He cleared his throat. "Nothing bad. You're strong and independent. To me, that means you like to get your own way."

"'Cause it's the right way," she answered sweetly.

Oh now she was flirting — in front of her whole family. That didn't feel right. They'd start asking questions she couldn't answer because even she didn't know what was going on.

"So you like strong women now, but maybe not in high school. You did break up with Monica Shaw all those years ago."

Brooke could almost see the wheels of memory turning in his head — how many women's faces did he have to go through to find the right one?

"Monica Shaw," he echoed, nodding. "She

91

still live here in town?"

"I just had dinner with her a couple nights ago. She remembers you."

"I bet. I was pretty preoccupied with . . . football back then."

Now it was her turn to chuckle. "You tell yourself that, soldier."

"You gonna keep calling me that?"

Though he spoke good-naturedly, something about the question intrigued Brooke. "I might. You have a problem with it?"

He paused, then shook his head.

She excused herself to return to the kitchen, where the prime rib awaited slicing on the stove. Again, she wondered if he was watching her, thinking about her, because she certainly couldn't forget about him.

Grandma Thalberg joined her and worked on the mashed potatoes. "Adam seems like a nice young man."

"Yep," Brooke said, concentrating on the task at hand — and hoping to dissuade her grandma.

"You two had a lot to talk about."

"We were talking about our grandmothers' exploits, nothing more. We're polite, Grandma, but we might as well be strangers."

"You don't have to be."

"We do. Let's just leave it at: It's nice to

talk to someone new." Nothing more complicated than that, she reminded herself. Something was going on inside her, a new question about her plans for her life, and she needed to focus on that, not a relationship.

The dining-room table was big and rough-hewn, a legacy from Brooke's great-grandparents. It seated the eight of them comfortably, and she found herself sitting opposite Adam, her brothers next to her, the widows next to him.

As they ate strawberry and walnut salad, the conversation ranged from the burned barn, to Thanksgiving, to the harsh early-winter conditions that might complicate calving season come January. Her dad, a veteran of Vietnam, brought up the current war, and though Adam did say he had sometimes visited the NATO base at Kandahar, he added little else. In fact, though he looked politely around the table as people spoke, he didn't contribute much. He made her quiet brother Josh look talkative. For a man who once boasted about his football receiving records, he had nothing to say about his service with the Marines. She found herself full of sympathy; she couldn't image what he'd experienced, what he'd seen.

Her father chewed a slice of prime rib, swallowed, then glanced at Adam speculatively. Brooke found herself tensing, even though she knew her father wasn't the sort to pry.

"So are you plannin' to stick around for a while, Adam?" Doug asked.

"A while," Adam responded.

Mrs. Palmer beamed. Brooke noticed that she hadn't touched much of her food except to push it around on her plate. She was a hearty woman, full of passion for life and people — and food. Sandy met Brooke's gaze curiously after noticing Mrs. Palmer's lack of appetite, and all Brooke could do was give a tiny shrug. She didn't know what was going on, but it certainly had something to do with Adam.

"You ride a horse, if I remember," Doug continued.

"I used to, sir," Adam answered.

Brooke looked between them, uncertainty making her frown. Where was her father going with this?

"If you're going to be here through the holidays, I could offer you some work as a ranch hand. I've been thinkin' about pullin' back some, maybe even be what they call semiretired." He grinned at Sandy, who looked surprised but not displeased.

Brooke shouldn't have been surprised that her dad was pulling back from his ranch duties to concentrate on her mom. Nate was in charge of the business side of the ranch and their investments, and she and Josh handled the day-to-day ranch operations. But semiretirement? She was bemused that he hadn't brought it up before now.

Her brothers each had their work passions — Nate for the business, Josh for his leather tooling. Hell, he'd begun to sell his products in town. The ranch was her love. She was a cowgirl, a barrel-racing champion, a rancher — like her dad. But was that all she was?

Adam exchanged a glance with his hopeful grandma. His face was impassive, and Brooke wondered what emotion he was feeling as he next met her gaze. And then she realized she'd be his boss, and all of these hot and achy feelings of desire that she'd just begun to acknowledge would have to be ignored. How would it look to her family if she proved herself so unprofessional as to chase after an employee? Doug was all business about the ranch. Distractions got cattle killed. Every head lost was money out of their pockets. She'd grown up with these words constantly ringing in her ears. And yes, things were better financially since Nate had begun expanding their investments, but

95

that didn't mean the day-to-day job was any easier.

"Sir, I appreciate the offer," Adam began at last, "but I can't mislead you. I've never worked on a ranch."

"But you ride a horse," Doug said. "You visited when your father hired on occasionally with us. Brooke and Josh can teach you what you need to know."

"Or," Mrs. Palmer began, "I could always use an assistant in my tarot business."

Brooke pressed her lips together to keep from laughing at her obvious ploy. She wondered what else was a ploy.

"Business?" Adam echoed dubiously.

"I didn't tell you about my plans, my dear boy? But of course, if you're workin' for Doug here, I'd understand."

"I don't think you have much of a choice, Adam," Josh said dryly. He glanced at Brooke. "Training a greenhorn. Think we can handle it?"

"We'll work him hard," Brooke said, finally looking at Adam and offering a polite smile. "But then, I'm sure he's used to hard work after being in the Marines. Now, if you'll excuse me, Grandma baked a cake that needs to be served."

As she rose, Doug slapped the table, his smile satisfied. "Then it's settled."

Though Brooke retreated to the kitchen, she could still hear his voice.

"We do work hard on the ranch, son," he said. "Ranchers don't take vacations, after all. But there was one time Sandy and I wanted to go down to Denver to see a show for the weekend —"

"And a Broncos game," Sandy interrupted dryly.

Brooke heard the chuckles as she picked up the chocolate-cake pan.

Doug continued, "So, Adam, we hired your dad to be here over the weekend to work alongside Nate, who was still in high school."

Brooke arrived back in the dining room in time to see Adam nod, but there was a tension in his shoulders that hadn't been there before. She knew his mom had been an alcoholic, but all she knew of his dad was that he seldom held down a job for long. Obviously taking care of his family wasn't that important to the man.

"So who'd like cake?" she asked from the buffet, where she began to cut slices and put them on small plates.

"Wait a sec, Cookie," her dad said.

With her back to the room, she closed her eyes and winced. She loved that nickname, but hearing it right after she found out she

97

was to be Adam's boss in what many would consider to be a man's world . . .

"So, Adam, your dad and Nate had a trailer-load of cattle and got a flat tire. While your dad was fixin' it" — Doug started to laugh, along with Nate — "the steers seemed to line up and" — he could barely get the words out now — "take turns pissin' on his head!"

It was a famous story in their house, and Mr. Desantis wasn't the only one it had ever happened to. But she was watching Adam's face, and although he forced a smile, it was obvious he had no good feelings for his dad.

Brooke set a plate of cake in front of Doug. "Okay, guys, shut up and eat."

Her dad was actually wiping away tears. But Sandy was watching her curiously, and Brooke went back to serving the cake.

"Okay, okay, I'm done," Doug said, his voice almost hoarse. "Adam, we'll feed you lunch every day, so no worries about that. You'll even have as much steak as you want for cookin' on your own. Get here at dawn tomorrow and work hard, that's all I ask. Come over to the business office first thing, and we'll fill out the papers."

"Yes, sir," Adam answered. "Thank you, sir." He started to eat his cake.

Brooke had to stop looking at him, had to

stop caring about his feelings. He might be in a world of hurt the next few days as he adjusted to life on the ranch, and it wasn't her job to sympathize. Her job was to get a good day's work out of him.

And stop thinking about him except as an employee.

CHAPTER FIVE

Adam got in a run before dawn, then arrived at the Silver Creek Ranch just as the sun crested the mountain peaks. He saw activity at the newer barn closest to the house, lights on inside against the gloom, horses out at pasture. It must be crowded in that barn, with the old one destroyed.

He found the ranch office easy enough, and Mr. Thalberg met him inside and offered coffee, muffins, then paperwork. Nate was already hunched over his computer, and he waved a good morning.

Adam was glad for the chance to work, to not twiddle his thumbs or elude another tarot reading. He loved his grandma, but too much togetherness had made him itch for some freedom. But he couldn't help gnawing over the fact that the Thalbergs surely hired him out of pity because his grandma had put in a word. He was a vet with no job at the moment, with little ranch

100

training. He would probably be a hindrance more than a help, but he was determined to work as hard as he could to prove to Mr. Thalberg that hiring him had been the right decision.

As for his attraction to Brooke, Adam was going to ignore it. The Marines had taught him honor, and that didn't include chasing after his employer's daughter — his boss.

Mr. Thalberg told him to head to the shed, the huge metal building where all the big trucks were stored, and that's where he found Brooke. She was outside the doors, standing on a ladder, head beneath the hood of a massive flatbed truck already stacked with bales of hay for feeding cattle. Some kind of crane was mounted on the flatbed, with what looked like a giant yellow fork attached, probably for picking up hay. Guess he wouldn't be riding a horse anytime soon, he thought, a little disappointed.

Brooke was layered up in cold-weather gear, from coveralls to at least a couple jackets, and a thick wool cap on her head. And then there were her high, all-weather boots. He looked at those, then dubiously down at his cowboy boots, already sinking into the winter mud.

That's when she chose to straighten out from beneath the hood, dipstick in her hand. She followed his gaze to his boots and shook her head.

"I thought you might not have the proper gear," she said. "There's an old pair of Nate's boots in the cab, along with some coveralls and a couple hats. That cowboy hat'll fly right off your head in this wind."

"Thanks." He looked past her. "You've already loaded the hay."

She shrugged. "I like to get an early start, especially since this retriever burns oil like crazy, and I have to keep checking it. And the stackyard would be a sinkhole of mud if I wait until the sun hits it. You'll figure everything out." Then she ducked back under the hood.

He studied her while she wasn't looking. He knew there might be men who thought what she did was unfeminine. He wasn't one of them. He could see the rope of her braid down her back and imagined what it looked like all spread out in chestnut waves around her shoulders.

Uncomfortably aroused, he opened the retriever's cab door and donned all his gear. By the time he was done, she slammed the hood down and walked swiftly back inside the shed. When she came back out, she got up inside the driver's side of the cab. He hopped up beside her.

"Where's Josh?" he asked.

"We drew straws," she said as she started up the engine. "I lost." She gave him a dubious glance. "I get to train the greenhorn today, and Josh gets to do some horse doctoring."

It was going to be an awkward day if her attitude was any indication. She started to drive down the bumpy dirt road, away from the buildings and out onto the rolling pastures enclosed with barbed-wire fence. He couldn't see grass for the white depth of the snow, and the wind swirled it across the windshield. Brooke drove like she could have done it with her eyes closed.

"We're feeding the yearlings first, farthest from the house," she said.

She stopped at a gate and just looked at him, one brown eyebrow lifted. After a second's incomprehension, he jumped out of the warm cab and into the cold, even more biting out there, where it came off the mountains with no trees or buildings to hinder it. He opened the gate, and after she drove through, he closed it again before getting back into the cab.

The several dozen yearlings looked like fully grown cattle but much smaller, steam rising as they breathed. Their heads came up when they heard the retriever coming, their lowing growing louder.

"They're expecting us," Adam said.

She nodded, pulled out a bungee cord, and affixed it to the steering wheel, then climbed out the door and onto the runner, leaving the cab driverless. The retriever was still moving, but now in a slow, wide circle.

She ducked her head back inside and gave a wicked grin. "You coming?"

Grinning back, Adam opened his door and clambered up onto the bed of the retriever. The bales took up almost all the space, and he could only hang on to the chains and pull himself on top of the double stack of bales. The ground looked fifty feet away.

"If you fall, make sure you push yourself away from the truck," she advised, still smiling. "Those are big wheels."

And he did fall, several times that morning as they ripped the string off bales of hay and together unrolled them so that they fell in a long, uneven line, startlingly green against the white snow. It was grueling work, each bale eight hundred pounds and frozen solid. The yearlings didn't seem to care as they chomped happily.

On the drive back to the truck shed for lunch, Adam glanced at Brooke with new respect. He might have been unloading cargo ships the last few months, but much of it was done by cranes and modern equipment. This was a more intense manual labor, and Brooke did it with ease.

She saw him looking at her. Her skin was red from the wind, tiny curls of escaped hair framing her face.

"What?" she demanded.

"You impress me."

She looked back at the road that only showed their previous tire tracks. "Surely you've seen some impressive women overseas."

"A few. You could handle yourself among them."

She didn't say anything, didn't look at him.

"You're blushing," he said.

Brooke felt the heat of that blush spreading across her cold cheeks. "I'm not." But she was. He sounded like he admired her strength. She didn't want to think that because it didn't lead anywhere she could go. "So tell me about the job you took after you were discharged. It must have needed strength because you handled yourself okay for a greenhorn. Or was it all that Marine training?"

"I worked in the shipyards on the coast of Louisiana."

"How did you get into that?" she asked with surprise.

"A buddy worked there before the Marines and went back. I had nothing better to do, so I went with him."

"You didn't want to come home to Valentine Valley?"

"Not really."

She glanced at him curiously, but his head was turned to look out the window. She could see his strong jaw, the silhouette of his throat and Adam's apple since he'd opened his coat. That alone was sexy, but she was able to overlook it. She turned back to the road. "But your grandma —"

"That's who I'm here for."

"And there was nothing else that made you want to come home?" She couldn't even imagine it — everything she loved was here, everything she knew. But there was a whole world out there, and maybe he liked the diversity.

Out of the corner of her eye, she saw him glance at her, brown eyes narrowed thoughtfully.

"Are you asking if there was a *woman* I wanted to come home for?"

She frowned, keeping her eyes on the road. "Of course not. After ten years?"

"I'm sure the grapevine would have been

buzzing if a girl had waited that long for *me*," he said with faint sarcasm. "There's a constant need around here to know everyone else's business. One of the reasons I didn't look forward to returning," he added.

She shrugged. "It can be good sometimes — or so I tell myself. I'm not a big fan of gossip even if I do share a juicy tidbit with my girlfriends now and then."

"Who are your girlfriends?"

Fair was fair — she was asking questions, so she had to answer some of his. "Emily, Nate's fiancée, and Monica, of course."

"Of course."

He must remember that she and Monica were best friends — maybe he even realized Monica told her everything — *everything* — he'd done while they were dating. Brooke hadn't appreciated his behavior at the time and had been indignant on behalf of her friend. But that was a long time ago.

"Monica's not married?" he asked.

"Nope. Surprised?"

"A little. I thought she was the marriage-and-baby type."

Brooke smiled. "I think she'd like to be but she hasn't met the right guy." She gave him a speculative glance. "Interested in picking up where you left off?"

"After ten years? No. I'm a different

person, and I imagine she is, too." He paused. "You don't seem to have changed all that much."

She stiffened, not sure if she should take offense. "I grew up knowing I'd be a rancher like my dad. And that's what I'm doing. I always knew what I wanted." But did she? a little voice inside her whispered. It was startling, even frightening, and she wondered where that voice was coming from. "I'm not sure it's flattering to be told I haven't changed."

"On the outside you've changed, maybe even in other ways I can't see."

Surprised, she looked at him again, and their gazes met and held for a long moment. Something hidden seemed to uncurl inside her, a sudden rising of desire that took her by surprise. He held himself so still, but it made her think of what strength he kept hidden, what emotions he restrained.

She glanced away. "Naw, I'm just me, Brooke the cowgirl. So did you quit your job to come here, or are you on vacation?"

"I quit. They'll take me back when I'm done here."

"Lucky you."

They rode the last ten minutes in silence, and Brooke told herself she was relieved. The wind had kicked up worse, and she was glad to be taking a break for lunch. When they parked the retriever, she wordlessly gestured with her head for Adam to follow her. They stopped in the barn because the dogs had gathered to greet her, and it was too cold to linger outside. They had three cow dogs besides Scout, who was usually with Nate. All three dogs greeted Adam with friendly reserve, and after a couple sniffs, with open enthusiasm, which he accepted affably.

"Let's get lunch," she said, not looking to see if he followed her. "My mom might have rung the bell while we were gone, but she also texted me."

"Modern ranch life," Adam said. "You don't have to feed me."

She glanced over her shoulder as she crossed the now-uneven, frozen yard, squinting against the wind. "It's part of the job, so be quiet and eat."

In the mudroom off the kitchen, they peeled their winter garments off in wet, dirty layers and walked in stocking feet into the kitchen. Her mom's wheelchair was pushed to the table, which spanned the many windows along one wall. Josh and Nate were already seated opposite each other, heads bent over their plates, although they did give twin waves while holding their hamburgers aloft. The ranch's part-timer, Lou Webster, seated across the table beside Nate, gave Adam an openly curious look. Lou had to be in his seventies, with bright blue eyes that peered out of wrinkly, leather skin, bald on top with a scraggle of white hair outlining the shining dome.

Sandy smiled. "Glad you two could join us. Not sure how everything tastes. Your dad insisted on cooking."

Brooke put a hand to her heart and pretended to reel. "I remember the last time . . ."

"Hey!" Doug called from behind the stove. "The recipe was wrong. In any case, it's hard to ruin hamburgers."

"I haven't tried the coleslaw yet," her mother said in a stage whisper. "But at least we have Grandma's leftover cake."

Brooke introduced Adam to Lou, who stood up and grinned as he looked Adam up and down.

"I was in Korea. Nice to meet a fellow vet."

Once again, no military talk for Adam, who simply shook Lou's hand, then sat down opposite him next to Josh. Brooke felt like scurrying all the way around the table instead of sitting next to Adam. She knew it would look stupid — it *was* stupid — so she sat next to Adam and helped herself to one of the burgers piled on a platter at the center of the table.

For a while, talk was concentrated on the ranch, from estimating how many of the cows were pregnant to which fence had to be repaired to Adam's first eventful day. Adam said little, eating as if he hadn't eaten in a long time, which amused Brooke. He'd done his best to act like feeding cattle was easy to learn, but she could tell by his appetite that he'd worked hard. He hadn't questioned her, hadn't tried to suggest doing something a different way, as some men might — hell, like *he* used to. Now he just listened to her instructions and followed her lead. He'd made mistakes — and his sore body would remind him of that by tomorrow — but he usually didn't make the same mistake twice.

Very different behavior than when he was in high school, she mused. She could remember when they'd been assigned to work in the same group on a history project. He hadn't wanted to put in the effort of leading, but he always had a comment on everyone else's work. He thought he was way too smart. Apparently, the Marines had taught him otherwise.

During a lull in the conversation, Brooke

111

said to Lou, "Too cold a day to expect any tourists, I bet."

Lou shrugged. "I'll hear the bell if anyone rings it, so yeah, I'll probably get other chores done."

Adam glanced sideways at her curiously, but since he had a burger at his mouth, she answered his unspoken question.

"We have a beautiful old sleigh from my great-grandparents' day. Dad had it fixed up last winter, and we started giving sleigh rides to tourists in the afternoons. We'll even do it in the evenings if someone makes a reservation. Otherwise, they just show up and ring the bell. There are signs in town advertising it at the community center, and we put some ads in the paper. But that's it."

"It's pretty successful," Josh said, after taking a swig of milk. "Nate's good with the advertising."

"The sleigh is actually a big draw," Nate added. "Josh did the leather tooling on the bench."

"It's beautiful," Brooke agreed. "And I take my turn driving occasionally when Lou can't. It's very relaxing, and I'm always surprised by the people I meet."

"She tries to pretend she's all into the solitary ranch life," Nate said in a teasing voice. "But sometimes I wonder."

Brooke laughed along with her family, but inside she felt a little jolt of surprise. What did he suspect?

Adam glanced at each of them dubiously. "Do you three get along this well all the time?"

"It gets a little sickenin'," Lou said, cutting himself a slice of cake from the pan.

"Oh, they've had their fights," Sandy added, leaning back in her wheelchair from her half-eaten plate.

Brooke frowned at how much of her mom's food had gone untouched. Her appetite didn't seem quite the same yet. She told herself her mom had just gotten home from the hospital, that the meds affected her appetite, so it was only natural . . .

And then she heard a guffaw, and realized all the men were laughing hard. She'd missed the punch line. Even Adam's eyes seemed bright with amusement although he hadn't given in to open laughter.

"What did I miss?" she asked, smiling.

Josh leaned forward to see around Adam. "Don't you remember how mad you were that Nate graduated from a pony to a horse?"

She rolled her eyes. "Not that story again. Let's not forget that I was, what, six?"

"Eight," Doug said, sitting down at the

other end of the table. "We caught you on Nate's horse about a mile from the house, clingin' to its mane, 'cause the saddle'd already fallen off."

"I wasn't clinging," she said patiently, then looked at Adam with a twinkle in her eye. "I was riding bareback, and my brothers still can't acknowledge my talent."

There was a collective groan from those same brothers, and though she grinned at them, she reached past Adam and smacked Josh on the shoulder. That pressed her up against Adam's arm, and she quickly pulled back, feeling suddenly flustered.

"Can you just let this stuff go?" she asked. "Now pass me the cake."

That evening, Adam fell sound asleep at the dinner table and awoke with a crick in his neck as his grandma was clearing the dishes.

He surged to his feet, feeling a dull ache settle in his lower back. "Let me help, Grandma."

She tsked. "I told you you wouldn't need to run for exercise."

"And I didn't listen to your warning. But it's a habit that's hard to break."

The other widows must have gone while he'd drifted off, and it was just the two of them at the kitchen sink. He wanted to lead her to a chair but already knew how badly that worked. She'd rather stand and tremble occasionally than admit to any weakness.

"So Brooke worked you hard," Grandma Palmer said, smiling.

"The ranch chores worked me hard," he amended. "They took it easy on me in the afternoon. I rode fence for several hours, looking for damage. A bull tried to escape, and I had to chase it back into the pasture."

"What happened?" she asked, staring up at him.

"I radioed Brooke, who brought the barbed wire for repairs. That was a challenge, considering the wind picked up."

"She wasn't with you?"

"She had me ride one way along the fence, and she went the other."

"She couldn't be avoiding *you*," Grandma teased.

Adam shrugged as he continued to wash and dry the dishes. There were moments during the day when they'd looked into each other's eyes, and it was as if things had shifted between them. She'd turned away faster than he did, so he was never sure. She was determined to be impartially in charge, and she *was* in charge. He wasn't about to forget that. She ordered him around a lot — which was what he expected of the girl he remembered — yet she still did her own half of the work with equal parts stubbornness and independence. She was obviously used to working alongside her brothers. Some of their quiet ways must have rubbed off on her, for she seemed to have lost the nervous need to chatter, which was a relief.

She was good at what she did, had all the knowledge and the skill to teach him anything he needed to know. Yet every time he glimpsed that strange softening in her eyes, he saw a mix of fierce cowgirl and vulnerable woman that was more appealing than he'd ever imagined.

But it was an appeal he had to resist. It was strange to have lunch with the Thalbergs and be so very conscious of not looking at their daughter more than he had to. And then she'd plopped herself down beside him, their shoulders occasionally brushing. He caught a tropical scent, like a Caribbean night, and wondered if it was perfume or shampoo. Just watching her peel off her winter clothes in the mudroom until she was down to tight jeans and an even tighter long-sleeve t-shirt was incredibly sexy. And then he'd noticed her earrings again, smaller for the workday, when he'd never cared about a woman's jewelry before. Was it because she was forbidden to him that he had to notice so much?

"Was it good to be back on a horse again?" Grandma asked.

Adam shook away thoughts of Brooke. "It's been a long time."

"You were good with your father's horse," she said quietly.

He nodded. "I know he sold it while I was gone. He had to, I'm sure," he added dryly.

She said nothing, and a look of such sadness crossed her face. She didn't often let him see those emotions.

"He'd lost his job," she began.

"Wait," he interrupted. "Grandma, I really don't want to talk about him. They're in my past."

"But don't you think —"

"No. I've spent ten years not thinking about them. And it was good."

She nodded and let it go. They worked silently, easy companions in the kitchen, and he tried not to imagine how it must feel to know the only daughter you raised had failed as a mother herself. He usually thought Grandma was too sensible to blame herself, but as she grew older, maybe it was more difficult. He had to make sure she knew how much he loved her, how much she'd been a mother to him more than his own. He told himself this wasn't because time was winding down for them — he couldn't face that, not after everything that had happened this year. He didn't want to be haunted by another ghost. Grandma would get better.

He played cards with the widows, amazed at how they had perfected the art of cheating on each other. Then he went to bed early, so Brooke wouldn't start work without him.

CHAPTER SIX

But it wasn't Brooke he worked with, it was Josh's turn to train the greenhorn. Once again, they fed cattle, and Adam felt a bit more in control. He never saw Brooke at all.

He did get a chance to spend time with Lou Webster that afternoon, familiarizing himself with the sleigh-ride business. Tourists parked in the main yard, by a sign marked SLEIGH RIDES. When they rang the bell, Lou came from the barn or truck shed, wherever he was working. After money was exchanged, the horses hitched, and the sleigh driven around, the guests were offered warm blankets. Adam climbed up and took the ride, memorizing the trails Lou followed, watching him handle the reins that guided the pair of horses, all while the old man instructed him in the art. When they left the open pasture and headed into a stand of trees beside the creek, he could hear snow plop from the branches, along with the cheerful jingle of the sleigh bells. Lou always had a story about the town when he was asked a question, and when the half-hour ride was over, their guests seemed genuinely pleased. After they'd gone, Lou spent another hour teaching him to handle the horses. By then, a young couple with a toddler arrived, and Adam did the driving, while Lou gave his advice.

On his third day at the ranch, he was with Brooke again in the retriever. This time a blizzard raged all around them, but hungry cattle still had to eat. Loading hay bales when you could barely see was a chore in and of itself. They perched on top of the bales on the bed of the truck, where the wind whipped by. This time Adam didn't fall, like he had the first day. He'd faced winter in the mountains of Afghanistan, and the heat of deserts — the weather was nothing new to him. But Brooke faced it every winter, year in and year out. He was too aware of her at his side as he mimicked her movements.

By the time they were finished at the second pasture, he couldn't feel the tips of his fingers anymore even though they were buried in gloves. Once they were both back in the cab, shivering as the heat began to seep up their legs, he tried to pull his gloves off, but his hands didn't want to work properly.

Brooke removed her hat, and he could see frost along her hairline where the hat hadn't reached.

She frowned at his hands. "Those are *your* gloves, not ours, aren't they? I was worried they weren't going to hold up to the job."

She scooted closer to him, tugged hard at his gloves until they came off, then clasped his hands together and put her own around them. The wind howled at the closed, frosted windows, the cattle bawled as they called each other to breakfast. But all those sounds faded as Adam found himself caught up in Brooke's warm touch.

She glanced up at him, and he didn't look away. Her dark lashes were damp from melting snow, her cheeks as pink as her lips from the cold. Her hazel eyes changed with her mood, and now they were almost green with an intensity that wrapped itself around him and wouldn't let go. His heart lurched. He didn't know if it was because he had forbidden himself from getting involved with her — or simply because it had been so long since he'd gone to bed with a woman.

And before he knew it, his mouth was on

hers. He didn't know who'd leaned forward first — and he didn't care. All his rational thought was swept away by lust. He tasted shared hunger, felt her mouth open to his. He met her tongue with his own, swirled around it, explored her mouth. He heard a groan of need and realized it was his.

Brooke was flooded by desire, hot and heavy in her veins. She wanted to fling herself against Adam and feel his body pressed to hers. She could imagine falling back on the bench, with him over her, all that masculinity overpowering with a delicious thrill.

She wanted to do all this on the front bench of retriever.

What was she doing?

She pushed against his chest, and they broke the kiss. They stared at each other, and his shock seemed as complete as hers.

"What was that?" she demanded in a hoarse whisper, then cleared her throat. "Why did you kiss me?"

"You kissed me," he whispered back.

He was looking at her mouth with hunger, and that felt so wonderful she almost fell into his arms again.

Wait, wait, she didn't want this to happen.

He seemed to come to his senses at the same time, and they both straightened back against their respective doors. How had rubbing his cold hands turned into such a hot kiss?

"I didn't intend to do that," he said at last.

"Me neither. And I won't be doing it again."

"No."

He spoke so quickly she winced. "Thanks," she said dryly.

He rubbed a hand down his face. "You know that's not how I meant it. This is a bad idea. We work together."

"I know. Forget it happened."

"I will."

They didn't look at each other the whole way back. Brooke's face felt hot with embarrassment — but the memories wouldn't stop. She could still taste him, still smell the soap of his morning shower. And he'd moaned, as if kissing her had been his wildest fantasy.

She realized that Adam had returned to Valentine, all silent and wounded and nothing like the brash, overconfident kid he'd once been. She'd noticed everything about him, from his uncomplaining hard work to the way he'd dismounted from his horse stiffly. She remembered the slight limp he'd had after helping rescue the horses. She wanted to know why — she wanted to know everything about him.

She'd been told lust could hit you right between the eyes, but hadn't believed it — Monica would say the magic of Valentine Valley finally had her in its grip. Not that she intended to find out what her friend would *really* say. She wasn't going to tell anyone about this madness. Surely she was reacting to the fact that she hadn't dated anyone recently, and Adam was close at hand, all masculine and soldierly.

When they were done feeding cattle and had returned to the ranch, Brooke was relieved when her father sent Adam home early because of the storm. She waved a good-bye without meeting his eyes, then went in to take a hot shower. She was going to curl up under a blanket in front of the fire and read a good book.

And not think about Adam.

But it was hard to relax when everyone else was trapped in the house, too. Even Nate didn't return to his cabin that evening. She wistfully wondered what it would be like to live alone — then grew angry with herself, especially when she was able to help her mom with dinner. They spent the hour laughing over the latest ranching story and planning the holiday crafts they'd make together. Brooke didn't need to be reminded how lucky she was.

When Adam arrived back at the boarding-house, he saw several cars parked out front, snow piling up on them in accumulating layers, depending on when they'd arrived. He let himself in the back door. Not wanting to disturb whatever committee meeting the widows were holding, he made himself a couple sandwiches and ate them at the kitchen table, munching on celery sticks at the same time. Someone had left a platter of brownies on the table, and he helped himself. If these were from the Sugar and Spice Bakery — and the widows were known to bring home goodies — then he knew why the place already had such a great reputation in just a couple months.

When no one came into the kitchen, curiosity finally got the better of him, and he opened the swinging door into the dining room. Now he could hear the murmur of voices, but he walked softly, peering into the front parlor without speaking. He saw two middle-aged women sitting opposite one another, magazines in their laps. But they weren't reading; they were discussing someone's new baby. Beyond them, he could see that the French door to the library was closed. Through the glass he noticed a man's back.

And then the man stood up, and Adam heard raised voices. The two women stopped talking and glanced uneasily at the library door. Frowning, Adam stepped into the parlor, but before he could go farther, Grandma Palmer opened the door and marched out, her cane thumping on the polished wood floor, showing more vigor than Adam had yet seen.

"Follow me, Sylvester," she called to the man behind her.

"Now, Renee," he began in a booming, lecturing tone, then came up short, frowning when he saw Adam.

The man was somewhere in his sixties, with curly gray hair and glasses perched on a sizable nose. Though he was overweight, he dressed well in a suit and trench coat, which seemed out of place in Valentine Valley.

The two middle-aged ladies also looked up at Adam, but with interest and anticipation.

"Is something wrong, Grandma?" Adam asked in a calm voice.

She beamed at him. "Adam, you're home early! How was your day, you dear boy?"

He gestured absently toward the window. "Stormy. But I haven't met your friend."

He looked pointedly at Sylvester, who lifted his chin defensively, then stuck out his hand. "Sylvester Galimi," he said, "owner of the True Grits Diner."

Adam shook his hand. "Adam Desantis."

"Staff Sergeant Adam Desantis," Grandma Palmer said with pride.

"Not anymore, Grandma," he said without breaking eye contact. "Is there something I can help you with, Mr. Galimi?"

"Your grandmother and I have a disagreement."

Adam's glance took in the other two women. "And you all came to discuss it together?"

"Oh, no, Cathy and Gloria are here to have their cards read. I told you about my little once-a-week business." She grinned at the two women. "Adam, Cathy Fletcher is the church secretary at St. John's and she used to be best friends with Emily's late mom. Gloria Valik is Monica's aunt and Nate's secretary. Have you two met yet?"

Adam nodded politely at the women, who looked him over without bothering to hide their interest.

"No, we haven't met," Gloria said. She had a darker complexion than her niece and the same wide, cheerful smile. "I work about nine to three, and this hardworking cowboy is there before me and long after. Guess I'll have to skip bringing my own lunch and eat with you, Adam, so we can get to know each other."

He nodded again, but his focus was still on Sylvester, who must have checked his watch twice while Gloria was speaking.

"Mr. Galimi, what's your disagreement with my grandmother?" Adam asked. "Did the cards say something you didn't want to hear?"

Smiling, both Cathy and Gloria turned to Sylvester with interest.

The man cleared his throat. "I did not come for this mystical nonsense."

Gloria gave him a sniff of disdain.

"Now, Sylvester," Grandma Palmer said, "there's no call to go offendin' me or my friends. Adam, Sylvester here is upset that the preservation-fund committee is supportin' a new, woman-owned business that's thinkin' of openin' a store in town. We've offered them a grant if they renovate a buildin' that's seen some hard times."

Adam narrowed his eyes. "And why would this upset you, Mr. Galimi, enough that you'd raise your voice to my grandmother?"

Grandma Palmer waved both hands in front of her, then caught her cane before it could fall. "That's just his way. You pay him no mind, Adam."

"There's just no call for that . . . sort of business," Sylvester blustered. "I wanted her to know that I'm not the only businessman who will stand against the committee at the next town-council meeting."

Though he didn't want to get involved, Adam couldn't help asking, "What sort of business?"

"Smut!" Sylvester erupted with indignation. "That's the sort of business your grandma is condoning!"

Grandma Palmer's once-booming laugh was now a weak chuckle. "Oh, Sylvester, have you even bothered to look at Leather and Lace's website? They sell pretty lingerie, and a town called Valentine Valley surely needs honeymoon clothes."

Leather and Lace? Adam thought, suddenly finding himself wanting to grin. But those muscles were still stiff with disuse. "That's an interesting name for a store."

"Interesting?" Sylvester barked. "Guess you haven't looked at the website either."

"My daughter has visited their store in San Francisco," Cathy Fletcher chimed in. "She brought me a lovely nightgown."

"There's more than nightgowns," Sylvester insisted, fists on his hips. "There are things our children shouldn't see when they walk past a storefront. You do realize what 'leather' means in the title!"

"I'm sure they won't put anythin' objectionable in the window, Sylvester," Grandma Palmer said patiently.

"You bet they won't because I'm going to make sure the town council knows that citizens object to this sort of business. They won't get a permit, I can guarantee you that."

He reached for his hat on the coffee table and put it on with emphasis. Adam thought the old-fashioned brimmed hat would go sailing away the moment the man stepped out the door. Sylvester closed it hard behind him, and when he was gone, the three women chuckled.

"That Sylvester," Gloria said, shaking her head. "I think it all goes back to Walmart. He's worried what they'll think of a 'smut' store in Valentine. He's always writing the company, trying to lure them to open a store here. He thinks it'll bring more customers to his diner, but he doesn't seem to care that it'll take customers away from places like Hal's Hardware or the Back in Time Portrait Studio. When I need something at Walmart, I have no problem driving to Glenwood Springs."

Cathy nodded.

Grandma Palmer's smile faded a bit. "But he does have a voice, and the mayor listens to him."

"That's because she's his sister." Cathy turned to Adam and spoke in a confidential tone. "But the mayor is more reasonable than her brother."

Grandma clapped her hands together. "I'm sorry for the interruption, girls." She turned to Adam. "You go on and eat lunch, my dear boy. The ladies and I still have some 'mystical nonsense' to attend to. If you have any more questions about Leather and Lace, you can always ask Brooke."

"Brooke?" He gazed at her in surprise, noticing that the other two ladies' eyes sharpened with interest. He had a sudden flash of memory, Brooke's arms entwined about him, their hungry mouths joined.

"She knows all about the store," Grandma was saying. "The owner first tried to buy Emily's buildin', but she decided to keep it and open the bakery. Speakin' of which, I brought some brownies home after I worked this mornin'."

"You went out in this?" he asked. He couldn't help remembering the sixties convertible she used to drive, not caring what it did to her hair. He didn't often see her drive through the trailer park because his mother would have a fit, but Grandma always made sure to look for him when he wandered the town. She let him jump right over the door to get in, which made him feel like a TV star. She'd buy him a snack and listen to him rattle on. He'd once been able to tell her anything — but not anymore. He couldn't hurt her like that.

"I've lived here my whole life, Adam," she said, smiling. "Rosemary drove the old station wagon, and we were very careful. But thanks for carin'. Now, are you sure you don't want to stay and have your cards read?" she asked hopefully.

"No, thanks, Grandma," he said a bit too quickly.

They all chuckled as he left. He didn't bother to tell her he'd already eaten. She might assign him a new chore, and he wasn't feeling in the mood. But as he returned to his room off the kitchen after helping himself to another brownie, he thought again about Sylvester Galimi's threats and hoped the man's behavior didn't encourage the widows to do something crazy.

The next day, Saturday, dawned with a perfect sky as blue as a robin's egg, but there were no days off when hungry cattle had to be fed. Adam wasn't surprised when he spent the morning balancing on hay bales on the back of the retriever alongside Josh rather than Brooke. She obviously hadn't been anxious to see him after their kiss, and he felt a little relieved.

And disappointed, too.

Lunch was uneventful, and Brooke puttered around the kitchen helping her mom with spaghetti and meatballs rather than sit at the big table anywhere near Adam. At one point, Nate gave her a confused frown, but Adam dug into his meal and ignored whatever her reaction had been.

Once again, he rode fence for the afternoon, glad to feel the peacefulness of a solitary ride with an amiable horse, Dusty, beneath him. On each side of the valley, mountains towered above him, looking as old as God and just as peaceful. He needed the view after a tired morning spent trying to get over his lack of sleep. For the first time since he'd come back to Valentine, the old nightmares of the war had invaded his dreams. At one point, he thought he came awake with a shout and could only hope he hadn't disturbed Grandma Palmer, who needed her rest. But no one had come to see what was the matter, and he was able to sink back into a sleep, where the enemy continued to hunt him.

In broad daylight, the dreams seemed distant and unreal, almost like the fleeting glimpse he had of Lou Webster driving the old-fashioned sleigh. It was something from another time and place.

He inhaled the cold, crisp air, smiled as Dusty tried to pick his way delicately through snowdrifts. Even one of the barn dogs had followed them, trailing along behind and exploring. Adam wasn't sure why the brindle-colored mutt, Ranger, seemed so interested in him, but he was.

And then suddenly a loud bang echoed between the mountains, and the sound made him flinch like he was still in the Afghani mountains. It took all his willpower not to fling himself from the saddle for cover. He shielded his eyes against the sun, and in the distance, he saw someone riding an ATV across the pasture rather than the road. The rider seemed to head right toward several dozen head of cattle that were minding their own business, snuffling through the snow. Adam stiffened, knowing none of the Thalbergs would have done such a stupid thing. He urged his horse faster along the fence, looking for a gate inside.

The motor cut out suddenly with another bang, and Adam realized that the rider had run into a fence post, tilting the ATV to an awkward angle. He could hear the guy attempting to restart the engine, even as Adam found a gate, pulling it open and closed without needing to dismount. He urged his horse into a gallop across the pasture, and at last the guy looked up.

It was only a teenage boy, and his frightened expression made Adam remember every greenie out of boot camp getting shot at for the first time. The kid gaped at Adam before flinging himself off the ATV and starting to run. By this time, the cattle were lowing loudly, stamping their hooves, starting to move toward the kid, who wasn't going to escape in time. Ranger went running toward the cattle, barking, and Adam followed to distract the dangerous animals. By the time they got the herd turned in another direction, the kid had hopped the fence and was long gone, leaving his ATV behind.

But it wasn't his ATV. When Adam inspected it as he pulled it away from the fence post, he recognized it as one he'd seen in the Thalberg truck shed. The kid had either meant to steal it, or had been using it for a joyride. And from the direction the kid had been driving, he suspected the latter. After all, in such a small town, how could a kid hide an ATV?

Adam slammed his body into the fence post to straighten it as much as possible before it could be replaced. He remembered his brief look into the kid's scared face. And suddenly he was that age again, doing stupid things because no one noticed him unless he did. His parents didn't care what he did, and if Grandma Palmer tried to get involved, she was shut out of his life for months. The worst he'd felt as a kid had been after he'd got caught joyriding, knowing he'd disappointed her. He might have gone into juvie except for Coach McKee's standing up for him. He'd been given a second chance.

Adam couldn't turn the kid in. Hopefully, almost getting caught taught him a lesson. He got the ATV started, and Dusty, used to the loud engine, amiably allowed himself to be led off to the side, while Adam drove slowly. He returned the ATV, with the busy Thalbergs not even noticing.

CHAPTER SEVEN

Brooke glanced at the list Nate had given her for supplies at the feed store. It was late afternoon, and the sun was already hovering just above the mountains, about to disappear for the day. She hadn't seen Adam yet, and running errands was giving her an excuse to get away before she did.

They were forgetting about the kiss — they'd agreed. It had been a momentary foolishness between two people who weren't dating anybody and just felt . . . an urge. Hell, he must have gotten his kicks with women once he got out of the Marines, and now being on his own back in Valentine was surely some kind of . . . celibacy he wasn't used to.

Josh was entering the office just as she was leaving. "I saw Adam by the truck shed," he said. "Take him with you. He could use some more cold-weather clothes. Did you see those gloves he has?"

"He didn't get new ones yet?" She frowned. "I told him yesterday . . ." She trailed off, shaking her head.

Nate glanced at her. "You sound like his mother."

She put her cowboy hat on her head and struck a pose. "I don't look like his mother."

Nate chuckled.

And then she realized what she'd agreed to. More time with Adam when they weren't working. When she could look at him and think sexy thoughts she had no business thinking.

She found him in the barn, rather than the truck shed, where he was unsaddling Dusty. Ranger, his new shadow, sat nearby, watching him with quiet adoration.

"So I hear you didn't get new gloves," she said.

Adam glanced up at her, giving Dusty a pat. The horse galloped back out to the corral to join his friends. Brooke regretted looking Adam in the eyes as she couldn't seem to break away. They studied each other for too long, until her skin was so hot it didn't feel like her own.

"It's a nice day today, so my old gloves are fine," he said. "I didn't get around to shopping during the blizzard."

"Then come on into town. I'm heading

for the feed store. You need more gear, and you can help me carry stuff."

He nodded. "Let me wash up."

"Meet me at my dad's going-to-town pickup."

One side of his mouth curled up. " 'Going-to-town pickup'?"

"It's just what it sounds like. The shiny new pickup doesn't get used for hauling manure like the others. He treats it with care. One of these days, I'm sure it'll be your job to wash it down."

"I see. Amazing the jobs there are on a ranch."

"You have no idea," she said, giving him a cheerful smile. "If my mom's flowers need weeding, that could be your job, too."

"Good thing it's winter." He found his Stetson and set it on his head. "I'll be back."

She couldn't help but watch him as he walked across the yard toward the office. His shoulders were broad beneath the heavy Carhartt jacket, but he'd removed his coveralls, so she could see his slim hips. He moved like a man confident in his body, a man who'd been well trained. She gave a little shiver.

She had the pickup warmed up in the yard by the time Adam returned. He got into the passenger seat uncomplaining, when she knew some men might not want a woman driving them around. He was pretty confident about himself, so that hadn't changed. She started down the winding dirt road, now covered in packed snow and gleaming with the occasional sheen of ice.

They were silent for the first couple minutes, but Brooke couldn't let tension build. They'd be together for days or weeks — who knew how long he was staying?

They passed the road leading down to the boardinghouse and her brother's cabin beyond. "So how's your grandma?" she asked, still curious about what the widow was up to.

"Except for being frailer than she used to be, she doesn't seem too sick, which I'm grateful for. She needs to eat more."

"I noticed that the other night. Her appetite used to be legendary." She wasn't about to tell Adam she had some suspicions. It was up to Mrs. Palmer.

He didn't make any effort to continue the conversation. She wasn't used to quiet men in her family, and certainly hadn't dated any. She drove across the bridge over Silver Creek, where the road became First Street. Past Main, she turned down Grace Street.

"I always like how the streets going this way were named after women," she said, then could have groaned at the inane conversation. In for a penny . . . "Mabel, Bessie, Nellie. It reminds me of the town's past."

"Uh-huh," he said, eyeing her.

There was a sparkle of amusement in his eyes that she didn't appreciate.

"Brooke —"

"We're here," she said, glad how close everything was in town. She practically jumped out of the pickup once she'd parked in the lot.

Adam glanced across the street at a large Queen Anne home, complete with a turret, that had been turned into a business. "The Mystic Connection. I've heard about it. So that's where Grandma got the crystals hanging in her windows."

"The tourists love it. Your grandma's a regular customer."

Adam gestured with his chin at the feed store. "Bet the ranchers love it, too."

Her lips twitched, but she wasn't going to smile. "Oh, you bet."

Inside, more than one old guy did a double take on seeing her with Adam, and soon two ranchers, Deke Hutcheson and Francis Osborne, friends of her dad and Nate, were giving Adam the third degree. She stayed out of it, her turn to be amused at his discomfort. He was at last free to find

141

some new coveralls and gloves, and a pair of winter boots that fit him better.

She could tell Adam was glad to leave when they made their escape. It was as if he didn't like crowds anymore. He'd always been with a group when they were young, whether with the bad kids before he'd been caught joyriding, or the football team, once he'd found true purpose in competition. He'd seemed to avoid his own solitary thoughts, and now that's all he wanted. It was almost . . . sad. Surely there was a middle ground for him.

They both carried bags out to the truck, then she opened the back end and they helped the stock boy load the bed with stuffed sacks. She and Adam got back in the cab and looked at each other. They'd go back home and keep working side by side. And suddenly, she needed a break.

"I need a donut," she said.

Main Street had yet to be crowded with the cars of people going to dinner, so she was able to find a parking spot near the Sugar and Spice.

"I know you don't want to see anybody," she added, "so you can wait in the truck if you want. I won't be long, and I'll even bring you something."

She left the engine on for warmth and

jumped out, relieved when he didn't argue or follow her, just crossed his arms over his chest and looked out at the Hotel Colorado. He'd turned into such a quiet loner, not her type at all, she told herself. She wanted a man with plenty to say, so she didn't feel like the one monopolizing every conversation. Not that she wanted that kind of man right now, of course.

She opened the glass door, a little bell tinkled, and she was hit by a wall of warmth and the smell of cinnamon that made her drool. A glass display case ran the length of the room on the left, where a restaurant bar had once stood. To the right, little clusters of tables and chairs populated the coffee corner. Though there were already Christmas lights circling the front plate-glass windows where cakes were displayed, inside, the bakery was decorated for Thanksgiving, with overflowing cornucopias along the top of the display case and bound corn stalks and pumpkins in the corners. In the center of each table, little Pilgrims and Indians stood side by side.

Nate and Emily had fallen in love doing the renovations of this place, Brooke thought wistfully.

The bell brought Emily bustling in from the kitchen. She gave a wide grin and a

143

wave, and Brooke chuckled at the flour-dusted apron she wore, with the logo, ASK US WHY WE'RE SUGAR AND SPICE. The first time she saw her grandma wearing it, she'd almost busted a gut laughing.

"Brooke!" Emily called in delight, drying her hands on a towel. She tossed it onto the back of a chair. "You need something in particular?"

She smiled, trying to settle her own tension. "I need a hit of sugar. A glazed donut should do the trick."

Emily laughed and went behind the counter to fetch one, and when she returned, she set a mug of hot chocolate down in front of Brooke, too. "There you go. Chocolate and donuts — we all need it sometimes."

Brooke sipped the drink slowly, then took a bite of the donut and closed her eyes. "Heaven."

The bell over the door jingled, and Monica entered, shaking the snow off her coat and tossing it over a chair.

"I saw your dad's pickup," Monica said. "Mrs. Wilcox has everything under control next door, so here I am." She bumped shoulders good-naturedly with Brooke as she sat down. "Ooh, a donut looks good."

Emily happily obliged.

"I noticed your truck running," Monica said. "You in a hurry?"

Brooke shook her head. "Keeping it warm for Adam."

Emily came back at that moment, and her gaze shot toward the door. "He's out there?"

"Yep," Brooke said, then took another bite of the donut. "He's come back far more unsociable than he used to be."

"Brooke!" Emily scolded, and marched to the door, flinging it open and gesturing for Adam to come in.

"What did I do?" Brooke asked Monica, feigning astonishment.

Adam ambled inside, the keys jingling in his hand as he took off his cowboy hat. He inhaled the delicious scents just as Brooke had done, then stood there, all decked out in cowboy-masculine in the middle of the feminine bakery.

"I was going to bring you a donut," Brooke reminded him.

"I know." He gave Emily a small smile. "But I really enjoy your brownies."

She laughed aloud, held up a finger, and disappeared behind the counter.

"Adam Desantis," Monica breathed quietly, then shook her head as if in disbelief as she eyed him up and down.

To Brooke's surprise, she felt a little

uneasy as Monica ogled the all-grown-up man.

Adam glanced at their table, and then his smile grew wider. "Monica Shaw."

"You look fine, Adam," she said, standing up.

"You do, too."

Brooke couldn't read his expression though he did look a bit surprised when Monica kissed him on the cheek. He sat down at their table, and when Emily returned with his brownie and more hot chocolate, Monica tsked.

"I can't believe you were going to sit out in that truck and not say hi."

Brooke eyed him, curious at his response. She hadn't asked him to come in, of course, and she felt a bit guilty.

He swallowed a piece of brownie even as he shrugged. "It's strange to live here again after all this time. I visited my grandma a couple times, and flew her to visit me, but being here every day . . . not sure what to expect anymore."

"You have friends, you know," Monica said.

He arched a brow. "Really? I don't need to look in on some of those guys I used to know."

146

"You changed for the better, why not them?"

"True."

"So you're a better man?" Brooke found herself joining in the teasing. "Still sounds pretty arrogant. Remember when you thought you could win the senior class presidency without a campaign?"

He glanced at her, his chocolate brown eyes warm with amusement. "I overestimated my appeal. Though I've always hoped I've changed for the better, I had a far longer way to go. Not saying I'm all that great even now."

"Humble," Monica mused slyly. "That's different."

He took another bite of his brownie. "I saw you come from next door, then I looked at the name. Congratulations on having your own business."

Monica grinned. "Thanks. It was a dream come true. How about you? What are you up to, now that you're a free man?"

He explained about being a longshoreman in Louisiana.

"Why didn't you stay in the Marines?" Monica continued. "Your grandma bragged all over town about your quick promotions."

He took a sip of hot chocolate so slowly that Brooke knew he was formulating a response. He hadn't really answered when she'd asked this same question a few days ago. And then it occurred to her that maybe he wasn't gallivanting about town because he didn't *want* to answer this. She couldn't imagine how a soldier began to talk about the horrible things he'd seen in war. And why should he tell them? They all might as well be strangers, for how little they'd kept up over ten years.

Softhearted Emily looked at him with so much compassion that Brooke almost nudged her under the table. A guy like Adam didn't want that from a woman — surely it felt too much like pity.

"It's hard to explain," he said slowly, his voice deep and impassive. "I just didn't feel a part of the Corps anymore."

Brooke looked at the last bit of her donut and found she couldn't eat it. She didn't want to think about the things he'd had to do, what he'd seen. And though he tried to keep every emotion from his voice, she thought he seemed . . . sad. Didn't Marines always consider themselves brothers for life?

Before anyone could make it worse, Brooke gave a determined smile. "So when did you become the silent type, keeping everything inside?"

The edge of his lip curled up in that little

way that she found so attractive.

"I finally learned not to talk when I had nothing to say."

"About time," she answered.

He met her gaze in almost a challenging way as if they were taunting each other. She swallowed and lifted her chin a bit, accepting the challenge.

He got to his feet. "Time to go, boss." He tossed some bills on the table, and kept them there even when Emily protested.

As Brooke rose, Monica smirked. "Boss. Now that's funny about our dear Brooke."

"I *am* his boss," Brooke pointed out, "and so are my brothers and my dad — poor Adam has lots of bosses."

As they reached the door, Monica called, "Oh, wait, Brooke, there's something I forgot to tell you." Then she noticeably paused.

Brooke tossed the keys back to Adam. "I'll be right there."

When he'd gone outside, Brooke turned back to her in curiosity. "What didn't you want to say in front of Adam?"

Emily laughed as she cleared the table. "You know her too well."

"Well," Monica said, "I wasn't certain you wanted your 'employee' " — she air-quoted the word — "here for this discussion. I thought I sensed enough sparks that I wondered if you'd changed your mind about dating right now."

"No sparks, no flame," Brooke said firmly. "I work with him, that's all. You're welcome to ask him out yourself."

"Oh, no, I don't relive the past, trust me."

"Whatever you'd like," Brooke said, her hand on the doorknob.

"I still think you should change your mind about dating. My brother knows this great guy —"

"Monica, you are a wonderful friend, but now's not the right time. Dating might be fun, but it could lead to a relationship, and that's just too much for me right now with my mom home from the hospital, the holidays, then calving season. Let's talk again in . . . March. Thanks for the donut, Em."

Monica lowered her eyebrows with speculation, but she didn't call Brooke back as she left the bakery.

As she walked across the snowy sidewalk, she winced inside. Were her thoughts about Adam that transparent? How embarrassing! She didn't even want to admit to herself — let alone her best friends — that she couldn't stop thinking about the man.

When she climbed up into the cab, she was relieved when Adam didn't ask what

Monica had wanted.

But as they drove down Main Street, he said, "My grandma says I'm supposed to ask you about Leather and Lace."

She gave a little cough. "Pardon me?"

"The store?" Once again, he had the faintest hint of amusement in his eyes. "She said it's a lingerie store trying to open here. And there's some backlash against it."

She frowned. "Really? I hadn't heard that."

He told her about Sylvester Galimi's visit to the Widows' Boardinghouse.

"Wow, a threat," Brooke mused, as she turned onto First and headed toward the bridge. "Not a physical threat. That wouldn't be Sylvester's style."

He gave that faint smile that she found so captivating, the one that seemed boyish and controlled and secretive all at the same time.

"He knew he couldn't push my grandma too far — or any of the widows."

"We all know how they respond to threats," she mused.

"That's what I'm afraid of. I thought I'd let you know in case your grandma displays unusual . . . symptoms."

"Hmm." She gripped the steering wheel, trying to consider what that might be.

"The widows probably don't know what

the store's really about," he said.

"Are you kidding? They know *exactly* what it's about. I was there when they went through every screen of the catalogue online. I covered my eyes when both our grandmas exclaimed with delight over a bustier. I could swear I saw Mrs. Ludlow put a teddy in her cart, but I didn't look too closely."

"Really?" he countered, obviously surprised. "A teddy? Why did you have to give me an image of what nice little old ladies might wear under their clothes?"

Brooke grinned.

"And how bad is it, that Galimi should be so upset?"

"There's a little . . . leather involved," she said, suddenly feeling hot and uncomfortable. She didn't want to talk about this stuff with a man she had no business kissing, but it seemed . . . exciting. She told herself to cut it out. "Some of the stuff might not be appropriate for window display, but Em has been to their San Francisco store, and she assures me their windows are tasteful and beautiful."

"So you're for it."

He was eyeing her too closely, and she was feeling way too cocky. "Of course. Every cowgirl needs pretty underwear to feel like

152

a woman under her muddy clothes."

In a low voice, he said, "You felt like a woman yesterday."

She swallowed hard, swamped by memories of the passionate kiss they'd exchanged in another truck cab. "Hey, that's crossing a line."

He straightened. "You're right. Sorry."

"Look, we don't have a relationship beyond work. Let's just pretend we're in high school again. You certainly didn't want anything to do with me then, so let's recapture those feelings."

"What are you talking about? The only thing I remember us clashing over was your insistence that I needed help with my homework. I was pretty offended."

"Offended? Why? Because I thought you were smart and you could do more and I wanted to help?"

"Whoa, wait a minute. You may have thought you were being helpful, but I smelled pity, and I didn't appreciate it. I'm getting enough of that from our grandmas, who must have schemed to get me this job."

"Pity?" she echoed, surprised. "I never pitied you, not even in high school. I saw potential, and thought you needed help finding it. You didn't take help from me, so obviously you found it from someone else.

Whoever it was, I'm glad. You've made your grandma so proud. She hardly pities you — unless it was because you were sweetly hanging around the boardinghouse to be with her, and she figured you must be going crazy. That's not pity. She was helping you."

He didn't speak for a moment. " 'Sweetly'?" he said, his voice once again laced with faint amusement.

She concentrated on driving across the snowy road winding its way between pastures toward the ranch. "Look, my family isn't pitying you either."

He ignored her insistence. "Your problem is that you're bossy and think you know everything, including how other people feel. That hasn't changed."

She pulled into the yard in front of the ranch house, the sun long gone, the last grayness of twilight still hovering about. She threw the pickup into park and turned to face him across the console between the two seats. "But I *am* your boss, and I *do* know everything."

Or so she kept telling herself because she wanted to fling herself across the console and kiss him. He infuriated her, he aroused her. All these emotions roiled around inside her until she could barely remember her promises to herself.

He put a hand on the console, leaning toward her, a light in his eyes that practically burned her, it was so smoldering.

And then she caught sight of movement on the front porch and realized someone was there. Good God, she'd almost been seen kissing him!

CHAPTER EIGHT

Adam's usual caution was deserting him where Brooke was concerned. Sparring with her was turning him on, overwhelming his normal good sense. It reminded him a bit of the battlefield, where you had to rely on your intuition but take risks. He leaned toward her, knew she wanted him to — then she gaped as she stared past him out the windshield.

"Someone's there," she hissed.

He saw the panic in her face and knew she worried about being seen doing something inappropriate with him, as if she feared being thought unworthy at her job. It softened something inside of him.

Both of them opened their doors and jumped to the ground. A shot of pain went up his thigh, and he silently cursed himself for forgetting to take it easy.

"Hi, Brooke, Adam!" Mrs. Thalberg called.

He gave a short wave.

"Hey, Mom," Brooke said too loudly. "Just got back from picking up the supplies."

"Good, good. I'm feeling well enough that I cooked supper tonight. Adam, care to join us?"

"Thank you, ma'am, sounds good."

"Is a half hour okay?"

"No problem, Mom," Brooke said. "We'll just finish up and be inside by then."

They put a few bags on the porch, then drove around the barn to the single-wide trailer that was used for storage. Adam didn't speak, and neither did Brooke, but he couldn't quite read the tension shimmering between them.

At the trailer, she unlocked the door, and he came up the wooden stairs behind her.

She turned around and gave a start. Then she sighed and said tiredly, "Did you have to agree to stay to supper? We're not doing so well here, you and I."

As he approached, she backed through the doorway. It was slightly warmer inside, but not much, so he shut the door behind him. He heard her fumbling for the light switch beside the door and caught her hand before she succeeded. Neither of them were wearing gloves, and the shock of skin-on-skin contact was electrifying. Just from touching her hand? he asked himself in disbelief.

"Your mom wants to cook for me from her wheelchair. I should say no?"

"I get it, I know, I'm just . . . upset. Let me turn on the light."

"There's a window right here," he said, his voice growing husky. "She almost saw us kissing in the pickup. Do you want her to see this?"

He turned her around and pushed her up against the door, wishing there were far less bulky clothes between them.

"Adam —" She whispered his name, then broke off.

The last light of day came through the window only faintly, but he could see her wide eyes staring up at him, imagined their hazel swirl of color that kept him so off balance. He didn't give her a chance to stop him, just leaned in and covered her mouth with his. Everything inside him knew it was wrong, knew he would be embarrassed if Mr. Thalberg discovered what he was doing.

And it didn't matter, none of it.

All he wanted was to taste her, to lick her lips, to meet her tongue with his own. She tasted of the sweetest sugar with a touch of chocolate.

She moaned and clutched him hard

against her. He buried his face against her hair, tempted to pull it down around him, but stopped himself. He nuzzled the sweet-smelling spot behind her neck, licked his way in a path down her neck. She tilted back her head, letting him do what he wanted. There was that citrus scent of summer nights at the equator. He inhaled deeply, letting the smell fill him.

He moved his hands up between their bodies until he reached the zipper of her coat. The sound of it slowly coming down was loud except for their frantic breathing. The coat parted, and he was able to slide his hands around her warm waist, feel the supple movement of her back as she arched with a gasp. He kissed every part of her face as he grabbed handfuls of her shirt in back, lifting up until he could slide his hands beneath to the hot, smooth skin.

They shared a groan and another kiss, and then she was fumbling at the snaps of his jacket, and he was so impatient he could have ripped the thing off himself. But he felt her hands up under his flannel shirt and t-shirt, caressing, skimming. Her fingers were slightly cold, sending a chill of excitement through him.

Against his mouth, she whispered, "We shouldn't be doing this."

"No." But he kept kissing her, over and over. He let one hand slide over the curve of her hip, palming her backside to hold her to him. He slid his other hand slowly up her front, tracing the line of buttons, taking his time in anticipation. He let the back of his knuckles brush over her breast and was rewarded with her groan.

"Adam."

His name on her lips was a breath of sound, of need, and he cupped her breast, pressed his hips against hers as he explored the thin bra that revealed the hard point of her nipple. He imagined the pretty underwear she'd mentioned, and he started to unbutton her shirt so he could see.

"Whoa," she said, suddenly putting her hands flat against his chest. "My mom is waiting for us."

He kissed her cheek, her brow, and murmured, "Is that the only reason you're stopping us?"

Her hesitation was the only answer he needed, and he kissed her again, deeply, before stepping back.

"Adam . . ." she began, even as she tried to zip up her coat.

Her fingers were trembling so much that he brushed them aside and zipped her up himself. Then he cupped her face in his hands and gently kissed her again.

"Oh, Adam," she breathed, sounding forlorn.

"I know. This is wrong, but I couldn't stop myself."

She flipped on the light and opened the door again. "You said it right the first time. This is wrong. It's only happening because we each haven't had anybody in a long time."

"I haven't said that. I have a different woman every week." He teased her and didn't know where that came from.

She stared into his eyes without any humor at all. "I don't think so. In fact, I don't think you've kissed a woman in a long time. And I'm convenient."

"You're not convenient," he said, following her down the steps to the back of the pickup. "Hell, this lust I feel goes against everything I think is right."

"I'm hardly flattered," she said, hefting a sack of mineral pellets over her shoulder and going back up the stairs.

He grabbed two of them and followed her. "Don't be like that. I can't do this because I work for your family, and I want them to trust me."

"Our reasons aren't too different." She dropped the sack onto the floor and watched

161

as he piled both of his on top. "You work for me. This has to stop. And it doesn't mean anything, Adam, you know that."

They finished unloading the truck in silence, then went up to the house. Brooke shivered as the light snow touched her hat, then the back of her neck, but she wasn't cold. Oh, no, she was hot and achy and aroused and frustrated. What had gotten into Adam, kissing her like that? Pushing her up against the door, his big body holding her there, his mouth hot on her neck, his hand on her —

She pressed her lips tight together, or she would have embarrassed herself with a groan.

Once they'd pulled off their coats and boots in the mudroom, Adam excused himself to wash up, and Brooke went into the kitchen.

It looked so normal, the big windows full of light, Sandy behind the counter enjoying the food prep. Brooke had heard often enough from her mom that feeding your family was an act of love. Brooke couldn't be surprised that it was one of the first chores her mom wanted to reclaim, but still, it gave her a lump in the throat just seeing the radiance of her smile.

"Before you say anything, I didn't go

crazy," Sandy assured her. "It's a simple meat loaf, nothing fancy. You can help me make a salad."

Her dad and Josh came in just as Adam returned, and the three men grabbed beers and started to discuss football. Brooke was a fan of the Broncos, so she chimed in occasionally as she chopped and started to relax.

Adam volunteered to help prepare the salad, and Sandy shooed him away. "We're almost done," she insisted.

Brooke was relieved. She was afraid she'd start blushing too much if she stood next to Adam. As it was, Josh gave her a curious glance at one point, and she gave him a curious glance back. When they all sat down to dinner in the kitchen, she hesitated, trying to decide if it was better to sit next to Adam or across from him.

Damn it all, he was affecting too much of her life, and she didn't like it. She took the nearest seat, and it happened to be next to Adam. Maybe that would be better than looking into his face, remembering how frantically she'd kissed him.

As they were eating, Sandy looked to Brooke. "Nate tells me they haven't set a wedding date because of Stephanie. How's Emily doing with it?"

163

"Okay," Brooke said. She noticed Adam glance at her curiously and thought it only polite to say, "A couple months ago, Emily discovered that Joe Sweet is her biological dad."

His eyebrows rose. "I remember the Sweet brothers. We went to school with them."

They'd been on the football team with him, she remembered. The Sweet brothers had worshipped at the altar of football and weren't too pleased that a "criminal" — their word — might harm their chance on the road to a state championship. But Adam's hard work had won them over.

"Joe had a teenage fling with Em's mom," Brooke continued, "but she left town without telling him she was pregnant. Joe was happy to meet Em, and so were the boys. But Steph . . ." Her voice trailed off.

Josh gave a sigh. "She's sixteen, but it doesn't sound like she's acting her age. Or maybe she *is* acting her age."

"Em thought things were okay." Brooke poured ketchup on her meat loaf. "But even though Steph is in the wedding, talking about it seems . . . stressful for her, so Em doesn't want to have that ruining their day. So she's waiting. I thought I'd talk to Steph."

Her dad frowned from his place at the

head of the table. "You think that's a good idea? Might make it worse to interfere with the natural way of things."

"She's taking a barrel-racing lesson with me soon. And heck, we're both bridesmaids. I could bring up the wedding and see what happens."

"That sounds reasonable," Sandy said. "You'll handle her as delicately as you need to."

Brooke smiled at her mom, feeling a rush of happiness at the support. "Thanks."

They ate in silence for another couple minutes, except for an offer of another beer from Doug, and Josh wanting the ketchup.

Sandy turned to Adam. "So, have you reconsidered living in the bunkhouse?"

Brooke almost choked on her meat loaf, and took a big gulp of milk before embarrassing herself. They'd offered Adam the bunkhouse?

And she was about to protest when some sort of sanity resurfaced, and she realized how she would sound. After all, if she didn't have any feelings for Adam, why should she care where he lived? They'd offered her the bunkhouse months ago, when Josh had first broached the idea of taking over part of the barn loft for himself, but she'd turned them down.

She glanced to the side and saw Adam's profile. He didn't look at her, but his hesitation spoke volumes. What excuse would he give for why he couldn't accept —

"Thank you, ma'am," he said. "I think this time I'll take you up on the offer."

Brooke forced a smile and continued eating, even as her dad clapped his hands together and grinned.

"I knew winter travel would prove to you how much easier it would be to live here," Doug said. "I told Sandy, 'Just give the boy time.' "

"Your grandmother won't mind, Adam?" Brooke asked, projecting deep concern. She had to try *something* to change his mind.

Adam glanced at her and shook his head. "I think I'm crowding her, and she's feeling like she has to entertain me. If she volunteers to read my cards one more time . . ." He gave an exaggerated shudder, making everyone laugh.

"Now, Adam," Sandy said, "she's pretty talented. She saw a lot of interesting things when she read my cards — not that I'm sharing. People swear by her!"

But Brooke could only think about Adam in the bunkhouse. It was a done deal, she saw with resignation. She was already working with him all day long, side by side. What did it matter where he slept?

But he would be *here,* where she could literally see him out the window — oh God, she really could see the bunkhouse right from her window.

"It's good that you have a place to live," she said. "The town has been thinking about that for returning veterans."

She could tell he stiffened at her words even though it was subtle.

"Oh, I forgot about that!" her mother said brightly. "There's a new committee that's been renovating houses for veterans. In fact, I think your grandmother — both your grandmothers," she said, looking from Brooke to Adam, smiling, "have been involved in securing grants. Adam, I'm surprised Renee didn't mention it to you."

Brooke wasn't surprised at all. Surely his own grandma knew how little he wanted to talk about his life in the Marines.

"No, ma'am," Adam said, his voice neutral. "But it's good to help people who need it."

But he didn't need anyone's help, she guessed.

Later, Adam insisted on clearing the table before he left, enduring teasing from Josh. When Adam was gone, and Brooke felt like she could breathe again, she joined her mother in the dining room to work on the decorations for the Thanksgiving table, little candy and cookie turkeys made with a flat chocolate cookie, a chocolate kiss, and mini M&Ms for the feathers. It was amazing how they actually stood up like little birds. Surely she wouldn't enjoy this as much as she did if she really was restless, looking for something else in life. With the snow falling outside, and gossip she and her mom exchanged, she felt a peaceful sense of the approaching holiday.

She'd been lucky that her parents had always been involved in her life. Before she knew it, she was telling her mom about the science fair years ago, when Adam's drunken mom had treated him so horribly.

Sandy put down the frosting she was using to keep the chocolate kiss and the cookie together. "That is just terrible. No wonder the poor boy thought so little of himself in those days."

"Thought so little of himself? I think he had the opposite problem."

"That's just what he showed the world, sweetie. He was proud even then." She hesitated. "It's hard to forgive his parents. They were pregnant at seventeen, and instead of trying to make a better life for their son, they wallowed in their self-pity. I

168

don't think either of them held a job down for long, and the way they used that boy to control Renee? Just terrible. Your father kept trying to help by giving Mr. Desantis work now and then, but . . . he had no discipline, could never last long. He'd either get too drunk to come to work, or lose his temper over something trifling. I wasn't surprised when Adam got into trouble himself. Who knows what would have happened if Coach McKee hadn't taken a chance on him. It's simply remarkable what Adam has accomplished."

Brooke reached out and took her mother's hand. "I was so lucky to grow up with the two of you."

Sandy blinked her suddenly wet eyes. "I know what you mean, sweetie. I feel very lucky, too."

Brooke would never do anything to disappoint her mom — no restless need for a change was worth that.

Brooke didn't want to be on the ranch when Adam moved in the next night — her family would help unload his pickup, giving her even more of a chance to look at him strangely or be caught alone with him. So she arranged a movie night with Emily and Monica.

That evening, she was walking across the lit porch when she saw Adam's truck arrive. He should have gone right to the bunkhouse, but instead he swung around in front of the porch, left the engine on even as he got out to look up at her with open admiration. He gave a low whistle, and she flushed with embarrassment and a secret thrill. Standing still, she let him look. She was wearing a dark sweater dress and leggings with knee-high boots. Her short wool coat was bright red, and her hair tumbled free around her shoulders. She always loved to dress up. She'd added more makeup than the mascara and lip gloss she normally wore to work.

"Damn, you clean up good," he said in a husky voice. "Who'd have guessed?"

"I'd throw a snowball at you if I didn't mind getting my gloves wet," she said, pretending to take offense.

"I like your hair down." He came to the bottom of the steps and reached up a hand as if to help her so she wouldn't slip.

Her heels were high, so she accepted the help. She still had to look up at him once she reached level ground. Even that made her feel all weak inside. There weren't many men she had to look up to. She disengaged her hand.

"You've seen my hair down," she said in disbelief. "I wore it to school that way . . . sometimes." Hadn't she? As an adult, she always let down her hair when she went into town for an evening's entertainment. But she'd been far less of a "girl" in high school.

"You always had ranch chores or barrel racing after school," he said. "Must have been easier for you to keep it up."

She was surprised he remembered that about her.

"I played basketball, too, in the winter." Now she was babbling. She should leave. But she felt . . . beautiful, the way he was looking at her. The moon was rising, and they were alone in the crisp, cold stillness, the light of the porch a beacon behind her.

"Another reason to keep your hair up," he murmured.

Then he touched her hair with his bare hand, sliding it into the gentle waves and spreading them out across her shoulder. She hovered like a hummingbird, yearning. When he stepped back, the ache of regret surprised her.

She sighed. "Why did you accept my parents' offer to live in the bunkhouse?"

"For exactly the reasons I said. It's more convenient, and I like living on my own."

"I've never done that," she found herself

admitting.

He gestured toward the house. "Why would you? Your family is here, and they're great. Your job is here. It just makes sense."

Then why was she thinking about it so much?

"I only started living on my own when I left the Marines six months ago, so we aren't that different." And then he grew serious. "I want you to know I didn't agree to the bunkhouse to annoy you. I gave it a lot of thought."

"I know." She gave him a tentative smile.

He nodded. "Have fun at the movies."

"I will."

And she did, even enjoying a late supper with the girls. By the time she got home, everyone was in bed, and she slipped into her own soon enough. Though she told herself not to, she turned her head and stared out the window. The moon hung bright in the sky, and she knew if she were outside, the stars would look like iridescent sand sprinkled across the blackness. And there across a small pasture was the log cabin where Adam lay. Snow blanketed the roof, and smoke puffed from the chimney. He'd started a fire, and the windows flickered with it. She imagined how cozy it must be.

She kept picturing herself lying in front of that fire with Adam. No matter how many times she told herself to cut it out, her crush on him just wasn't going away.

CHAPTER NINE

Adam looked out his window up at the main house, and knew when Brooke was home by the lights going on in her window. Though she passed in front of it several times, the curtains were gauzy, and he couldn't see much.

He stood there for a while, holding his beer, enjoying the silence. Not that the boardinghouse had been rowdy, but there was something peaceful about the ranch. He was hoping it inspired dreamless sleep, but if not, at least he wouldn't disturb anyone if he had a nightmare. They'd been fading gradually over the six months since his discharge, but sometimes, in the half sleep just before wakefulness, he still felt like he was back there, on patrol, in danger, calling in the air strike that had been the biggest mistake of his life. He shook the memories away quickly.

To his surprise, Grandma Palmer hadn't

even been upset about his moving out. And then he'd seen the glance that passed between her and Mrs. Thalberg. Those two widows were going to find *something* to meddle in.

Brooke's light went out, and the ranch house settled into darkness. And then he saw the other light he'd missed, the one in the barn. It was almost midnight — was a horse ill?

Shrugging into his coat and hat, he walked through the yard, his boots crunching on the frozen ground. He went into the dark barn with the horses crowded into each stall, but no one was working. Most of the small herd roamed on the horse pasture and never came inside. He heard several dogs whine a greeting, but none barked, now that they knew him. Ranger came bounding toward him, tongue hanging out of a dog-smiling mouth, and Adam rubbed between his ears. A door at the far end was open — one that was usually closed. He realized he'd never gone in there.

"Hello?" he called before approaching the doorway.

"Adam?"

It was Josh's voice, so he went inside and was surprised to find him at a workbench, a mallet and some kind of tiny chisel in his hand. He was bent over a shaped piece of dyed leather. Adam's gaze swept the rest of the room, obviously a workshop, with floor-to-ceiling shelves along the other walls.

"Can't sleep?" Josh asked, looking up with his usual smile.

"I saw your light. I had no idea you did this in your spare time. I'm not even sure what it is."

"Leather tooling."

Josh gestured over his shoulder at another bench where projects were laid out in various stages of completion. There were belts, wallets — and a lot of purses. All had been intricately carved and colored in various patterns: simple geometric shapes, swirling vines and flowers, soaring eagles.

"You're good," Adam said, returning to the main workbench.

"Thanks. I've got orders to fill, so I'm usually in here most evenings. My work's on display at Monica's shop."

"The 'and Gifts' in Monica's Flowers and Gifts?"

Josh chuckled. "Right. Local artists and craftspeople sell there on consignment. Seems my purses are very popular with the ladies." He wiggled his eyebrows, then bent back over the leather.

Adam laughed. "Mind if I watch for a bit?"

"Pull up a stool."

Adam did so, studying how Josh used different tools to bring out a three-dimensional image of a daisy in the leather.

He worked in silence for a while, then spoke without lifting his head. "Sorry if my sister can be a pain."

Adam tensed but spoke impassively. "What do you mean?"

"Give her some time. Her bossy ways will calm down. You're her subordinate, so I imagine you bear the brunt of it." Josh looked up at him. "She seems to be going through something. She'll work it out — she always does."

"I'll remember that, but honestly, I haven't seen any problems."

"Then you must be used to strong women. Oh, wait, your grandma is one of the widows, too. That explains it."

Adam smiled. The widows were a much better topic of discussion with Brooke's brother. "I hope lining themselves up with Leather and Lace doesn't cause them problems."

"I've been hearing rumblings about that store in a few places. Nate says the guys who drink coffee at Hal's Hardware aren't too pleased. Seems Sylvester is lining people up to speak at the next town-council meeting."

"Do you think our grandmas will be cowed by a bunch of men?"

They shared a grin.

The next day after school, Brooke met Stephanie Sweet at the barn. The teenager had driven over, pulling her horse trailer, then led out her horse, already saddled.

Brooke went into the barn to saddle her own horse, and found Adam and Josh shoveling out stalls. Steph stepped inside, probably to do some ogling, so Brooke introduced her to Adam.

When Steph left the barn ahead of her, Adam said quietly, "So this is Emily's sister? The one who's causing all the wedding problems? Hard to believe."

Brooke smiled. "I know. She's a nice girl — most of the time."

"You going to interrogate her?"

"Of course not. My mom trusts me to handle her, so you should, too. Now get back to work," she added with mock sternness.

Josh leaned on his shovel and eyed them. "Damn, but you're a taskmaster."

She grinned and waved at her little

brother, turning on her heel and sauntering outside.

She and Steph mounted and rode toward the corral, where she'd set up the barrels in their cloverleaf pattern. Steph had sworn last time that she was going to clock a faster time galloping around the barrels than Brooke in her record-setting days, and Brooke had to grudgingly admit that day might come soon.

"That Adam guy?" Steph said. "I'd heard about him being here, but didn't know how hot he was."

Brooke grinned at her. "Is he? I guess so."

Steph, her blond ponytail bobbing behind her, rolled her big blue eyes. "You guess? Come on, Brooke, he's a *Marine*!"

"Well, we went to school together, so I still think of him as that boy who used to annoy me."

"I'm not twelve," Steph said. "Most boys don't annoy me anymore."

"Most? Is there one in particular you find least annoying?"

Steph shrugged and looked off into the distance, but Brooke thought she might have detected a blush. She went back to her own memories of the days when boys were a mystery she just couldn't figure out. She'd always been a tomboy in high school, and had only blossomed as an adult, when she realized how much better she could feel about herself when she wore pretty clothes and paid attention to her hair. Although heck, with Adam, she hadn't done any of that, and somehow she was — irresistible.

"I have a lot of different friends," Steph said. "There's the Chess Club that meets at the community center. It's pretty fun."

"You play chess?" Brooke asked in surprise.

Steph laughed. "No way. It's not really a chess club — it just *started* as a chess club. Then they threw some parties, and kids realized they could hang out and do other things together. But we kept the name. It's kinda funny."

"What do you do there?"

"Some volunteer stuff around town — shoveling, raking, painting, stuff like that. We hold a dance a couple times a month, go hiking, and sometimes we go to Aspen or Glenwood Springs."

"It does sound like fun."

"We're supposed to let anyone in," Steph continued, "but there are these idiots in school, led by Tyler Brissette."

Brooke felt that the name seemed somehow familiar. "How are they idiots?"

"They get in trouble a lot, causing problems in class. They even got kicked out of the Rose Garden in town for hanging around too late."

"Maybe they don't have enough to do, and the Chess Club would be good for them."

Steph pulled a face. "I don't know about that."

"They sound bored if they're hanging out in the Rose Garden with the tourists."

That got a giggle out of her.

"I don't know," Steph said at last. "Maybe Tyler's only going to get worse. His brother just got out of jail this week."

That's why the name had been familiar, Brooke thought. Cody Brissette had gone to jail for arson last year, and now he was out? She looked at the ruins of the old barn near the corral they'd be practicing in. The firemen had said it was an accident, and Cody hadn't been out of jail, yet . . . It made Brooke unsettled.

"So you think Cody will influence Tyler to be worse?" Brooke asked.

Steph shrugged. "I don't know. I saw Cody a day or two ago, and he seemed . . . really different. Kinda quiet, you know?"

"I'm sure jail can change a person. Bet Tyler's feeling bad about his brother."

Steph stayed silent for a moment. "Yeah,

maybe you're right. It's gotta be hard having your brother come home from jail, where he doesn't have a job and everyone knows what he's done." She stared at the ruins of the barn with her own troubled expression.

Time to lighten things up.

"Guess we're lucky with our brothers, huh?" Brooke asked.

Steph relaxed and grinned back. "They're okay."

"You're lucky to have a sister. I'd give anything to have one."

Steph's smile faded, and Brooke thought, *Uh-oh.* But she had to find a way to bring Em up. She wanted to be a bridge between the two sisters.

Brooke held up a hand. "I know, I know, we haven't known her that long. But she's become like a sister to me."

"Well, she's marrying your brother," Steph reminded Brooke with faint sarcasm.

"You're right. And you and I are going to be bridesmaids together. Has she told you the color for the gowns?"

Steph shook her head.

"Me neither. I asked her if it was a secret, and she said she just couldn't decide. Guess we'll have to help her. Speaking of Em and your Chess Club —"

Steph gave her a look that said *How are you gonna connect that?*

"— maybe you could go to the bakery and get some snacks for your meetings. I'm pretty sure your sister would give you a discount. Heck, she might offer a box for free."

Steph looked away. They'd arrived at the empty corral, so she mumbled, "I'm not gonna bother her. She's got enough to think about with the *wedding.*"

As Brooke leaned over to open the gate, she winced at the sarcastic emphasis on "wedding." Okay, enough of that. Hopefully, she'd planted some seeds. Once they'd gone through, and she closed the gate behind Steph, she gave the girl a challenging look. "We've got a little thaw today, so the ground will be muddy. After a warm-up, let's see how fast you can go."

Steph brightened immediately and trotted her horse over to take the starting position.

After the lesson and Steph's departure, Brooke was oating Sugar before letting her loose in the pasture with the other horses when Nate approached her.

He glanced out in the yard, where they could just see the taillights of Steph's horse trailer disappear down the road into dusk.

"So . . . how'd it go?" he asked, leaning

oh so casually against a stall.

She eyed him with amusement. "Steph is going to be a champion someday, if I have anything to say about it."

"You know what I mean."

"I thought you didn't want me talking to her?" Brooke asked innocently. "You know, I might goof things up worse."

"I didn't say that. And I know you can't keep your mouth shut. So how'd it go?"

She smiled. "Okay, I guess. She didn't want to talk about Em or the wedding much. I just brought up the gowns we might wear as an 'us bridesmaids' kind of thing. I suggested the Chess Club go to the bakery for their snacks."

Nate's brows lifted. "Chess Club?"

Laughing, she explained the misleading name.

"That was a good idea," he admitted.

"Don't look so surprised," she said lightly. "I do have them now and again."

He reached around and tugged her braid. "I know."

She swatted at his arm, and he just grinned. When he walked away, Brooke couldn't help staring after him and shaking her head. It was rather amusing how desperate her playboy brother was to get married.

■ ■ ■ ■

After helping a couple tourists park in the right spot for the sleigh ride, Adam almost walked into the barn when he caught sight of Nate and Brooke talking. He backed out again before they saw him. Nate had assigned him some mechanic work in the truck shed, and he wasn't quite done.

When he saw Nate leave the barn, he went in and found Brooke hanging up her tack.

She glanced at him and shook her head. "Surely you're not interested in how my talk with Steph went."

"Not really. I don't have too many fond memories of the teenager I was."

"I think you're being too hard on yourself. You straightened out . . . some."

He shrugged. "And your brother may want to get married in a hurry, but it's not like he's spending his nights alone."

Brooke laughed. "No, but they don't live together. He loves her and wants to be with her." She tapped his chest as she walked past him out of the tack room. "Don't tell me you're complaining about spending your nights alone."

"Not me. It's peaceful."

"Then why are you bothering me?" she

185

asked in a lighthearted tone. "Tomorrow's Thanksgiving, and I have lots to do." She moved to the barn door and paused. "Did my mom invite you to Thanksgiving supper tomorrow night?"

"You don't want me to be there," he said, knowing it was for the best.

She didn't deny it, only met his gaze then, and as usual, he couldn't look away. He could get lost there, forget where he was — forget what she wanted. He wasn't sure he knew anymore what *he* wanted from Brooke.

"But I don't want you alone on the holiday," she admitted at last.

"Alone?" He smiled. "When I have the widows?"

She visibly relaxed. "So you'll be with your grandma then."

"For the afternoon. Then I hear the widows are coming to your place. I'll convince my grandma to come, too, so I can have some peace and quiet."

"You seem to value that," she said, putting her hand against a wooden beam.

"I do. When you've spent ten years shoulder to shoulder with other men, and you never do anything alone, even the most private . . . well, let me tell you, that log cabin is mighty peaceful."

"I'm glad." A sly smile curved her mouth. "Once upon a time, you never went anywhere alone, if I remember correctly."

He grunted.

"Ah, so you can't disagree. What did you need that posse for? Proof of your popularity?"

He had no choice but to smile. "I can't deny that. It made me feel good to have guys who thought I was cool. It was something I definitely didn't get at home."

She winced. "I'm sorry, I didn't mean to imply —"

"Naw, it's okay," he interrupted. "I did have a childish view of friendship then, that friends would do whatever I wanted, back me up, whatever I said. It took the Marines to show me that I was the one who had to prove I was good enough, to show that I would give my life in loyalty to my brothers." He thought of those brothers, of Paul and Eric and Zach, and so many others who'd died because they believed he couldn't make a mistake.

She stared at him solemnly, as if sensing his troubled thoughts. "Adam?" she began uncertainly.

He waved a hand. "Sorry. Lost my train of thought. Have a good Thanksgiving, Brooke."

■ ■ ■ ■

Thanksgiving had been hectic but wonderful, Brooke thought, as she finished up the last of the dishes with Josh. The day had been filled with football, turkey preparations, then a great meal. Nate and Emily had been practically glued together all day, arms around each other or holding hands, making Brooke feel happy but a little jealous. They looked into each other's eyes and saw a future together. It must be so wonderful to be a part of that.

But not right now, she reminded herself. She had to figure out some things on her own, without the complications of a romance.

Adam's grandma had come to dinner dressed as a Pilgrim, making everyone laugh. Brooke had thought that Adam was probably relieved not to be seen with her in her outlandish getup.

But that wasn't fair. He loved her and tolerated all her eccentricities. She knew Mrs. Palmer had been more a mother to him than his own.

She kept thinking about Adam as she wiped down the tables, turned out the kitchen lights, and went to her room. Nate and Emily had left, escorting the widows home, and Josh was out in his workshop. Her mom had been tired though she protested it wasn't true, so her dad had retired to their room with her.

And Brooke was left to stare out her window at the bunkhouse. The lights were on low, firelight flickering.

Had he eaten supper? During the meal, she'd thought of him just across the way, and as if reading her mind, Mrs. Palmer had told her Adam had promised he was going into town for a bite. Wistfully, Mrs. Palmer had added she hoped Adam could find some nice young people to be with.

But Brooke stared at the bunkhouse and wondered if he'd lied about going into town.

She remembered the spartan condition of the cabin when she'd bandaged Adam's face after the fire. Did he have anything in there but his clothes? And then she imagined what his Thanksgivings had been like growing up, with two parents who didn't care about him, let alone worry about making the holiday special for him. He'd gone into the Marines, where Thanksgiving was spent far from Mrs. Palmer, his only true family.

And Brooke had agreed that she didn't want him at Thanksgiving dinner. She groaned aloud at her selfishness.

Without questioning what she was doing — or why — she put together Thanksgiving leftovers, kitchen and bath towels, soap dispensers, condiments, and some snacks. She didn't feel sorry for him — he would hate that. But he'd moved onto her family's property, and it was Thanksgiving.

Bundling up, she left the house quietly and walked across the yard, carrying her bags, with only the moonlight as her guide up the lane between pastures. The wind swirled around her and stole her breath, and she was shivering even under her coat when she walked across the porch and knocked on his door.

He opened it so fast she was startled.

He let his breath out and ran a hand through his hair. "Sorry, I heard footsteps and . . . old habits."

She stared at him, dressed in jeans and a t-shirt. Behind him, he had a roaring fire going in the stone hearth.

"Can I come in?" she finally asked.

He backed up, and once she was inside, shut the door. He looked down at the bags. "Going somewhere?"

"Here." She kicked off her boots and carried the bags to the kitchen table.

He followed her. "I don't understand."

"You didn't go anywhere for supper, like

you promised your grandma, did you?" she asked, throwing her coat on the back of a chair and beginning to unpack.

His silence was an answer.

She glanced at him. "You didn't want to see your grandma as a Pilgrim?"

He winced, a smile beginning to curve his lips. "Oh believe me, I saw."

"You must have been traumatized. So I brought you some leftovers. And . . . other stuff."

He glanced at the bags, then said with amusement, "Housewarming gifts?"

"Oh, please." She turned her back and started unpacking, and felt vindicated when he picked up one of the plastic containers.

"Leftovers, huh?" he said. He loaded up a plate with turkey, mashed potatoes and gravy, stuffing, corn, and peas. After heating it in the microwave, he plopped a healthy scoop of cranberry sauce on the side. "Can't eat any of it without cranberry sauce," he said, his tone very serious.

"Oh, I agree."

She wasn't going to sit and watch him eat; it just seemed too . . . intimate. She put away the towels and condiments, noticing the bare refrigerator — except for a six-pack of beer, of course, and a carton of orange juice. Oh, he had food stacked on the counter — beef jerky, packaged cakes, and donuts.

"I just moved in," he called from the table. "That's what I could get at the gas station. I'm going to the grocery store tomorrow. I just didn't want to deal with the holiday crowd yesterday."

She wasn't certain she believed him. "They even sell fruit at gas stations, you know."

"Not all of them. I love those little packaged donuts. Hard to get overseas. And thanks for the towels. Grandma Palmer left me a bag of them, and I forgot to bring them. So I just grabbed one from the barn."

She shuddered. "That's disgusting!"

"They'd been washed," he protested mildly.

With nothing left to put away, Brooke sat down opposite him at the table. "I admit I was surprised when your grandma didn't drag you to our house tonight."

"She tried. I finally told her to go work her wiles on the other vets in town. She keeps talking about those houses they're renovating. She knows I'm not interested."

"She just wants you to stay," Brooke said quietly. She knew that the old woman was using every trick in the book to make that happen.

He glanced at her briefly before closing his eyes in bliss over a bite of stuffing. Eventually, he said, "I'm here now, and that's what matters." His look sobered. "I've been keeping an eye on her. I actually talked to old Doc Ericson, who told me she's fit as a fiddle."

That lessened the guilt Brooke was feeling about hiding her suspicions. At least Adam knew his grandma was healthy.

"Now, did she make Doc tell me that?" he continued. "Who knows? But I'm here and willing to help. All I can do is trust that she'll come to me when she needs me." He swallowed a bit of stuffing with his eyes closed. "So how did your mother handle the hectic holiday?"

"We didn't let her do too much, and after all these years, she knows not to push herself. But . . . I found myself watching her a lot, you know? Trying to enjoy each moment." She looked away, her face hot. "God, that sounds morbid."

"It sounds smart," he said.

When he put his hand on hers, she pulled away and gave him a polite smile.

"Let's find the pumpkin pie," she said. "I need seconds."

She brought out the pie, and his eyes went wide.

"It's a whole pie," he said almost reverently.

"Blame my mother. She insisted we make far too many. I snuck this one."

"I love pumpkin pie for breakfast. To hell with donuts."

She couldn't help laughing as she cut two slices and plated them. Holding up a can of whipped cream, she gestured with her hand for his approval.

"What more do you want of me?" he demanded. "I'm already salivating."

After squirting way too much whipped cream on her slice, she carried the can and her pie over to the worn couch in front of the fire and sank into it. Adam followed and sat beside her.

"Are you keeping this to yourself?" he asked, grabbing the can to use it.

"No, I share. I just might need more."

They ate the first few bites in reverent silence.

"Maybe you won't visit me anymore," Adam said at last, setting down his plate, "but I feel you deserve the truth."

She eyed him. "What truth?"

"I had many fantasies when I was overseas about the things I could do to a woman with whipped cream."

She swallowed heavily and just stared at

him. "I can't believe you're telling me this. What balls. I might never come back."

And then they both dove for the can. She got her hands on it first, laughing in triumph, but with impressive strength, he flung her back on the couch and straddled her to get the can back. He loomed over her, and she was breathless from laughing and trying to hold his arms away from her.

He squirted a dot on each cheek, then examined her face as if he were a painter. "Very nice."

She groaned, and when she tried to wipe off the cream, he dropped the can and gripped her arms at the wrists, slowly raising them over her head.

Her smile died, and all of her amusement seemed to combust inside her, morphing into the powerful desire for him that was never far from her thoughts. She lost her breath as he leaned over her, then shuddered when he licked the whipped cream off each of her cheeks.

"You taste good," he whispered.

"That's not me, it's the cream, you idiot," she said, her protest lacking any firmness.

She couldn't move beneath him although she tried to get her hands free. It was the strangest, most erotic thing that had ever happened to her. She was used to being in control, even on dates. But with Adam, she was helpless . . . helpless to resist even though she should. She should tell him to stop — and he would.

With his weight on her hips, and his hands holding on to hers, she was arched beneath him, and she saw his gaze go to her chest. It sent a rush of hot pleasure surging through her.

And then he kissed her, and she opened her mouth with a groan as he invaded her. Since he still straddled her, she could feel his erection hard against her stomach, and she arched up to feel even more.

"Let me go," she whispered, as he kissed his way down her throat.

He did immediately. "I shouldn't have —"

"I didn't say to stop kissing me!"

She grabbed him and pulled him back down on her. Now she could put her arms around him, her hands deep in his wavy hair as she held him to her.

"God, you smell so good," he said, taking little nips at the skin down her neck. "Every time I get near you, I think of hot nights on an island somewhere, torchlight in the distance, you and me in the sand."

"Wow, soldier," she said with a hoarse chuckle, as the image flooded through her, heating her. "I didn't know you had such an imagination." She moaned aloud as he moved down her body, kissing his way to each button of her shirt and undoing them.

"Every time you wear one of these Western shirts," he said against her stomach, "I think of doing this." Then he spread the shirt wide. "Pretty underwear, just like you promised."

Her bra was pink and lacy, but she didn't wear it for long. Soon he pulled her to the end of the couch and knelt between her thighs. She was naked above the waist, and he was still fully clothed. He stared at her breasts, and when she arched her back, offering them, he went still.

"Are we really doing this?" he asked hoarsely. "Stop me now if you have to, but not later."

"It's just sex," was her answer. "We're not getting all serious, and no one is going to find out. Can you live with that, soldier?"

He put his hands on her bare waist, and she swayed forward, until the tips of her breasts brushed his t-shirt.

He groaned. "I can live with it. Can you?"

"I'm the one with my clothes half-off." She pulled his t-shirt up over his head and admired the curve of his muscles, the scattering of light brown hair, the flat of his stomach with the sexy ripple of abs leading down into the waistband of his jeans.

They came together, hot skin to hot skin, and kissed with long and deliberate intent. She wasn't going to change her mind. She locked her legs about his hips and rubbed herself against him. When he bent her over the arm of the couch, she felt deliciously abandoned. The first kiss on her nipple made her cry out, and he took it at a slow pace, teasing her until she was squirming, until at last he opened his mouth on her breast and took much of it inside.

She moaned his name. Never had she felt this hot for a man. She didn't know if it was because he seemed so forbidden to her, or she attached no meaning to their relationship, so therefore no pressure. Whatever it was, it made her feel free to enjoy herself without thinking, without judging, things she didn't often do.

He kissed his way down her stomach, unbuttoning her jeans. His mouth followed the zipper's slow retreat, his tongue darting in to tease her to even greater heights of desire. He paused with her jeans caught around her thighs to taste her, and she couldn't take it anymore.

She shoved him onto his back beside her, and let her jeans and thong fall to the floor. She leaned over him, reveling in the passion that made his half-closed eyes smolder. "Off with your jeans, soldier."

He shrugged out of them easily. She saw the scars crisscrossing his right thigh, a few puckered and still red, others beginning to fade. And now she knew why he occasionally limped. She didn't remark on them, knew he wouldn't appreciate it.

He swung her into his arms, and she gasped and clutched his shoulders.

"Put me down! You'll hurt yourself."

"The day I can't carry a woman to my bed . . ." he murmured.

She thought he'd toss her onto the bed and jump in, but instead he set her gently on the edge, pulled her braid around to the front and began to loosen it.

"I've wanted to do this from the first day I saw it beneath your hat," he said, his voice husky with reverence.

She couldn't say anything past the wonder that felt like a little knot in her throat. And then he combed his fingers through the long waves of curls and brought them around her shoulders to hide and reveal her breasts.

"God, you're beautiful," he murmured.

She tried to tell herself that any guy getting laid was going to say that, but . . . she believed he meant it. Then he reached into a drawer and pulled out a condom.

"A soldier's always prepared?" she asked, smiling.

"Especially when he's been out of the country a long time. He's always hoping."

She drew him back onto the bed, and for the first time, he lay full on top of her. She loved the feeling of being pressed into the mattress, aware of strong bone and hard muscle beneath fiery skin. They kissed again, over and over, rolling about with abandon. She licked his nipples as he'd done hers, explored his body until he couldn't take it anymore.

"Do you want to ride, cowgirl?" he asked as he lay tense beneath her questing fingers.

"Oh, yes." She took him inside her from above, undulating on top of him, feeling the upward thrust of his lean, strong hips.

And she was lost.

CHAPTER TEN

Adam looked up at the incredible view of Brooke Thalberg, her lean, supple body in charge, guiding him as she wanted. Her breasts were high and full on her rib cage, bouncing with each thrust. Her hair was a chocolate waterfall all around her body, and her face was intense as she sought her pleasure.

The sight alone could have driven him over the edge, but he held off, waiting for her. And when she came, he rolled her onto her back and drove into her, meeting her orgasm with his own before she was even finished.

Shuddering, panting, he braced himself on his elbows and buried his face in her hair, smelling coconut and pineapple, a far cry from a Colorado winter.

At last, he lifted his head and looked down at her. She was staring up at him a bit wide-eyed, and he knew how she felt. What the hell had just swept over them both?

"Are you all right?" he asked, kissing her cheeks and her chin and her fluttering eyelids.

"Oh, believe me, I feel incredible."

"And I agree you do."

They were still joined, and he felt as well as heard the rumble of her laughter. He slid to the side, gathering her into his arms and resting among the pillows.

"Adam," she began tentatively, "I know we shouldn't have done that, but I don't regret one bit of it."

"Me neither."

"And I don't want you to think I planned this, plying you with pumpkin pie and whipped cream."

He kissed her again. "The taste of it on your lips drove me wild."

She seemed so natural about the whole thing, unembarrassed, uninhibited. He wanted to take her all over again.

"And I don't think you took advantage of me," she continued. "I'm a big girl, and there are two of us in this bed." She looked up at him, her expression sobering. "We can't have any kind of relationship, Adam. It will look so bad to my family — you're my employee, and I'm your boss."

"I know. Your father trusted me to work

for him, not to seduce you."

She groaned. "Can we not bring up my father? And can we not pretend that I'm a delicate flower you had to persuade to 'give myself' to you?"

"Okay. You said you wanted no one to know what we've done."

"No one," she said, her expression serious, even as she brought up a hand to cup his whiskered face.

"This is — I don't know what you call this between us —"

"Lust?"

"God, yes, but otherwise . . . Adam, it can't be any more."

"You're saying this one time will be all I ever have of you?"

"No, I'm not saying that," she said too quickly, her gaze lingering on his chest.

The more distracted and unfocused her expression became, the more Adam could feel satisfaction seep through him. "We're going to do this again."

"I — I don't think I could stop myself," she admitted breathlessly. "This will be our secret, something just for us."

Relieved, he started kissing her. When he slid his hand down between her thighs, she stopped him.

"No, I've got to go. It's not like I can

spend the night when my parents are right in the next building." She sighed. "I still have to worry about this when I'm twenty-eight years old."

"When can I see you again?"

As she got out of bed, unabashedly naked, she grinned wickedly, and said, "Tomorrow morning as we feed hungry cattle."

After a quick stop in the bathroom to dispose of his condom, he followed her, saying, "That's not what I mean, and you know it."

She found her bra and put it on, along with her underwear, a lacy little thong the same bright pink as her bra. Who'd have guessed what she had on under those cowboy shirts and jeans?

He stared at her, openmouthed, then groaned. "I won't be able to wait long to see *all* of you again."

"This is a secret, which means we can't plan anything." As she pulled up her jeans, she shot him a look. "I think spontaneity can be exciting."

He found his own jeans and donned them, not bothering with the top button. He pulled her to him and kissed her again. "Anything with you is exciting. But I'll be patient."

"Patient — and distant," she added in a

mock-severe tone, waving her finger in front of his face.

He caught it in his mouth and nipped her. "Just don't go wagging that cute ass in front of me every chance you get."

She pulled on her coat, grinning. "This cute ass will do whatever it wants. I'm the boss, remember?"

After one last smoldering smile, and an appreciative look down his body, she disappeared out the front door. Adam went to the window and peered through the edge of the curtain. She faded into darkness across the yard, but nearer the house she came back into the light. He watched her until she opened the kitchen door and was gone.

Then he sat on the couch, dropped his head back, and closed his eyes. He hadn't seen *that* coming. But damn, what a lot to give thanks for.

Her request to keep things simple was for the best. He knew he had too much baggage to bring to any deeper relationship, and that would really be burdening the Thalbergs too much.

It was just sex, safe and protected, and no lies involved. No one was going to get hurt, and he'd never let Brooke suffer any embarrassment because of him. She was a proud woman, doing a man's job. No way was he going to let her family think anything bad about her. She didn't deserve that.

And then he realized there'd be no risk at all if he just stopped seeing her outside the job.

But he wasn't going to do that.

As Brooke left the house in the morning, driving her Jeep into Valentine, she realized that last night with Adam, she'd forgotten her annual Black Friday shopping trip to Aspen with Monica, and hadn't told him about it. It would be Emily's first time.

But Brooke hadn't exactly been thinking when she'd been with Adam. Every response had been physical and overwhelming. Sex with him had lived up to the heated imaginings she'd had the last couple weeks. After looking out the window at the bunkhouse and savoring her memories, she'd fallen into the deepest, most relaxing sleep and awakened in the morning feeling utterly . . . delicious. Satisfied. She had a little secret, something all her own that had nothing to do with her family. And Adam was passing on through, so she did not have to worry about something permanent happening. That was too much to think about right now.

She'd missed this intimacy with a man. It

was only sexual intimacy, but that was just fine, she told herself. The worst part was feeling like a teenager, having to sneak back home.

As she drove away, she glanced at the bunkhouse one last time, and a faint uneasiness stole some of her contentment. The place looked so lonely, just like its new resident. She had her friends to hang out with, and he'd always had his, including the brotherhood of the Marines. But he seemed to have become a loner, and she wondered what had made him that way. Was it her place to suggest he go into Valentine and find some of his old friends? Steph's brother Chris Sweet had gone to school with them — he'd been on the football team with Adam though he hadn't been in Adam's bad-boy posse before that.

But no, she wasn't his girlfriend. She couldn't talk to him about problems in his life. Yet she was a talker — no way could she avoid conversations with Adam. He'd just have to understand that.

Now that he lived so close, would she see him coming and going, perhaps even into town in the evenings? But no, Adam seemed to focus on work and his grandma, where she enjoyed being out with people, too.

Or did she just enjoy getting away from

the ranch?

She tried to tell herself that everyone needed a break from their job, but the ranch was more than that — it was a way of life. She couldn't believe she'd try to escape that — it would mean that everything she thought she loved about her life was a lie. She'd just helped Emily find a new direction — the bakery — so for Brooke to discover that she herself was feeling a bit uncertain was a blow.

After a long day of shopping and good food in Aspen, Brooke and her friends stopped in at Outlaws for some dancing. She had done her best not to think about Adam because she wasn't going to tell Monica and Emily about him, but at the honkytonk, he was never far from her thoughts.

Sitting in a booth, having a beer to cool down after dancing with the other two women, Brooke snacked from a bowl of popcorn on the table.

"Well, you're getting some looks tonight," Emily said, glancing over her shoulder where two guys at the bar were staring at them. She had to speak loudly to be heard over Miranda Lambert belting out a mournful tune.

Brooke and Monica followed her gaze, then shared a groan and quickly pretended their bottles of beer were very interesting.

"They're Derek and Chad, two guys we went to school with," Brooke said. "Actually, they used to be in Adam's posse."

She wanted to wince — she hadn't meant to bring him up that day, and had been successful — until then.

Emily gave her an interested look. "You said Adam straightened himself out with the help of football. How about them?"

Monica shook her head. "Both have been divorced already, and Derek doesn't see his kid enough. Bad news."

Emily looked at both Brooke and Monica. "It never ceases to amaze me how much you small-town people all know about each other."

Brooke risked another glance at the two men. That could have been Adam if he hadn't been sentenced to community service as a football manager. But, of course, there were many men who would forget about community service when it was over, and go back to their old lives. Adam hadn't.

It was men like Derek and Chad that made Adam none too eager to renew old acquaintances. But he'd found new friends on the football team. Wasn't he curious about them? She thought about getting out her high-school yearbook and perusing the

faces. Adam would want to know who —
and then she stopped herself. If Adam was
interested, he'd do something about it. He
wouldn't welcome her interference.

He just welcomed her into his bed.

Her face got all hot, and she told herself it
was because of the dancing. She'd never
kept this kind of secret from her friends.

As if reading her mind, Monica mused,
"You know, you've got a handsome man
right on the ranch to distract you every day."

Brooke shrugged and gave her a bright
smile. "We work together. It's not like that.
Maybe *you* should ask him out."

"Nope; I already said, he's my past."

Brooke took another sip of beer, then
changed the subject. "Hey, I've got something interesting. You know this mess about
Leather and Lace? Mrs. Palmer says she
predicted there would be problems when
reading her cards."

Monica and Emily gave a collective groan.

"She brought her cards to Thanksgiving.
Good thing Adam wasn't there," Brooke
added, shaking her head.

"He didn't come to Thanksgiving?" Monica asked.

"He celebrated with the widows at the
boardinghouse."

"Wonder why he didn't celebrate with

you?" Monica eyed Brooke with speculation. "I mean your family, of course."

"He's become a loner — strangest thing," Brooke said, keeping her voice light. "He said after the Marines, he needs a little peace and quiet."

"At the boardinghouse?" Monica said, her expression one of incredulity.

Trying to speak nonchalantly, Brooke said, "My dad invited him to move into the bunkhouse. So he's got his peace and quiet."

"Good for him," Emily said.

But Brooke was trying not to watch Monica, who was eyeing her with too much interest.

"The bunkhouse?" Monica echoed, elbow on the table, chin propped on her hand.

Brooke summoned her acting skills. "Yep. He moved in a few days ago. He's still a loner. I barely see him but for work."

"Twelve hours a day," Monica mused.

Emily looked from Monica to Brooke in confusion. "Is there something I'm not seeing?"

"I don't know, is there?" Monica asked innocently.

Brooke smiled and shook her head. "You're thinking too hard, Monica. Adam and I weren't attracted to each other in high school, and there'll be no relationship

211

beyond work now." And that wasn't even a lie — oh, she was good.

"If you say so."

Monica gave her a last, searching glance, and Brooke threw her hands wide, as if she didn't know what Monica expected of her.

"But back to Leather and Lace," Emily said. "Are we going to go to the next town-council meeting? The widows need our support."

"Of course," Brooke said. "And that way, maybe we can head off the preservation committee's counterresponse."

"You really think they'll try one of their stunts?" Emily asked, her blue eyes going wide.

Monica and Brooke shared another glance and a grin.

"Oh, believe me," Brooke said, "this is like waving a red cape at a bull."

That was the last beer Brooke allowed herself as she spent another hour dancing. She even danced with Chad because, what the hell, she liked how his appreciative look made her feel sexy. Then he opened his mouth, and she remembered why they didn't get along.

On the drive home, she found herself going slowly along Main Street, looking up at the apartments over the stores. Many now had single candles in their windows, or icicle lights. Monica and Emily each lived above their stores. More and more, it seemed wrong to Brooke that she was twenty-eight and living with her parents. But her job was right there — and so was her mother, who needed her. Now wasn't the time to start changing things just because she was feeling restless. But . . . was she supposed to put her life on hold? After all, she didn't even know what kind of life she wanted anymore.

As she pulled into the yard beside the ranch, she glanced at the lit windows of the bunkhouse and felt a hunger that was so overwhelming, she knew she wasn't going to follow up on it. Sex wouldn't make her uncertainties go away, and she didn't want Adam to think she was crazy about him.

There wasn't a TV in the bunkhouse, but Adam didn't mind. He read until he fell asleep each night, which was usually pretty early. If he'd had a TV, he wouldn't have noticed when Brooke's Jeep crunched the hard snow outside, he wouldn't have gone to the curtain to catch a glimpse of her.

Her hair was long and wild tonight. He knew from a casual question to Josh that Black Friday shopping was a tradition, but it would hardly go so late at night. She'd gone somewhere else that evening — a date?

The shot of jealousy took him by surprise. He hardly needed to remind himself of the rules he'd agreed to where their nonrelationship was concerned. It seemed all of his emotions were coming back to life, welcome or not.

He went back to the fridge and pulled out the pie for a late-night snack. He'd stocked up on groceries. Although he wasn't the world's best cook — the Marines had fed him, after all — he'd learned a thing or two when he was still a kid, and his parents had been too drunk to care about feeding him. He made a mean omelet, and his spaghetti was always perfectly boiled.

But he had the pumpkin pie, and thought of Brooke, and what other parts of her body he should have decorated with whipped cream.

He was going to get himself all riled up at this rate.

And then he heard a scratching at the door. He wasn't proud of how quickly he jumped up, and this time it wasn't because of any military habit. Had Brooke decided she had to see him and didn't want to knock for fear it would carry across the pasture?

Adam opened the door wide, already feeling satisfied — but there was no one there.

And then he looked down.

Ranger, the cow dog, was sitting on his haunches on the porch, looking up at him with a wide doggy grin. His ears went back, and he gave a little whine.

Sighing, Adam squatted and rubbed between his ears. "What's up, boy? You lonely?"

Ranger gave another whine and licked his face.

Adam sputtered. "Okay, okay, you can come in for a visit. Let's see how muddy you are, first."

He used the barn towel on the dog, then Ranger happily trotted around the living room, smelling every corner, then lifting his nose to the edge of the table.

"Not my pumpkin pie," Adam warned.

Ranger seemed to sigh, then, after a cursory inspection of the bedroom, curled up on the rug before the fire.

"I know the barn is warm enough for you," Adam told the dog.

Ranger's tail thumped, but he didn't lift his head.

"Oh, all right, you can stay here for the night."

But soon, Adam regretted his decision, because the dog took up more of the bed than he did.

■ ■ ■ ■

The nightmare started like it always did, a typical patrol in-country, asspack, canteens, and six rounds of live ammo bouncing around his torso, his rifle in his hands like a part of his body. That rifle was so real, but everything else around him was a dreamy blur, a torn picture of Paul's girlfriend moving in and out of focus, Adam picking up an unusual stone for Zach's son.

Then artillery rounds landed too close, the impact like a belch of air from the earth, the explosion shaking the ground, sending rocks to slice flesh. Adam's voice sped up and slowed down as he called in fire support, but the enemy's position wasn't attacked. Instead, the bombs fell on them, screaming out of the sky from the jet long past them. The dead and dying were like bright blood on hunks of meat. Dragging his mangled leg, he felt the weight of Eric as he pulled him behind the shelter of rocks, but the man's face was already lifeless. The smell of smoke and death swirled around him, the heat of flames as hot as his damaged thigh.

And that was always where he woke up, his mind filled with regrets and recriminations and a desperate plea to God to turn back time so he could save them all. But the true nightmare was what he discovered later, that they'd dropped a 500-pound bomb rather than a 250, altering his calculations, and men had died.

He was breathing hard in the dark, and Ranger whined softly in confusion. Adam closed his eyes and put his hand on the dog's silky head.

He had to let them go, he told himself in sorrow, his friends, the men he'd watched war movies with before being deployed, drinking beer until they'd yelled Semper Fi like idiots. They were dead, and he was not. They'd want him to go on living his life, to forgive himself. But no one had ever told him it would be so hard without them.

Ranger gave a sad whine and leaned against his thigh in a companionship as old as time.

CHAPTER ELEVEN

The next morning, Brooke met up with Adam near the truck shed. The air was slightly warmer, the sky clear blue, and they stared at each other for the first time since they'd made love. Brooke thought she'd feel nervous or even guilty, but it wasn't that at all — she felt . . . excited and aroused at the thought of having a secret lover. They both slowly smiled but knew they were too out in the open to acknowledge any other emotion. She could still feel his hands on her, his mouth —

She was thankful her dad and brothers weren't around because surely her cheeks were blazing red, she felt so overheated.

"You should have come to see me last night," he said in a low voice.

Brooke hadn't thought her blush could spread, but it did. "I went dancing with the girls and got home too late."

"There's never a 'too late' for us."

"You'd think differently in the middle of a hardworking morning."

"If you say so — boss."

The gleam in his eyes gave her wicked thoughts. She shook them clear and held out the weekly newspaper. "Did you see the *Valentine Gazelle*?"

"Nope. Something I should know about?"

"Your grandma's on the front page, along with mine."

Frowning, he unfolded the paper so quickly that she had to grin. They looked at the picture of the three widows smiling sweetly into the camera.

"They appear so innocent," Brooke said, shaking her head.

The article was entitled "Valentine Valley Preservation Fund Committee Backs Controversial New Business."

She waited while he scanned the article. The reporter explained what Leather and Lace was, and how the owner would be coming to the next town-council meeting to explore getting a permit for the store. The article quoted Sylvester Galimi and his opposition on "moral grounds," then the rest was devoted to the widows' knowledgeable discussion about the freedom to do business, the antiwomen bias of some people in the town, and the variety of lovely clothing

219

items tourists as well as townspeople could buy from the new store.

"Antiwomen bias?" Adam repeated.

Brooke shrugged. "Could be. It's women who own and frequent the store, after all."

"Says who? I might be a customer."

"And I thought my underwear was pretty enough," she whispered, looking over her shoulder. No one was around.

"I like to give presents to the women in my life. Grandma Palmer —"

Laughing, she hit him in the arm. "Let's not go there. I just wanted you to know in case there's some kind of backlash against your grandma in town. Not that you go into town . . ."

"Sure I do. I went to the grocery store, didn't I? I've even played pool at Tony's Tavern."

"Not since you've been living in the bunk-house."

"Keeping an eye on me, Brooke?"

"How can I not? I can see your cabin right out my window."

"How convenient. Maybe I'll buy some binoculars."

"Hey, enough of that. In the retriever, soldier."

He gave her a slow inspection, his eyes sexy and knowing. "Yes, boss."

They worked as a unit in the stackyard until the hay bales were balanced two high in a long row on the bed of the truck, then they started down the road toward the first pasture to feed. Adam opened a thermos, and the smell of steaming coffee permeated the cab. He offered her a sip, then took one himself.

"You know how I mentioned my conversation with Steph Sweet?" Brooke asked. "She talked to me about this group of bad kids who are causing trouble — nothing too terrible, some graffiti, hanging out too late at night, that kind of stuff. Although one kid's brother just got out of jail doing a year for arson."

"That could have been me," Adam said, his voice impassive.

"I told her she should ask this boy's brother, Tyler, to join the teen group, that maybe he was bored and needed something to do."

Adam arched a dubious brow at her but said nothing.

"All right, maybe I'm being optimistic here, but she seemed to dwell on this kid, like she felt sorry for him. And I couldn't help thinking — what makes some kids, like you, straighten out, and others not?"

He took a thoughtful sip of his coffee. "In

some ways, I think it was luck that I tangled with the right person. It was Coach McKee's car I stole, and you could have blown me away when he showed up at my hearing. I thought he was there to make sure they put me away in juvenile hall to teach me a lesson. Instead, he spoke up for me, said I was a good kid and deserved a second chance."

Unspoken, but plain as day, was the knowledge that no one except his grandma had ever called him a good kid. She remembered in seventh grade when a teacher had assumed he'd been the one to throw food in the cafeteria, without a shred of proof. He'd just accepted the punishment without protest, as if he knew not to bother. Could that kind of thing be a self-fulfilling prophecy? Brooke's stomach tightened with sadness. When your own parents treated you like dirt, it was hard to think otherwise about yourself. "I bet your grandma was at the hearing, too."

He gave a wry smile. "Front row. I was embarrassed to have her see me like that, knew she was trying not to cry, and for the first time realized that my actions affected someone else. She had an encouraging smile for me, and I knew I hadn't lost her love." He looked away.

Brooke had to swallow hard as the love between grandmother and grandson warmed her. "So Coach McKee put you on the football team?"

"As a manager. You have to earn the right to play. No matter how sarcastic I was about my 'job,' Coach McKee never took offense. He kept track of me just as he did the rest of his players. And by tryouts the next season, I was convinced I was just as good as any of his team." He glanced at her mockingly. "I thought rather highly of myself."

"No!" she said, looking at the road as she drove but putting a hand to her chest. "I'd never have thought that after spending some time in your bed."

"I'd pinch your ass if you weren't driving."

She stuck out her tongue at him. "So go on with your story."

"There isn't much more to tell. I started from the bottom and worked my way into a starting position. I took some ribbing, but after my parents, there isn't much that some kid could say that would affect me. I felt driven to prove Coach wasn't wrong about me. I'd never worked so hard. And there were rewards, too. Guys who'd never given me the time of day started listening to me.

By senior year, I was one of the team captains, and being in charge, being respected, felt good. I'd never had that before."

She listened to his quiet voice, and occasionally looked at him to see his expression unfocused, as if he saw the past.

"But then how did you go from that to the Marines? It's a big jump."

"I thought about college, and maybe I could have gotten a football scholarship to a small school — I wasn't a Division I prospect. But I'd have had no money for books or travel or clothes, and frankly, going to school more just didn't appeal to me. You neither?" he asked her.

She shook her head. "Nate went to college and learned everything about business and animal science. It seemed . . . repetitive to learn the same stuff."

"That was the opinion of an eighteen-year-old girl. What do you think now?"

"I guess I still feel that way," she said with a shrug. "His skills help him take care of his part of the ranch. My skills are out here, under the sky, with the animals. Do you wish you'd chosen differently?"

"No. Once Coach suggested the military — he was a vet himself — something seemed to click inside me. And Grandma

Palmer was so proud I had a direction in my life at last."

"You had more than a direction — you must have been driven. Your grandma told us you'd been promoted through the ranks to staff sergeant at a young age."

He shrugged.

And then . . . nothing. It took everything in Brooke not to ask him specific questions when it was obvious he was keeping so much inside.

"So what you're saying," she said at last, "is that this Tyler kid needs some good people in his life. I kind of told that to Steph, suggested she invite him to join her teen group. I'll let you know what happens."

She didn't feel hurt that Adam didn't confide in her — they didn't have that kind of relationship. But . . . she was worried about him.

Late that afternoon, Adam thought he was going to the Widows' Boardinghouse to have dinner with his grandma. Instead, she met him at the door, leaning on her cane, her dress full of browns and yellows and oranges, because to her, it was still the Thanksgiving holiday.

On the porch, Adam did a double take. "Grandma?"

"Help me with my coat, dear boy," she said, holding it up to him as he stepped inside the kitchen.

He took the coat. "I thought we were having dinner."

"We are, but I'd like you to take me into town and make an evenin' of it. Won't that be nice?"

He helped her on with her bright red coat, and he tried not to smile as it clashed with her dress. "Um . . . okay. Do you have a place in mind? I didn't dress real fancy," he said, looking down at his jeans, t-shirt, and fleece beneath his winter coat.

"You've got cowboy boots on, don't you?"

"Yeah," he said, puzzled.

"That's fancy enough for Valentine Valley. You bring that truck of yours around to the stairs, and I can step right in."

He did, and before he could get around to the passenger side, she already had the door open, which sort of surprised him. It was pretty heavy. As he held her elbow, she settled inside, then beamed up at him from beneath her immaculately combed blond wig. She'd put on some makeup, which made her seem more like herself. He had a quick thought that she hadn't lost any weight since he'd been home, considering how little he'd seen her eat. He'd have to pay more attention.

"Now get in, boy, we can't dawdle!"

He chuckled, determined to enjoy whatever she had planned.

And that wasn't dinner, at least not right away. After they crossed the bridge into town, with the sun behind the snow-tipped mountains and the last gray lighting the day, she kept telling him to turn left and right, until they'd zigzagged through practically every block.

"Grandma, surely we've seen every restaurant by now. Pick one."

At last, when she'd directed him to turn onto Fourth, a block off Main Street, she said, "Stop here!"

He drove up to the curb and looked around. He didn't see a restaurant, but across the street was a nightclub called Wild Thing, and La Belle Femme, with women's clothes in the window. "Is this a good parking spot for a restaurant I don't see?"

"No. But do you see this buildin' here?"

He turned the other way and saw an old Victorian three-story home with a steeply sloped roof all around at the top, carved stone above each window, and especially large plate-glass windows on either side of the front door. A weathered FOR SALE sign had been driven into the snowbank near the road, as if the place had been for sale a long time.

"It used to be the funeral home until they found a buildin' more suitable to their needs," Grandma mused.

He wondered what that could be — and then he remembered the last time he'd been in a funeral home, six months ago. His chest felt heavy with sadness, but for the first time it didn't seem so crippling, so permanent.

Suddenly, a light went on inside the building although they couldn't see in through the frosted glass.

"Right on time," Grandma said with satisfaction. "Let's go in."

He caught her arm. "So we're not going to dinner?"

"Oh, of course we are! I love the True Grits Diner."

"You mean that place Sylvester Galimi owns? Is he going to be happy to see you, after that newspaper article?"

"Of course he will. Sylvester values money above all else, and we'll spend some there."

Adam ducked down until he could see out her window. "Then who are we seeing here?"

"Why, the future proprietor of Leather and Lace, Miss Whitney Winslow. This is the buildin' she wants to buy."

"You have an appointment, and you didn't bother to tell me."

She looked at him over her glasses. "I thought you were accompanyin' me tonight, Adam. You never told me you had to approve our schedule first."

"I don't like surprises, Grandma, but I'm happy to go wherever you'd like."

"Not like surprises? Did your admirals tell you everythin' that was happenin' in your wars?"

"Admirals are in the Navy, Grandma."

"You know what I mean. You're used to surprises, Adam, and I'm a woman who likes to offer them."

He sighed. "And I love you for it."

She squeezed his cheek as if he were four. "I know you do. Now let's go inside. You'll enjoy meetin' Whitney."

Oh, would he? he thought suspiciously. She leaned on his arm and her cane as she walked up the stairs, one at a time, then rapped smartly on the door.

The woman who answered gave Grandma Palmer a friendly smile, then glanced with barely masked surprise at Adam.

"Hello, Mrs. Palmer, it's so wonderful to finally meet you in person."

Whitney Winslow was stylishly dressed in slim black pants and a white-and-black-patterned silky-looking top. Adam suspected her clothes wouldn't look out of place in Aspen. Her black hair hung in various lengths to her shoulders, framing intelligent, gray eyes. If someone could radiate determination, it was Whitney, with her slim back as straight as a Southern finishing-school graduate.

Grandma Palmer beamed and took the other woman's hand. "Such a pleasure, Whitney, such a pleasure. Allow me to introduce my grandson, Adam Desantis."

Adam shook her hand gently because his own palm was full of calluses, and hers felt like she'd never done anything more physical than typing at a computer.

Whitney's smile was nothing more than polite, and he found himself relaxing. At least she didn't seem to know that his grandma might have several motives for their evening.

Whitney spread her arms wide as if displaying the place. "Mr. Deering, the real-estate agent, left me the keys to give us some privacy."

"That Howie Junior, so thoughtful."

Adam remembered Howie — or "Deer" as they'd called him on the football team, for his fast speed at running back. If memory served him, he'd even dated

Brooke in high school, but Adam seemed to remember hearing it hadn't gone too well. Though Deer had been fast on his feet, he was clumsy as an ox with girls.

"So what do you think?" Whitney asked, turning around slowly.

Adam saw a large bare room with a fireplace on one side, and huge, plate-glass windows facing the front porch. An intricately carved banister followed stairs up to the next floor. There were two doors at the rear.

"I plan to take out the wall into the dining room for one big showroom," Whitney explained. "The fireplace will make it seem so intimate."

So will the lingerie, Adam almost said. But it was none of his business. He strolled around to peer into the kitchen and dining room while the two women went on and on about the lingerie catalogue online, until his ears were burning at hearing words like bustier and teddy come from his grandma's lips. He wondered if Brooke had seen his grandma order something online but spared his feelings by not telling him.

"I can't tell you how grateful I am for your support, Mrs. Palmer," Whitney said. "We should have no problems."

Grandma glanced at Adam as her smile

231

dimmed a bit. "Well . . . that might not be true, my dear Whitney. There are some people in town who've heard you're inquirin' about a permit, and they're not too happy."

Whitney turned a baffled expression on Adam, then back to his grandma. "But . . . I have two other stores, and I've never had a problem."

"I heard about the one in San Francisco," Grandma said. "Where's the other?"

"Las Vegas."

"Ah well, there you have it." Grandma shook her head. "They're big cities, and Valentine Valley is a small town with some small minds who can easily influence the rest of 'em."

Whitney's expression turned pensive, and she rubbed her upper arms as if comforting herself.

"But don't worry, dear," Grandma said in a cheerful voice. "You're not alone, as you can tell from that newspaper article."

Whitney frowned. "Article?"

Grandma opened her purse and pulled out the folded *Valentine Gazette.* "So be at ease, knowin' you have help. We'll be there to back you at the town-council meetin'."

Whitney sighed. "I didn't know I needed help."

232

Grandma gave Adam a look, and he tensed with expectation.

"Now that we've put your mind at ease," she said, "why not a tour of Valentine Valley? Adam here, would be free to —"

He held up a hand and interrupted. "Sorry, Grandma, but I haven't lived here for ten years."

"Yes, yes," Grandma said, nodding. "And you do work long hours at the ranch." She smiled up at Whitney. "I'll give you the tour myself one of these days."

And Whitney would get to hear every detail of Valentine's history — just what she needed, Adam thought, hiding a smile.

"We're going to the True Grits for dinner," Grandma was saying. "Care to join us, Whitney?"

Dammit, she was arranging his dates now.

Whitney brightened. "I would love to! And I'll bring along my portfolio with sketches for next year's line. I'd like to hear your opinion."

Adam could have groaned. Not more lingerie talk with his grandma!

CHAPTER TWELVE

Brooke was just setting the kitchen table for dinner when her cell phone rang and she saw Monica's ID. "Hey, Monica."

"Are you busy?" Monica asked.

"I'm fine, thanks," she teased, "and nope, not too busy."

"I think you better come to the True Grits."

Brooke frowned, holding a cup motionless above the table. "Why?"

"It's so crowded no one can get in, and people are saying Mrs. Palmer's in there with the owner of Leather and Lace. More than one whisper has gone around that Adam's in town at last — and he's in there with them."

Brooke remembered hearing about Mrs. Palmer's last battle with Sylvester Galimi at the boardinghouse — and she'd gone to the man's diner? "Are you there now?"

"Nope, I'm at my store. If I couldn't get

in, I'm not standing out on the street. It's freezing! Park near me, and we'll run down together."

"I'll be right there."

When she pulled into a parking space near the flower shop, Monica came rushing out the door, parka already zipped, fur hood falling to her eyebrows.

"I've got Karista to cover for me," Monica said, referring to her teenage part-timer. "Wait!"

She ran next door to Sugar and Spice and leaned her head inside. Emily came out a moment later, wearing a long wool coat and tucking a scarf around her neck.

"Who's covering for you?" Brooke asked, as they walked across Third and headed past Espresso Yourself, which was ominously empty.

"Mrs. Ludlow."

"So she's not in there raising hell with the other widows?" Monica demanded.

"She's just fine hearing all about it later. Brooke, she said *your* grandma is home doing paperwork, so it's only Mrs. Palmer in the eye of the storm."

As they passed Hal's Hardware, Hal was standing outside, the red tip of his cigarette reflected in his glasses, eyeing the crowd the next block over in front of the diner. When he saw them, he quickly put out the cigarette. *Nice, a fireman who smokes,* Brooke thought with amusement.

"Do you know what's going on?" Hal asked, as they hurried past him.

"Nope," Brooke said over her shoulder. "Except I hear one of the widows is involved."

"Aah." Hal nodded as if that explained everything.

By the time they reached the next block, Brooke was relieved to see it wasn't a huge crowd gathered outside the True Grits but only a few people looking in the plate-glass windows, which were outlined in red and green Christmas lights. Glad she was tall, Brooke peered over their shoulders to see a full crowd filling the booths and counter, people milling between the tables.

She marched to the door, and just as she reached it, a woman near the window said, "Good luck getting in there."

Brooke didn't recognize her, which was always a surprise in Valentine. "You must be from out of town," she said.

The woman, plump even in her winter coat, with a fur hat over hair that seemed too red, crossed her arms over her chest and looked perturbed. "I drove in for the day from Glenwood Springs just to see the

Christmas lights and decorations. I thought I'd have an inexpensive meal — but look at this place!"

"It *is* the holiday weekend," Emily said gently. "Try Carmina's Cucina two blocks back toward town hall. Good food and not too expensive."

"Thank you," the other woman said, then put her hand in the arm of an older man who wore a long-suffering expression, and marched off.

Another person at the window turned out to be Chris Sweet, Emily's brother. Unlike Steph, the brothers were rather intrigued to have a new sister. He worked the ranch with his father and occasionally helped out at the family's Sweetheart Inn. His blond hair beneath his cowboy hat had darkened since the summer, and he kept his hands shoved in his fur-lined jacket. He'd been a couple years behind Brooke at school — but on the football team with Adam, she remembered.

Emily gave him a hug. He kept an arm around her shoulders as she shivered.

"Do you know what's going on?" Emily asked.

"Nope, but I heard Adam Desantis is inside. I was fixing to say hi, but . . ." He gestured with his head toward the diner. "Guess it'll have to be another time. You ladies going in?"

"Someone's got to," Emily said with conviction. "If the widows are up to something . . ."

Chris backed away, raising his gloved hands palm out. "Then you're braver than I am. But I might hang out and see the fireworks."

Brooke opened the door and began to push her way past the broad shoulders of several ranchers in stained Carhartt jackets. There was some grumbling, but when they saw who she was, they let her pass through.

"Nate with you?" Francis Osborne asked. His mustache, twirled at the ends, couldn't hide his thinly pressed lips.

"Nope."

"A shame, he could have stopped this. It's — it's unseemly."

She sighed and came to a halt as she looked into the diner, all sleek chrome and red-upholstered booths. A display case near the hostess station showed off mouthwatering cakes, pies, and cheesecakes — many from Sugar and Spice — but Brooke ignored their allure. Handfuls of women walked between booths, talking and chattering in voices that kept increasing in volume as they strove to be heard over each other. Mrs. Palmer stood in the middle, both hands resting loosely on her cane, watching it all with motherly pride.

The center of attention was clothing sketches done in watercolor affixed to cardboard backing, propped up at the back of many of the tables and booths. No, not regular clothing — lingerie. Occasionally, Mrs. Palmer pointed at a sketch with her cane, then glanced guiltily behind her, as if she didn't want someone in particular to observe her perfect balance.

And then Brooke saw Adam, seated in a booth and eating as if he didn't really care what was going on around him. Brooke skirted the crowd of excited women of all ages, noticing that some of the older men were frowning and grumbling to each other. Waitresses in khakis, white buttoned-down shirts, and fifties soda-jerk hats were threading through people as best they could, clearing their way with heavily laden trays.

Brooke nodded to each call of her name and slid into the booth opposite Adam. "What the heck is going on? I get a call from Monica, and it sounds like the town is up in arms!"

He glanced at her mildly and finished swallowing. "This apple pie is incredible."

"It's mine," Emily said, grinning as she took the seat at Adam's side, and he gave her room.

"It can't top the brownies, but it's close."

Brooke interrupted, "We're not here to discuss the food!"

"Sorry." He wiped his mouth with a napkin from the silver dispenser near the wall. "I'm not sure how this all took on a life of its own. One minute Whitney was showing us the portfolio of her designs for next year —"

"Whitney?" Monica said, pushing Brooke farther into the booth with her hips.

"Whitney Winslow, the owner of Leather and Lace." Adam ducked his head side to side, trying to see through the crowd of women, then pointed. "That's her, next to my grandma."

Brooke put an arm across the back of the booth as she swiveled to look behind her. Whitney was thin and elegant, looking the picture of a boutique owner from San Francisco. She was talking animatedly to Julie Jacoby, the redheaded summer hostess from the Halftime Sports Bar, who must be home from college on Thanksgiving break. They seemed to be discussing one of the sketches of a long-legged woman in a black bustier, wearing black boots up above her knees.

"How did all these sketches come out?"

Brooke asked, starting to feel uneasy. Men and women sat in booths or gathered in twos and threes, some looking affronted or worried. She recognized most of them, even the ones she didn't see regularly enough to know their names. A few were obviously tourists, some so in love they couldn't stop holding hands even though they sat side by side. Valentine Valley tended to do that to people for some inexplicable reason.

But she wasn't going to let it do that to her, not right now. And then Adam's boot touched hers, and lingered. She didn't meet his eyes. He was her secret, and she wasn't going to share him. It was more exciting than she could have imagined.

Adam slouched back in the booth. "Grandma had me take her to the building Whitney is thinking of buying. We broke the news to her about the resistance among some of the townspeople, so Grandma invited her to dinner."

"Here?" Brooke asked, baffled.

"I made it a point to say it might not be wise. We haven't seen Galimi yet, so I'm hoping that means he's gone home for the day. Whitney had promised to show her next year's sketches, and before I knew it, Grandma was passing them around. It's getting kind of loud, isn't it?"

241

"And people can't get in the door," Monica said, giving Brooke a worried look.

"I think we're pressing our luck hanging around this long," Brooke said. "Let's you and I collect the sketches before Sylvester makes an appearance."

No sooner had they all started to get out of the booth, then a man roared, "What the hell is going on in here?"

The rumble of voices died to a murmur as heads swiveled. Coming to her feet, Brooke could see that Sylvester must have just emerged from the swinging doors leading into the kitchen. He normally wore a suit every day, but he was in shirtsleeves now, his tie loosened, as if he'd been working in his office. He was red-faced with anger, and Brooke wouldn't have been surprised to see steam covering his glasses.

Mrs. Palmer limped toward the counter with the help of her cane. "Good evenin', Sylvester," she said, her thick Western twang making her sound innocent and cheerful all at once.

"Are you here to disrupt my business just to punish me for disagreeing with you, Renee?" he demanded, looking around to make sure people got the point.

Brooke exchanged a glance with Adam, whose expression was no longer amiable but one of cold intensity.

"Heavens, no!" Mrs. Palmer said, her wrinkled face full of surprise. "We came to enjoy your staff's fine cookin'."

"Then what's all this?" he demanded, coming around the counter.

He stopped in his tracks when he saw a sketch propped on the first booth table — a woman in a bra and thong so tiny . . . and what was obviously a leather collar around her neck.

Brooke winced.

"That — that's —" he sputtered, "that's — pornography!"

Voices rose again, this time the indignant ones.

"My children are here!"

"Where are your morals, Renee?"

"Whose filth is this?"

Brooke rolled her eyes and said to those around her, "Oh, please, your children can see lingerie at Walmart!"

Nobody was listening to her.

Whitney stepped forward, chin raised, to stand beside Mrs. Palmer. "My name is Whitney Winslow. These sketches are from my company, Leather and Lace."

As gasps and cries of recognition filled the air, Brooke saw her brother Josh shoulder his way through the crowd by the door.

Their glances met across the room. His incredulous frown said, *What's going on?* and she splayed her hands in the air on either side of her head, implying, *Beats me, but I'm panicking!*

Sylvester literally backed up a step from Whitney, as if she smelled unpleasant. It was so over-the-top, Brooke could have laughed.

"You're the young lady — young . . . woman responsible for this pornography?" Sylvester said, gesturing wildly to the sketches.

"They're not pornography," Whitney said, smiling her disbelief.

Brooke looked around at the women who'd just been excitedly examining Whitney's work. Most stood behind her resolutely, but a few had melted into the disapproving half of the restaurant. Julie, who'd been talking to Whitney moments before, quietly began to gather up all the sketches.

"Now, Sylvester," Mrs. Palmer began, firmness overtaking the joviality in her voice.

Whitney interrupted. "These sketches are samples of my collection, underwear, nightgowns, robes. I don't know what the big deal is —"

"The 'big deal,' Miss Winslow, is that we

don't need your racy kind of store in our town."

"But this is Valentine Valley," Whitney said, her voice growing cooler. "I've done my research. Why do you think I picked your town? You're all about weddings and engagements and romance. And so is lingerie."

Across the room, Josh was watching Whitney, his easygoing expression turning into admiration. He gave Brooke a nod as if to say, *She's handling herself just fine.*

Julie brought the sketches to the booth. From beneath the table, Adam produced a large leather case and zipped the sketches away inside.

"People can buy it in brown paper packages off the Internet if they like," Sylvester continued righteously, "but they don't want to see it displayed where innocent eyes will be watching."

"My window displays are tasteful and beautiful," Whitney responded with indignation. "There would be nothing inappropriate."

"So you say now," Sylvester responded, "but once you own the building, you'll reveal your real agenda, corrupting the morals of our children!"

Whitney's face went red, and her mouth

dropped open.

Mrs. Palmer's eyes had gone cool with distaste. "That is unbelievably rude, Sylvester, to call our guest a liar."

"This is over," Adam murmured, and pushed forward to his grandma's side. He tossed some money on the counter. "For our bill, Harriet, darlin'," he said to the older waitress in her fifties, whose buttons on her too-small blouse looked like they might pop at any second. "Time to leave before anything worse is said."

Brooke noticed he emphasized a deep drawl he didn't normally have, and Harriet's eyes softened. More than one woman was giving him the once-over, and Brooke could hear, "That's Adam Desantis," from several booths and tables.

"I'm not leaving," Whitney said to no one in particular. "I've been insulted, and I want this man —"

"The name's Sylvester Galimi!" he said clearly, hands on his hips.

"— to hear me out."

Nothing good was going to come of this, Brooke knew. But Whitney didn't know her — why would she listen? Mrs. Palmer was with Adam at the rack by the front door, busily trying to find her coat.

Voices were rising again, with people on

each side beginning to argue with their relatives or neighbors. Carrying the portfolio case, Brooke reached Whitney's side at the same time Josh did.

"Whitney, you don't know me," Brooke began, "but Mrs. Palmer's like my own grandma, and I've known Adam forever. Why don't you follow them before this gets worse?"

A look of frustration and worry wrinkled her forehead. "But I can't let this man —"

"Ma'am," Josh said, his deep voice smooth and full of the West. "I'll escort you. You can't accomplish anything with these hotheads all riled up."

Looking up at him, Whitney's eyes widened, and she seemed to forget what she was going to say, except for a weak, "But my coat . . ."

Brooke grabbed it from the booth they'd just left and followed Josh and Whitney, as a path cleared for them to the door.

Whitney tried to turn back. "My sketches —"

Brooke handed the case over, and Whitney's expression melted from anger to sadness as her gaze swept the room. Then Josh tugged, and she allowed him to lead her through the door.

Out on the street, Brooke zipped up her

coat and saw everyone else doing the same, their breaths puffs of mist. The last Peeping Toms called their good wishes to Mrs. Palmer even as they hurried down the street, shoulders up around their ears from the cold.

Chris Sweet was still there, and as Mrs. Palmer was slowly buttoning her coat, he called, "Adam?"

Adam turned around, his forehead lowered in confusion. Then his expression cleared, and he stuck out a hand. "Chris, good to see you."

"So what are you up to?" Chris asked.

The two men exchanged a brief summary of their current workdays, and when Chris heard that Adam was working as a ranch hand, they started trading cowboy stories. Brooke saw her brother Josh tip his hat to Whitney and walk away down the street, whistling.

Whitney looked forlorn, staring into the brightly lit diner window like a kid who didn't get any Christmas presents.

Mrs. Palmer patted the woman's arm. "Don't worry, dear. We aren't defeated yet."

"I didn't know there was going to be a battle," Whitney said sadly. Then she took a deep breath and straightened her shoulders. "But I won't be defeated, not by such ignorant people. Somehow, I'll find a way to show the town what I'm about, and what I'd like to do to help the women of Valentine feel their prettiest."

"Good for you, dear," Mrs. Palmer said approvingly. "Now let us take you where you're stayin'."

"I'm at one of the Four Sisters B&Bs. I can walk — it's not far."

"But it's cold," Adam said. He raised a hand to Chris, who was already heading toward the street. "We'll drive you." He tipped his hat to Brooke, Monica, and Emily. "Good evening, ladies. Brooke, you need a ride home?"

"I have my Jeep, thanks."

"Grandma, my truck's right in front. Whitney, let me put your portfolio in back."

Brooke couldn't help watching, a smile on her face, as Adam herded the two women away like a cow dog.

"I gotta tell you," Monica said, pulling up her hood, "that man sure is different."

Brooke hugged herself and started to walk. "I guess. Have you guys eaten dinner?"

"Nope," Monica said, "but Just Desserts across the street is looking mighty good."

Emily groaned. "Much as that looks good, I think I need some real food first."

"Wait, let's go the other way," Brooke said. "Mexican?"

"You're on," Monica said. "What about that scene of melodrama?"

"I felt so bad for Whitney," Emily said. "She seems very nice. We never spoke when she was looking into purchasing my building, but I wish I'd had the chance to introduce myself."

"I think you'll get your chance," Brooke said, linking arms with both her friends for warmth. "With the widows at her side, I won't be surprised if she goes on the offensive."

CHAPTER THIRTEEN

Once they'd dropped off Whitney at her B&B, Adam drove his grandma slowly through the town streets. Snow had begun to fall softly, muffling the occasional car and emphasizing the beauty of the Christmas decorations. Now that Thanksgiving was over, people seemed to have spent the weekend decorating Main Street when they weren't shopping, stringing lights from tree to tree like in the movie *It's a Wonderful Life*. Each old-fashioned lamppost had a large outline of a poinsettia jutting out toward the street, all lined with red lights for the petals and green for the leaves.

When Grandma didn't say anything, he eyed her with concern. "Are you feeling okay? Was this too much excitement for you?"

"I'm fine, Adam," she said briskly. "I am simply so furious with Sylvester Galimi." She hesitated. "And with myself. I never thought things would . . . blow up like that. I was so convinced we'd tweak his nose a bit maybe, but . . . oh dear. I've made things so much worse for Whitney."

"Sylvester already planned to do that, Grandma. Tonight, he just got a head start."

"But . . . he was so ugly about it. I never imagined he could insult a young lady like that, when he knew nothin' about her."

"Maybe he's got some reason he's so upset about lingerie, like he caught his dad wearing it."

Grandma gasped, then they both laughed. He was glad to ease her unhappiness, even if only for a while.

As they approached the end of town just before the bridge over Silver Creek, Grandma suddenly pointed. "There's one of the houses being renovated for veterans. Oh my, the new sidin' looks lovely."

"I'm surprised you never brought this subject up," Adam said. "I heard about it from Mrs. Thalberg. It makes me suspicious that you're up to something." More than one thing, truth be told, but he was a patient guy. He hadn't missed how she'd forgotten to use her cane a few times at the diner. He loved her crazy ideas — he loved her. He realized he wasn't going to leave her again.

"Your suspicions are plain wrong, Adam Desantis. You don't want to discuss your military life with me, and I thought mentionin' the veterans' housin' plans might upset you."

"I'm not a fragile doll, Grandma," he said. "If your committee has an interesting project, you can tell me."

Even if he didn't do anything about it.

When there was a soft knock at the cabin door late that night, Ranger put his head up, ears alert. Adam could have vaulted the couch to get to the door.

Brooke stood on the porch, smiling. Innocently, she said, "I'm just dropping something off . . ."

He pulled her inside, closed the door, and put her up against it so he could give her a proper kiss. Her lips were chilly, her coat bulky between them, but she still felt incredibly good, especially when she sank her hands into his hair and held him to her.

Behind him, Ranger gave a woof.

When they came up for air, she looked around Adam. "So you've got other company."

"Ranger decided I shouldn't be alone at night since you've deserted me."

"It's been two days," she said, laughing as

she put her hands on his chest and pushed.

"Two long days where I get to see you and not touch." He backed up a step as she took off her coat and hung it on one of the hooks beside the door.

Her smile faded as she regarded him. "Is our undercover secret not working for you?"

"I didn't say that. I'm just all hot and bothered from those sketches, and I almost threw snowballs at your window."

Brooke moved toward the fire, petting Ranger, then holding out her hands to the warmth. "I don't know why you're hot and bothered — they're not pornography." She sent him a smile.

"I don't need pornography. You'd turn me on wearing cowboy boots and hat and nothing else."

She held out a hand to him and he joined her in front of the fire. He shooed Ranger away and sat down on the rug, back against the couch, and pulled Brooke down to sit between his legs. She leaned against him with a sigh of contentment.

"I did feel bad for Whitney," she said quietly. "That was an ugly thing Sylvester said."

"He was just spouting for an audience. He's got to recruit for the town-council meeting after all."

"How did she act afterward?"

He pulled the band off the end of her braid, then ran his fingers down through her dark brown hair until the wavy curls spread freely down her back. "You saw her. She's not giving up. And it was only a couple blocks to her B&B. She didn't say much in the car."

"Your grandma must have been steamed."

"Partly. And then she blamed herself. She never meant any of that to happen."

"I'm sure you reassured her," Brooke said, tipping her head back and snuggling beneath his chin. "I saw you and Chris talking. You know he'd be happy to reintroduce you to people."

"We'll see. I also heard about another teammate today. We used to call him Deer."

She laughed. "I haven't thought of that nickname for Howie Junior in I don't know how long."

"If I remember correctly, he dated you in high school." He nipped the side of her neck with his mouth.

"Oh, yes, you should be jealous. I'm always attracted to men who tell everyone our private business."

"So he ran at the mouth about as fast as he ran with a football?"

"Maybe faster. Guess that's why I like you."

She twisted her head as if to glance at him, but he could only see her profile.

"You seem pretty good with secrets," she continued.

He wasn't stupid — she was talking about more than their sex life. But he wasn't going to burden her with his problems. "Deer never said much to me about you. What did he have to say to other guys? If he got to first base or not?"

"That about covers it. We didn't last long, so that was all the baseball we played. But he's a nice guy, even if he's no longer able to run quite so fast."

"Hmmm, first base," he said, nuzzling behind her ear. "I got there the moment you walked in the door." Then he slid his hands up and over her breasts, cupping their fullness. "Second base."

She gave a soft gasp that was nearly his undoing, arching her head back to his shoulder. He kissed his way from her earlobe down to the collar of her shirt, while he gently rubbed her nipples through her clothes.

"A thin bra," he said.

"Not quite as impressive as the ones in the sketches."

"Let me be the judge of that." He slid one hand down and cupped the warmth between her thighs. "Third base."

"Oh, please," she said breathlessly. "You call that third base?"

"Is that a challenge?" In an instant, he had her on her back on the rug, her hair spread all around, her face glowing with the firelight and her good, sweet nature.

Sweet? Brooke? He would never have thought that before. She was clearly addling his brain. But then he was taking off her clothes, and his brain shut down altogether. Her Western shirt unsnapped in front, and so did her polka-dotted bra. He spent endless minutes worshipping her breasts, kissing and licking, aroused by every helpless gasp and moan she emitted. She couldn't lie still, pulling at his clothes until at last he yanked off his t-shirt. But he wasn't in a hurry, not this time. He wanted to explore.

Unbuckling her jeans, he tugged them very slowly down her hips, revealing her sexy curves and the indentation of her belly button. Her long thighs were next, and at last he had her completely naked but for her thong, so lacy and delicate he wanted to stare at it a while longer.

And then he started at her feet and kissed his way up along her smooth, feminine muscles. He parted her thighs and mouthed her through the silk, and she cried out. Just a few strokes of his tongue, and he made her come, shuddering.

"Inside me," she whispered, tugging at his belt buckle.

He stood up, said, "Be right back," and went for a condom. When he returned, she was completely naked, reaching for him. Then he covered her body with his own, there in front of the heat of the fire, and entered her so slowly it drove them both crazy. He took his time, luxuriating in long kisses, rounding his back to lick her breasts, bringing her ever higher, until, when his thrusts increased, and she came again, he let go of his restraint and joined her.

When he could function, he eased to the side, propping his head on one hand and caressing whatever he wanted with the other.

At last she murmured, "I guess I should go. We're taking the sleigh out to cut down a Christmas tree. Family tradition." And then she winced, as if she regretted her words, and rushed on. "Nate suggested we take photos and use it for publicity for the sleigh rides."

"You don't have to explain," he insisted. "I spent my life hearing about other people's families. I'm used to it. And don't even think about inviting me. It would make certain people suspicious."

"You could get your own tree, you know."

"I'll think about it."

When he closed the door behind her after a long kiss good-bye, the place seemed lonely without her. He didn't think a Christmas tree would help.

The following Tuesday afternoon, Brooke stood inside the barn, waiting for Steph to arrive for her lesson. The wind blew like breath across ice, and snow, although light, was falling at an angle. She was tempted to call the girl and cancel, but then she could see the pickup and horse trailer come slowly down the winding road toward the ranch.

By the time Steph had her mount ready, the snow had only increased.

"Brooke, can we please ride?" Steph pleaded. "I thought about it all day."

"Was your holiday that stressful?" Brooke teased.

When Steph only smiled halfheartedly, Brooke hesitated to press her.

"Okay, let's give it a try. We haven't had that much snow accumulation today."

They began to ride toward the corral near the burned barn. They were both wearing caps and scarfs to bundle up their heads, and Brooke felt relatively warm. She glanced at Steph, whose face was lifted as if to take in the serenity of the Elk Mountains. Their bodies moved gently with the gait of the horses.

"So what happened at Thanksgiving?" Brooke asked, then added, "If you don't mind the question." She knew Emily and Nate had been there for lunch before joining the Thalbergs for dinner. She felt a little ache for her friend, who so desperately wanted her happily-ever-after.

Steph shrugged. "It was okay. I know you're asking about Emily, and she was fine."

"Please tell me she told you about bridesmaid gown colors, because curiosity is driving me crazy! You may not know it to look at me, but I love pretty dresses."

That got a smile out of the girl. "Naw, we didn't really talk about the wedding, and that was part of the problem."

Brooke waited, when she wanted to say with exasperation, *Isn't that what you wanted?*

"I felt like . . . it was my fault people don't discuss it, and I don't want to be the cause of all that tension. My mom said I wasn't, but she's my mom."

Faith Sweet was smart about people and surely knew what her daughter needed to hear. Maybe Steph needed to figure things out on her own.

"Then if your mom said that, why don't you just trust her and not worry about it? I saw Emily and Nate for dinner, and they were just fine."

"Good," Steph said absently. She slid her gloved hands along the reins over and over, never tugging, but like a nervous habit.

"So tell me about the Chess Club," Brooke said. "Any new members?"

Steph glanced at her, and a slow grin made her shake her head. "You just want to know if I asked Tyler Brissette to join."

"Guess I'm not very subtle."

The girl gave an exaggerated sigh. "All right, yes, I told him about the club. At first he was all, 'That's for nerds,' but I told him it wasn't like we really played chess or anything."

"Hey, I like chess," Brooke protested. "Not that I play regularly, but I have. My nerdy habit is reading."

Steph rolled her eyes, but admitted, "Yeah, I read Harry Potter when I was a kid. And I like *The Hunger Games.*"

"I've read both those series. They're very good."

"Anyway, I didn't think Tyler would come. And I'd asked him the day before Thanksgiving, and who knew if he'd even remember. Then yesterday, after school, he and a couple guys came to the community center. I was shocked!"

Steph's blue eyes shone, and Brooke found herself wondering if this was more than an attempt to help a troubled classmate.

"Well, how did they do?" Brooke demanded.

"Some of his friends called it the Chest Club, like they thought they were so funny. Anyway, we didn't have a big trip or anything planned, but we all hung out and played pool and Ping-Pong and Wii. He just watched for a while, but he's pretty good at pool. I didn't really talk to him much or anything," she added quickly. "But he was cool about the whole thing."

"Much as pool and Wii sound fun in the winter, do you have any outdoor events planned?" Although right now, when the wind picked up, she was wishing she had worn her coveralls. She wasn't so sure *anyone* should be outside, including the horses, whose ears twitched with each gust.

"We try to go snowboarding together at least once during the season."

"And is everyone able to afford that?"

Steph frowned. "I never thought about it before. But Tyler and his friends . . . I'm not so sure." She glanced at Brooke as if embarrassed. "I don't want to make anyone feel bad."

"Then can I make a suggestion? What about if you come here to ride? I can give lessons to those who don't know how, and we can do a trail ride or even a sleigh ride."

Steph grinned. "That sounds awesome!"

Brooke was surprised to find herself equally excited. She'd enjoyed giving the occasional lesson to barrel racers like Steph, and the chance to help improve the skills of other teenagers sounded like a good challenge.

The corral fence suddenly loomed in front of them in the snow, and she realized that the weather had grown too bad. "I think we're going to have to cancel, Steph. I'm not sure you can even see the barrels."

The teenager released a big sigh. "Guess you're right."

They guided their horses in a circle and headed back the way they'd come. Brooke trusted the horses to find their way if things got worse.

Back in the barn, after rubbing down and oating the horses, then putting away the tack, Brooke insisted Steph couldn't drive in that weather, so the girl came inside for dinner and some Trivial Pursuit before the weather had cleared enough for her to drive home. It was an old game, but Brooke had grown up playing it.

After Steph was gone, Sandy sat at the dining-room table and studied her. "You were really good with her."

Brooke blinked in surprise and pleasure as she picked up a bowl now empty of chips. "What do you mean? She's a nice kid — what was difficult about it?"

"I don't know, but some people can be impatient — including Steph herself — but when she got frustrated about not knowing a lot of the answers in the game, you were able to head off any problems. You'd have been a good teacher."

"Why . . . thanks," Brooke said. "Dealing with teenagers one-on-one isn't so bad. I can't imagine controlling a whole class of kids."

Sandy grinned. "Guess you'll find out if the Chess Club takes you up on your offer."

"Didn't I tell you you're in charge that day?" Brooke teased.

Sandy waved a finger at her. "Not this time, sweetie. You're on your own."

■ ■ ■ ■

The next afternoon, Adam was getting a lesson from Josh on repairing leather tack when Nate came into the workshop looking for him.

"You could have called my cell," Adam said, smiling as he rose to his feet. "What can I . . ." His voice trailed off as two other men crowded behind Nate, trying to see in.

"You've got guests," Nate said, wearing a wry grin.

"Hey, Adam!" one of them called over Nate's shoulder.

Adam thought he recognized them, but the light from the workshop didn't quite reach, and he didn't want them crowding Josh and asking questions.

"We can finish up later," Josh said. "You go have fun with the boys."

Nate and Josh seemed to know something he didn't. But he wiped his hands on a rag and went out into the open area of the barn between stalls.

"Remember these guys?" Nate asked in a dry tone of voice.

"It's Derek and Chad," said one man, reaching out to shake Adam's hand.

"Derek and Chad," Adam repeated, shaking the other man's hand, too. They weren't from his football-playing days but from before, when he'd been joyriding in cars and getting in trouble. He'd avoided them junior and senior year, when the two of them had been tag-teaming each other in detention and even the occasional suspension. Who was he to assume they hadn't straightened out in the past ten years?

Nate excused himself with a touch to the brim of his Stetson, buttoned up his coat, and left the barn, closing the door behind him.

Adam turned to the two men. "What can I do for you guys?"

"Nothing," Derek said. "We just heard you were in town and thought we'd be neighborly." He had dark hair that crossed a line into a mullet, curling out from beneath the back of his baseball cap.

Chad constantly smoothed the patch of sparse brown hair on his chin and gave a nervous twitch of his shoulders. "So you're out of the Marines?"

"Yep."

"Had enough killing?" Derek asked.

Adam frowned. "I'm not sure what you're trying to say."

"Oh, we know you were 'serving your country' and all that," Chad added. "But it's gotta be tough."

"It was. What have you two been doing with yourselves?"

"We both tried getting married," Derek began.

"To each other?" Adam asked innocently.

"Naw!" Chad looked offended. "We're not gay. We got divorced from *women.* Derek's even a dad."

Poor kid, Adam thought.

"We work for Sweet Brothers Construction," Derek continued. "Good jobs and lots of building going on from Glenwood Springs to Aspen."

"Good for you."

"We didn't know you were a cowboy," Chad said, a bit too slyly, as if it had been rehearsed. He braced a hand on the door of a stall, then pulled away when Brooke's horse, Sugar, tried to nip him.

"I wasn't. But the Thalbergs offered me a job as a ranch hand while I'm in town. I'm learning a lot."

"Is Brooke teaching you?" Chad asked, then sent a significant glance at Derek.

Adam didn't know how he was supposed to miss that, but if they thought they were hiding something, then whatever. "Sometimes. Why?"

"Chad had a dance with her the other

night," Derek said. "They looked pretty good together."

Adam arched a brow in surprise and just waited.

Chad rocked back and forth on his heels, wearing what he probably thought was a woman-magnet grin. "Think you can call Brooke here so we can say hi?"

Their bravado should be laughable — but Adam wasn't laughing. "So basically, you're using me to get to Brooke?"

Derek's brow wrinkled. "Don't see how anyone's using anyone. We came to see you *and* Brooke."

"But I'm supposed to somehow . . . smooth your way?"

Chad and Derek exchanged grins. "That's mighty nice of you," Chad said.

"Not today, boys. I have to get back to work."

They looked confused but eventually left after Adam had to refuse them a second time. Hands on his hips, he watched them go, then turned and went back into the barn.

Josh was coming out of his workshop. "They left? You could have gone with them, you know."

Adam grimaced. "They stopped maturing in high school."

Josh cocked his head. "I heard them mention Brooke. Why didn't you call her?"

"Because she wouldn't want to see them."

"Really? Good luck with that." Josh grinned and returned to his workshop.

Adam went to search for Brooke and found her in the truck shed, starting and restarting the engine of the ATV that the teenager had stolen. "Is something wrong with it?" he asked, hoping he wouldn't have to mention the kid.

"No, I thought it hesitated when it started, but it seems fine now."

Adam was relieved. "Just wanted to let you know that Derek and Chad from the old days stopped by."

She grinned, climbing off the ATV and grabbing a rag to wipe her hands. "So they tracked you down. I thought they might."

"It was only a ruse to see you. I sent them on their way."

Her eyes widened briefly. "You did? Why?"

"I knew you wouldn't care to see them. They're losers."

"I know that — and I can take care of myself. Besides, maybe I'm interested in one of them." She met his gaze, and suddenly a rueful grin appeared. "Well, okay, maybe not. But regardless, it's up to me to choose, so please don't act in my place." She touched his arm as she moved past him toward the tool bench.

Adam went outside and took a deep breath of the cold. He'd acted as her protector without even thinking about it. Protecting people had been his job for ten years, but still . . .

He was already acting like Brooke was his, as if they had some kind of a relationship. Would that be so bad? he wondered, thinking of his promise to move forward in life rather than linger in pain and regret.

CHAPTER FOURTEEN

Friday evening, Adam went to spend time with his grandma, and once again, she was waiting for him at the door wearing her coat. He couldn't see what outrageous dress she might be wearing, and that had him worried.

"Where are we going now?" he asked patiently.

"The Silver Creek Community Center," she said, smiling at him. "I'm entertainin' the Chess Club this evenin'."

Adam blinked at her suspiciously. "Doing what?"

"Readin' their cards, of course!" She held up a little drawstring bag. "I'm goin' to teach them about the mysteries of tarot, too."

Shooting pool and having a beer might be more enjoyable, but this night was his grandma's. He followed her into the community center, an old brick factory that had been converted for the town into meeting rooms and even a large reception room for small weddings and other events. Grandma told him about the huge deck where people gathered for the Music to Eat By programs during summer lunches. In the reception room, he saw various small booths along one wall, advertising local business like music quartets and romantic picnic baskets made to order. Someone worked hard to play up Valentine Valley's romantic reputation.

But his grandma kept walking at a slow but steady pace, and as he studied her gait, he noticed she wasn't acting quite so feeble as she had been the first week or so of his arrival. She must think he was completely under her spell — and he was, he admitted to himself. He followed her into a slightly smaller room, with kitchen cabinets and appliances in one corner, pool table, Ping-Pong table, a large-screen TV, and groups of comfortable couches and chairs.

And then he saw Brooke, Emily, and Monica huddled over trays spread on the kitchen counters. Brooke was dressed in black jeans, a patterned top, and a sexy leather jacket. Her brown hair hung loose though pulled back from her face. He realized he was staring, when his grandma stepped into his line of vision, unbuttoning her coat. He helped her take it off, then hid a wince as he saw her dress patterned with stars and moons. Where did she find these clothes?

Brooke glanced their way. "Hi, Mrs. Palmer!" she called, then, "Hey, Adam. Guess Nate didn't keep you forever."

Adam smiled. "Yeah, I finally got it right."

Monica wiped her hands on a towel. "Got what right?"

"I couldn't manage to cut a cow from the herd and rope her. Nate needed to doctor her. I probably galloped through that herd a hundred times, but he insisted I needed to learn."

"It must have taken hours," Brooke said solemnly. "Adam's a slow learner. Maybe he's even saddle sore."

Monica and Emily both laughed, and Adam tolerated being the butt of their jokes.

"So when do the kids arrive?" he finally asked, when the women headed toward the kitchen.

"Anytime now," Brooke called back.

"How did you guys get involved with this?" He followed them, while Grandma Palmer limped away to claim a small square table and spread out a glittery cloth.

"Steph heard about your grandma's many

273

talents through her own mom," Brooke began.

"Faith is into all the mystical stuff," Monica confided. "Steph, not so much, but they were looking for a fun guest, and who's more fun than your grandma?"

"I offered to provide refreshments," Emily said, coloring a bit.

He understood why. She was eager to become closer to her new little sister and probably relieved and excited that Steph had accepted.

"So what do we have here?" he asked, checking out the spread that covered the counters.

"Little samples of everything," Emily said, coming to his side. "Help yourself."

Everything had its own little paper cup for display — little cookies, mini cupcakes and cheesecakes, and squares of her delicious brownies. He went for one of those first.

"I'll try the others later," he promised.

"So you're sticking around?" Emily asked in surprise. "I couldn't even get Nate to come, and he's engaged to me."

"I guess a grandma can be more persuasive than a fiancée." He paused. "Brooke's told me a bit about your problems with Steph."

"She has?" Emily asked, her blue eyes round.

He shrugged. "We're together most of the day, and we talk to fill the time."

Emily looked past him, wiping the concern off her face and replacing it with a cheerful smile. Adam turned his head and saw the teenagers arriving in groups of twos and fours, staying clustered together. Someone turned on music, and the beat thumped through the room. None of them approached the adults at first, as they hung up their coats and spread out around the Ping-Pong or pool tables.

Then Grandma Palmer waded right into the center of them and started talking.

"I really like her," Emily said, her voice wistful.

Steph came toward them, smiling up at Adam. To her credit, the smile only dimmed a little when she turned to Emily.

"Thanks for making the food," Steph said.

"I'm glad you asked."

"How much do we owe you? We keep money in our budget for snacks."

"No, please, it's my treat. Think of it as advertising, right?"

"Well, okay, thanks." She turned away.

Emily gave a quiet groan and closed her eyes. "Advertising," she murmured, her voice laced with disgust. "I couldn't have just said it was a gift?"

"She might not have taken it," Adam said.

"But it sounded . . . all business and professional, not like she was my sister and I'd do anything . . ." Emily's voice trailed off.

Adam felt awkward. Should he pat her on the back?

She cleared her throat. "Sorry."

Brooke approached and bumped shoulders playfully with Emily. "Don't worry, it'll be okay. At our lesson the other day, she said she felt sorta bad that it might be her fault you didn't discuss the wedding on Thanksgiving Day. Baby steps, right?"

"She said that?" Emily's sad expression turned hopeful.

"And she came to you for the food — that was my idea, too," Brooke added.

"Oh, Brooke, I'd hug you, but it might make Steph think you're conspiring with me."

"Well . . . I am."

Emily put a finger to her lips. "Shh!"

Adam smiled at Brooke, enjoying how easily she found a way to encourage her friend and make her feel better. She was a protective woman, he knew, especially about her family, but also the other people in her life.

Monica broke out the sodas, and Adam helped set them out on various tables, but then he retreated, knowing the kids would feel more comfortable pretending he wasn't there. Many of the girls had already gathered around Grandma Palmer, who was holding court in a quiet, but firm voice. He remembered her booming laugh, bigger than life, embarrassing his mother but not him. He could always hear his grandma from across any football field. He hoped to hear that booming voice again soon, but he couldn't very well spoil her plans.

The adults stood near the kitchen while the kids played games. Gradually, almost all of the girls but Steph clustered around his grandma. In between laughter, there was an occasional "oooh" of recognition as she talked about the pattern of the cards.

Steph was sitting on a stuffed couch near the TV, talking to a boy whose back was to Adam.

Brooke grabbed Emily, and said quietly, "That must be Tyler. He's the boy I told you about, that she asked to join the Chess Club. Guess he and his friends have been in some trouble."

Emily frowned. "I heard her mention a boy during the week, but didn't realize he had . . . issues."

"Lots of kids have issues," Brooke said, then glanced at Adam. "Remind you of anyone?"

He nodded. "Yep. And someone gave me a chance to turn myself around. But she should be careful until he does make some kind of effort."

To Emily, Brooke said, "Since she's already mentioned him to you, perhaps you can ask her how it went, helping him, I mean. Hey, it's something to talk about."

Emily nodded, then asked, "Can I change the subject?" She gestured to Monica and brought her over. "I have some news to tell you."

"Should I leave you ladies alone?" Adam asked.

"No, I won't banish you to the corner by yourself." Emily smiled up at him. "As it is, it's pretty easy to notice you'd rather be with us girls than the kids — or your grandma."

Monica and Brooke both chuckled.

"Hey, I'm not about to let my grandma think I put stock in her wacky musings. I'm glad she has a hobby, but I don't have to believe in it. As for the kids, they'd rather be with each other than me."

"Oh, come on, you remember what it was like to be one, don't you?" Monica demanded.

Brooke was watching him silently, and he guessed she understood what he meant.

"Of course I remember being a teenager. Some of it I wish I could forget."

Brooke glanced at Monica. "Like a couple dates he had . . ."

"Hey!" Monica said, hands on her hips. "I get your implication, Brooke Thalberg!"

"Do I need to step between you ladies?" Adam asked mildly, even as the two women grinned at each other. "But Monica, Brooke is right in one sense — I'd like to forget the way I treated you. If you'd accept my apology, I'd appreciate it."

Monica waved a hand. "Oh, please. If I had to apologize for every stupid thing I did as a teenager, I wouldn't have time to work. Of course you're forgiven. But that doesn't mean Steph and her friends don't have something to learn from you."

"I don't know about that."

"Wait, wait, I didn't get to tell you my news!" Emily cried, then looked around at the teenagers and lowered her voice. "Nate and I have decided to move in together."

Monica practically squealed as she gave her a hug, and although Brooke also fell into the hugging line, she gave Emily a worried look afterward.

"This isn't some kind of proof to Nate that just because you haven't set a date —"

"No, no, nothing like that!" Emily interrupted.

"Because he's a big boy, and he loves you enough to wait for whatever makes you happy."

"Thanks for that," Emily said with a soft smile. "But no, I want to be with him. I don't need to wait for the wedding. But I had another reason to tell you the news — would you mind helping me pack and move?"

Brooke grinned. "What are friends for?"

Adam watched the three women chat happily about Emily's plans and realized they shared a bond of friendship that was just as close as family. They'd created this themselves, something he wasn't ever going to do by hanging out at the bunkhouse alone each night. It was hard to be happy, really happy, when his men — his brothers — were dead. That's what he'd been telling himself for months now.

But he *was* happy — being with Brooke was making him happy, whether at night wrapped up in their secret, or during the day, working at her side. He looked at the teenagers, so involved in their own lives, oblivious to what might await them out in the world. He remembered those days, when the world had seemed full of possibilities. It could be that way again for him.

After the teenagers had gone, and Brooke wiped down the last table, she approached Adam, who was helping his grandma into her coat.

"Did I mention how much I love your dress, Mrs. Palmer?" Brooke asked, smiling.

"It catches the young people's attention, of course," the older woman said. "And that's often the first battle."

"Did they enjoy your readings?"

"I think they did. Oh, they giggled a bit, and the boys rolled their eyes, but some of them left here feelin' more calm about their future, and that's all you can ask."

Brooke looked up at Adam and found that having to keep herself so friendly and neutral around him was much harder than she'd thought. They worked together much of each day, even had lunch together, but there were so many people around them at the ranch, and everyone was busy. She could concentrate on her work, or her discussion of work, and include Adam as a coworker rather than a lover.

It was much more difficult being around her best friends — who knew her so well —

and Adam's grandma, and finding a way to be pleasant and friendly, although not too friendly. She kept almost touching him, or leaning against him, all because of the physical intimacy they'd been sharing. It was making her tense, and she was glad the evening was almost over.

She put her acting skills to use and smiled up at him. "Josh and I came to town together earlier, and I told him to take the truck, and I'd find a ride home. Adam, would you mind?"

"We'd love your company, dear!" Mrs. Palmer said, patting her arm.

When the maintenance worker arrived to lock the doors, they all left, waving goodbye in the parking lot. The drive to the Widows' Boardinghouse passed quickly, and Adam helped his grandma inside. As he got behind the wheel again, Brooke jumped into the front seat and saw Mrs. Palmer's purple drawstring bag.

"Whoops, she left her cards," Brooke said. "I'll be right back."

She dashed up the kitchen stairs and opened the door without knocking, as she always did. To her surprise, she found Mrs. Palmer still in her coat, the cane on a hook by the door, a giant plate in her hands as she ate voraciously. At the community grandma to herself in response and hope that Mrs. Palmer had it right.

center, she'd picked at her food like an injured bird.

Brooke came to a stop, unable to hide her grin. "Ah-ha, caught you!"

Her guilty expression gave everything away. "Oh dear. You already knew?"

Brooke nodded. "I didn't share my suspicions with Adam."

The widow put a hand to her chest. "Thank goodness."

"Why don't you tell me what's going on?"

With a sigh, Mrs. Palmer crossed to the table with her usual brisk gait and set down her plate. "I've been . . . exaggeratin' a bit. I was desperate to get Adam to visit and perhaps stay. Oh, every year he flew in for a couple days, or he had me come visit him, but these last six months since his discharge . . . I've had a bad feelin'. Even my cards were tellin' me somethin's wrong. You see, I never got to be with him all that much when he was a child. Funny, isn't it? He lived right here, but his mother, my only child, resented how close he was to me. She used me when she needed me, and when she wanted to punish me, she didn't let me see Adam."

Her voice broke a little, and Brooke felt a pang of answering sadness that brought tears to her eyes.

Mrs. Palmer held up her hand and gave a trembling smile as she went on. "I was her reward to him. When he was good and docile and did everythin' around the house, he was allowed to visit me for a night. His clothes were too small and smelled like cigarette smoke" — she bowed her head and had to lay her hand on the table — "but if I gave him new things, he and I were both punished."

"Oh, Mrs. Palmer," Brooke said, putting her arm around the woman's trembling shoulders. "How terrible for you."

Mrs. Palmer stiffened and composed herself. "Not nearly as terrible for me as for Adam. He lived a neglected childhood, and I couldn't do a thing about it. He almost ruined his life, but with the kindness of other adults, he found his way. Somethin's wrong now — and I can help. Let me keep helpin', Brooke, dear. Don't tell him I'm well, or he might get it into his head to leave, thinkin' I don't need him." Her voice dropped to a whisper. "But I do need him. It's been so wonderful havin' him home."

Brooke didn't need to think long. "I won't say anything, I promise."

Mrs. Palmer briefly closed her eyes. "Oh, thank you. Now you better go before he gets suspicious." She looked around frantically.

"Ah, here's Connie's coffee cake. Take some to your mama, and that'll be a good excuse for dawdlin'."

After she'd put half on a paper plate and covered it in foil, their hands met as they exchanged the cake.

"Thank you so much, Brooke," Mrs. Palmer said. "I hope the lies don't weigh on you."

"They won't." But she wondered . . .

When she climbed back into the pickup truck, Adam looked at her with concern. "I almost came in. She didn't fall, did she?"

When he studied her closely, she only gave him a bright smile and stared out the windshield. "Nope, she just wanted to give my mom some coffee cake."

On the drive home, she thought about her promise to remain silent. It wasn't hurting Adam to think his grandma was getting feeble. She was in her late seventies and not the same as she used to be. And Brooke was getting lots of practice misrepresentin' herself, lately.

But if she had any doubts, all she had do was conjure up the images Mrs. Palm had evoked, of Adam so neglected a child. She knew he was keeping someth from her, something that weighed on She would keep this truth about

CHAPTER FIFTEEN

Sunday afternoon, Brooke drove into Valentine and parked in the alley behind Sugar and Spice. She knocked on the back door, and Emily let her up the rear staircase to her second-floor apartment. Brooke walked down the little hallway, past the two bedrooms and the galley kitchen into the long room that was part dining room, part living room. Monica sat folding boxes from flattened cardboard into usable containers.

A huge picture window overlooked Main Street. Emily had several fake candles in the windows, little ceramic Christmas decorations on the tables, and a Christmas tree in the front corner. The decorations actually looked handmade, to Brooke's bemusement.

Emily sighed. "Guess I should have waited on the tree. But I like to have one the weekend after Thanksgiving."

"You and Nate can cut down another one

at the ranch," Brooke said, putting her arm briefly around Emily's shoulders. "Leave this one here. I imagine you'll be up here occasionally during the workday, right?"

"Of course," Emily said, obviously relieved. "Smart thinking." Then she sat down on the couch beside Monica and let her shoulders slump.

"Okay, what's wrong?" Brooke demanded, coming to sit in the chair across the coffee table from them.

Monica put down the packing tape. "Spill it, girlfriend."

"Poor Steph," Emily began.

Brooke thought of the girl driving that horse trailer from one ranch to another, across town. "She didn't get in an accident, did she?"

"Oh, no, no — it's actually her . . . friend, Tyler."

"They looked pretty close Friday night," Monica said. "Like more than friends."

"I know," Emily said grimly. "And that's what makes it worse. My father said he caught Tyler joyriding on one of his ATVs at the Sweet Ranch. He ran into a rock hidden under the snow and bent an axle. His 'friends' abandoned him on other ATVs, also stolen, but later found undamaged. Dad was pretty upset. He couldn't just let

288

him go — there was damage done."

"Of course he couldn't," Brooke soothed. "Tyler has to learn the consequences of his actions."

"So Dad called the sheriff, and a deputy took Tyler away. I didn't want Steph to hear this as a rumor, so I went to her privately and told her what had happened. She started to cry, and begged me not to tell our father she'd been seeing Tyler. She believes he can come around and that she can help him, but if Dad forbids it . . ."

Brooke groaned and ran a hand down her face. "Oh, this is my fault. When she first told me about Tyler, I suggested she invite him to the Chess Club. I practically threw them together."

"You couldn't have known, Brooke," Monica said with sincerity.

"It's not like they've done more than hang out a few times," Emily insisted. "But . . . Steph likes him and wants to help. I understand her — hell, don't women *always* want to help? But I was so relieved she confided in me that I promised my silence without thinking things through. I did insist that the moment I thought Tyler could hurt her, the secret was done. And she agreed and hugged me and thanked me and said Tyler was trying to get away from a bad group of guys, and she wouldn't go anywhere with him, only see him at school —" It was her turn to groan. "I'm a sucker. Who knows if he's lying to her? How can I keep something from my dad when we're only just getting to know each other?"

Brooke leaned forward, elbows on her knees. "Tyler *could* be lying to her — we all know that."

Monica looked from Emily to Brooke. "And we all know someone who really was trying to get away from a bad crowd, and who stole a *car*, before getting his act together."

"But as long as Steph doesn't go hang out with this bad crowd of Tyler's," Brooke continued, "I don't think it'll hurt your dad too much for you to keep Steph's confidence. If she trusts you, she'll tell you things, right? If she's mad at both you and your dad, she might be worse off."

"Do you think so?" Emily asked with hope.

Brooke tried to infuse reassurance in her smile. "She's a smart kid. I think you can give her the benefit of the doubt. *She* wasn't joyriding, after all."

"You're both making me feel better," Emily said. "All right, I'll cut Steph a little slack. But I'll keep an even closer eye on her."

"From Nate's cabin?" Monica asked innocently.

"Maybe Steph and I can have a sleepover!" Emily said, as if she hadn't heard.

Brooke and Monica exchanged an amused glance.

Brooke woke up to a foot of powder up on the hills Monday morning. She and Josh had a long-standing deal, alternating who got to go skiing and enjoy the occasional powder day in Aspen. They took turns covering for each other, and today it was her day to take off.

Josh and Adam had already loaded down the retriever with enough hay for the first couple pastures, and they'd be dropping mineral pellets as well, later on. She felt a little guilty — but not that guilty.

Carrying her skis over her shoulder, she ran into Adam in the yard.

"Aren't you the ski bunny?" he said.

He gave a slow, thorough examination of her body with half-lidded eyes. She was wearing pink ski pants and a blue shell.

"Those pants nicely accent your ass. I'll be thinking about it all day."

She felt a rush of heated memory, and

they kept staring at each other. It had been a few days . . . She found herself wishing she could invite him to go along, but besides the fact that he was working, she had their "no dating" rule to remember. And maybe he didn't even know how to ski — after all, it wasn't like his family had had the money. She imagined how it must have felt to know so many of your friends were doing what you couldn't. And here she was, rubbing his nose in it again.

But Adam was smiling at her, that cleft in his jaw so masculine, his eyes alight. She knew if she got closer, she could see the gold flecks in their centers . . . but no, she wasn't getting closer.

"Hey, you should have told me in the feed store that Josh's belts were for sale there," he said. "I would have liked seeing the display. He told me all about it."

"He's getting so popular. Have you been in Monica's Flowers and Gifts? He's got a whole display all to himself. He's even considering an offer from an Aspen boutique."

Adam gave a low whistle. "Impressive. No wonder your dad hired me. Sounds like Josh could hit the big time."

"I hope so!" She glanced down at Ranger, sitting patiently at Adam's feet. "Your constant companion nowadays?"

He lowered his voice. "Don't worry, you have first dibs on my bed."

And then they were looking at each other again, yards apart, but the air between them seemed to smolder.

"Come to me tonight," he whispered.

Almost breathless, she whispered back, "I promised I'd go out with Monica."

"No problem," Adam said, rubbing his hands together. He looked over his shoulder and saw Josh heading for the retriever. "Gotta go. Have a fun day."

Brooke sighed and turned away, only to see Nate coming out of the truck shed.

He glanced at Adam, then her. "Everything okay?"

"Of course."

"Is he going skiing?" Nate asked.

"And desert his post? Incur your wrath?" The she lowered her voice. "You know, he probably didn't ski growing up."

He nodded, then arched a brow. "All concerned for him, are you?"

To her surprise, she felt more excited than nervous as she protected her secret rebellion. She'd never really had one before, an actual experience her family didn't share and couldn't express an opinion on. And she liked it. "Look, he's a friend who's going through some tough times."

Nate nodded. "You're right. Have fun today."

She almost let out a sigh of relief.

It was a strange day for Adam. He hadn't realized how much he looked forward to spending part of each day with Brooke. Even if they didn't feed cattle together, they had lunch as a boisterous group with her family, and more and more, he'd begun to feel at ease, even with her protective brothers. Yeah, he was keeping a secret, but they were all adults, and it was none of their business what their sister did.

He liked the different sides of Brooke he saw, from a woman unafraid as a bull charged her, to one who spent time on the household pursuits that her mother enjoyed, to the woman who enjoyed dressing up in pretty, figure-hugging clothes for an evening. He even appreciated her bossy side.

At lunch, Adam found out that Lou Webster, the ranch's part-timer, had come down with the flu. Nate asked Adam to take over being "on call" for the tourists, and sure enough, every time he got involved in a chore, the bell would ring. He wasn't too nervous about handling the team on his own because he'd been practicing. The worst was the trip he took with a couple newlyweds, so wrapped up in each other they barely listened as he pointed out features of the landscape, an ice waterfall down a mountainside cliff, several deer bounding through a far pasture. Instead, thinking he couldn't hear them, they murmured together about their dreams of the future, the children they would have, the home they wanted to save up for.

Adam had spent the last six months without any dreams. People usually had the next goal they wanted to achieve, and he'd gotten in the habit of never thinking beyond today. He'd thought he was too damaged for a family life, but he remembered Zach's rocks, and how he'd made sure to send them home to the boy from his father. That was a family connection he'd help make even when he was at his bleakest. Maybe there was hope for him after all.

Back at the house, the dreamy young couple strolled hand in hand to their car, and there was another parked alongside it. A man was getting out, as if waiting for his return.

"Adam Desantis? Is that you?" He came forward, hand outstretched.

Adam met him halfway to shake, knowing he looked familiar. He wore a bulky parka and jeans. His brown hair receding a bit above his temples might have made him look older but for his freckled, cheerful face.

And then the name clicked. "Deer, good to see you."

Howie Deering Junior reddened, then glanced behind him as if to cover it up. "Haven't heard that nickname in years. My wife will laugh. I'm not quite as fast as I used to be."

A short, chubby woman with a toddler by her side was taking a baby out of a car seat.

Adam suddenly felt old. "Two kids, Deer? Has that much time passed?"

"I started young, I know," Howie said. "While you were off being a macho soldier, I settled into the family real-estate business. Tame stuff, I know you'd say."

"Tame sounds good to me."

"Give me a sec." Howie hustled to his wife's side and took the toddler's hand, then said to his wife, "Tara, I'd like you to meet an old classmate of mine, Adam Desantis. He just got out of the Marines."

Adam didn't bother to offer his hand to shake — hers were burdened with a wide-eyed baby who looked unable to walk yet. Tara had freckles like her husband, but bright red curly hair that the toddler had obviously inherited. His hat was falling off of his head, and he soon tossed his mittens, too.

"Howie!" Tara scolded the little boy.

Adam glanced at the older Howie, who spread his hands wide and grinned.

"My mom would have killed me if I didn't use the family name."

When Howie III had his hat and mittens on again, Tara smiled at Adam. "Nice to meet you. I heard you call Howie 'Deer.' So you were on the football team with him?"

Adam nodded. "We were both on offense, though he was much faster."

Howie glanced at Adam ruefully. "I bet it's the other way around now."

Tara blushed. "With the kids, it's so hard to find time to exercise. We both work and feel guilty for taking any time for ourselves."

"That's why we brought them for a sleigh ride today," Howie added. "A nice family outing."

"Then let's get started," Adam said.

Adam actually enjoyed the ride. Howie and his wife appreciated all the little tidbits he told them about the ranch and the town. They, in turn, explained it in simpler language to their son. The baby was so good, never making a peep, just staring wide-eyed. The toddler was thrilled when several deer bounded across their path.

When they arrived back in the yard, and Tara was putting the kids back in the car as it warmed up, Howie came back to Adam.

"You doing anything tonight?" Howie asked.

"Nope," he said, glad to feel interested again.

"There's a pool tournament I've entered at Tony's Tavern. Very informal, nothing big. You'll see lots of people you know. You could stop by. It starts at seven."

"Thanks, I'll see you there."

After a day of skiing, Brooke stopped at Monica's, who insisted she come to the pool tournament at Tony's and look for men. How could Brooke say she had her own already? So after Monica put long ringlets of curls in her hair, she donned her evening makeup and a tight little dress with high leather boots.

Brooke quickly realized what was going on as Monica innocently introduced her to LeVar Kirk, a friend of her brother, who was in the family plumbing business in Carbondale. He was a tall, lanky black guy with good arms he showed off in a polo shirt even though it was almost winter.

Before she could even comment on his name, he said, "Yeah, my dad was into *Star*

Trek, and I'm not so upset about it any-more."

At least he made her laugh although she wasn't laughing when Monica disappeared, leaving her alone with LeVar. Soon he began to tack "babe" on to the end of everything he said to her, like it was his pet name for her after one hour together. She should probably leave, but she didn't want to hurt his feelings, and the music was good, and heck, she knew almost everyone in the pool tournament.

Since he was betting on the pool game in the back room, she offered to get him a beer. She was waiting for her order when she saw Adam walk right past her, eyes on her ass as she leaned on the bar.

He did a double take of recognition, then his gaze flew to hers. They collided, and the vivid awareness was more than any man had ever made her feel.

"Don't say it," she said in a low voice.

He gave a slow grin, and in his eyes she could read, *I recognized you by your ass.*

He elbowed his way to stand beside her. "Hey, boss."

"What are you doing here? I thought you were hibernating in your cabin for the win-ter."

He shrugged. "Met up with Deer Deering

today when he brought his little family for a sleigh ride. He invited me to watch him play. Am I late?"

"They just started. I'm getting a beer for a friend, then heading in."

"A friend?" he echoed, cocking his head, that sly smile playing on his mouth.

"A friend of Monica's brother," she explained patiently. "I have been set up, and Monica seems to have disappeared. I don't want to be rude," she quickly added. "We're just watching the tournament with everyone else."

"Guess I'll leave you to it, boss." Wearing a devilish grin, he tipped his cowboy hat and moved back out through the crowd.

"Boss," "babe," she had lots of names tonight, she thought, giving a reluctant smile. She glanced over her shoulder, where she could just see Adam saunter into the pool room. Damn, he looked good from behind. The evening had just gotten more interesting — and more dangerous, she reminded herself.

As she carried two bottles of beer into the back room, LeVar came up to her with a grateful, "Thanks, babe," before slurping down some beer.

"So how's the tournament?" She had to raise her voice to be heard.

"Some guy named Howie Junior is up next."

"I know him." She looked around the bar. "In fact, I know most people here — except you. So tell me about your family business."

She dipped her lukewarm fries in ketchup and listened, but her gaze kept roaming to Adam. He stood with Chris Sweet and Howie Junior — she couldn't imagine calling him Deer. Adam was listening with only an occasional laid-back comment, as expressive Howie talked about something and used his hands the whole time. Once Adam had to pull his beer back, or Howie would have knocked it to the floor. They both laughed.

Something inside Brooke eased at this evidence that Adam was trying to meet people again. She didn't want to watch him stay hunkered down in his cabin every night, letting whatever was bothering him fester.

But it was a little harder to watch the women begin to gather, like they were seagulls, and he was the only snack food on the beach. Amber was a couple years older than Nate, divorced with three kids of her own, but she haunted the bar looking for the next guy. Nicole was a year or two younger than them, and had been in the

4-H club with Brooke, relentlessly cute and cheerful, and knew just how much cleavage to show to hook a man's interest. Then darkly exotic Shannon, way too young for him, arrived to the women's admiration party, moving sultrily to the music, as if she'd lure Adam to dance.

"Hey, babe, who you looking at?" LeVar asked, craning his neck to follow her line of vision.

"A guy who works as a hand for us. He's just out of the Marines, and the ladies are welcoming him tonight."

She thought about what it would be like if Adam were her date. Maybe he would have taken her dancing, and she'd let him lead her anywhere he wanted to go.

But it was Shannon who was pulling him into a corner to dance, and Brooke lost track of him in the crowd. A good thing, because she was worried her lustful look might give her away.

"Wow, this guy plays an impressive game of pool," LeVar said excitedly.

It was her turn to follow where he pointed, and she saw a slim man playing pool with a prosthetic arm. He'd had a special piece made for the end to rest his pool cue on.

"Scott Huang," she said. "We go to the

same church. I wonder how good he is at pool."

"I'll let you know."

LeVar walked away from her to get a closer look, without asking if she wanted to go. She had no problem with that.

And then she saw Adam standing alone, watching the disabled vet play pool. His expression was so impassive, it was a little scary.

She approached him and nudged his arm. "Scott's pretty good, isn't he?"

Adam nodded and glanced at her while taking another sip of beer.

"He works for Outdoor Tours here in town. They do everything from take guests on rugged cross-country ski weekends, where you camp outdoors, to fly-fishing weekends in the summer, where guests are catered to like royalty. His specialty was rock climbing."

Adam studied her. "Why are you telling me this?"

"You looked interested. It took him a while after the Army, but he found himself again. He's an incredible skier, and he still leads mountain-biking expeditions. There's lots of stuff he can do. You know that veteran's housing project I mentioned? He's the next recipient."

"Hey, babe!" LeVar suddenly called as he worked his way back across the room.

"Babe?" Adam whispered, amusement laced through his voice again.

Without glancing at him, she murmured, "Maybe a little sexier than 'boss.' "

"So I should use 'boss' at more intimate moments, is what you're saying."

"Shh!" But she wanted to laugh.

When LeVar arrived, she introduced them, and they shook hands. For the next ten awkward minutes, the discussion ranged from the pool tournament, to the plumbing and ranching businesses, to the Denver Broncos. Not the Marines, of course.

LeVar finally glanced over his shoulder toward the pool table. "Next game's up. You want to go watch, babe?"

He started away, and as Brooke politely moved to follow him, Adam whispered, "I think he forgot your name."

She bit her lip as another bubble of laughter threatened to erupt.

Two hours later, when a winner had been declared and her feet were killing her, Brooke politely declined LeVar's offer to walk her to her car — and his cell-phone number. As she was donning her coat beside the front door, she saw a poster she hadn't noticed before. In bold colors it said,

"Come to the December 8 town-council meeting. Stand up for freedom in America. Stand up for Freedom of Choice, of Business." And in little letters at the bottom, "sponsored by the Valentine Valley Preservation Fund committee."

Great. She was going to have to attend.

After Brooke had gone, Adam thought how hot she'd looked, her dress hugging every curve, but no hotter than she looked first thing in the morning going out to feed cattle.

Guess he found her hot no matter what.

He extricated himself from the tavern without a woman on his arm and started to drive home. He passed the house being renovated for Scott Huang. *And I thought I came home with scars.*

Brooke's jeep was already in the yard when he arrived, but she didn't come to him. He missed her, and knew it wasn't just about the sex. He was feeling more for Brooke than she wanted him to feel, but he didn't regret it.

CHAPTER SIXTEEN

Late the next afternoon, before he could change his mind, Adam drove into town and stopped at the house renovation project, a two-story cottage with dormers jutting from steep gables and decorative trim along the front porch. Scaffolding was built along one wall as people worked on the siding. Several pickups and minivans lined up along the curb. When Adam knocked on the front door, a middle-aged woman on the scaffolding ducked her head beneath the porch roof to look at him.

"Go on in," she said with a smile. "We're glad for the help."

Inside, there were a couple people working on the trim in the living room, including an old guy in his seventies with a bald dome of a head and scruffy white hair circling the base. But he still had a white beard and mustache, and this was how Adam recognized him.

"Coach McKee?"

The man straightened a bit slower than he used to, his grin broad. "Adam Desantis. How good to see you, boy."

Wiping his hands on a rag, he came toward Adam and they shook hands. George McKee was still a big man, barrel-chested, but a bit more stooped with age. He'd done a couple years early on in Vietnam, and he still had the bearing of a man who took care of himself — and who didn't take "any guff," one of his stock phrases as a coach.

"I heard you were back in town," Coach said. "I was starting to think I'd have to track you down. Want some coffee?"

"Sure, thanks."

Coach led him into the kitchen, where a big pot had been brewed. The room was obviously finished, all done in light woods, with a big picture window overlooking a snowy backyard with a swing set.

"I saw the man who'll get this house last night," Adam said after accepting a steaming styrofoam cup.

"Scott Huang, yes. His family will put that swing set to good use. Three little boys."

"How many other houses are in the works?"

"Three in various stages, from the initial sale or donation to one that's being moved into this weekend. You're working for the Thalbergs, right? They donated one of the houses."

Adam blinked, and a brief sense of unease touched him. "That was decent of them."

"Sure was. Doug's a Vietnam vet — you knew that, right?"

"It might be part of the reason he hired me," Adam said dryly.

"Maybe." Coach's eyes twinkled. "Those Thalbergs, they care about the community. Your grandma's a part of the Welcome Ceremony. Good people, those ladies, although they had some strange ideas about how to welcome the vets and their families into their new homes."

"Why am I not surprised?"

Coach chuckled. "They were convinced every home should have a puppy, the perfect welcome gift from the preservation-fund committee. It took a while to talk them out of it."

Adam smiled. "Even without a puppy, this is a good program. So do the vets have to pay a mortgage?"

"A small one, but nothing compared to what the final product is worth. All of our time and most of the renovation supplies are donated." He paused. "So you're out of the Marines?"

Adam's smile faded a bit as he nodded.

Coach looked at him way too astutely, but only said, "Your grandma bragged about you making staff sergeant. I hope you knew the great honor."

"I did, sir."

Coach shook his head. "Hard to believe you ever doubted yourself as a commander of men."

Once it would have been hard to hear that, but Adam was trying to honor the memories of his friends rather than avoid them. They deserved that.

"By your senior year, you had the football team in lockstep. I just knew. But then again, there was a time where you didn't want anyone telling *you* anything."

"Yes, well, now that I'm working at the Silver Creek Ranch, I have a lot of bosses telling me what to do."

"Fair people, of course, so I'm sure it's no hardship."

"Speaking of family, I was overseas when I heard about your wife's death, sir. I'm very sorry for your loss."

His expression sobered. "Thanks, son."

"She was very kind to the team. I'll never forget those meals she coordinated for us before every big game."

Coach smiled. "She was good at getting

all the moms involved." Then he winced. "Sorry."

"No, don't worry. I've long since come to terms with my mom's selfishness." Adam took another sip of his coffee and realized it was the truth.

"Still, her death was a terrible thing. A fire like that . . ."

"Her own fault," Adam said. "Thanks for being there at the funeral for my grandma when I couldn't fly back in time."

"Oh, please. The way that woman looked after me when my wife died? She and the widows organized two *months'* worth of delivered meals, and they visited me several times every week. I'd do anything for her. I don't know if I ever told you, but back when you stole my car —"

"Borrowed it," was the automatic answer Adam had always given when he was on the football team.

Coach grinned. "Okay, okay, 'borrowed' it. It was your grandma who came to me before your court appearance and encouraged me to attend."

Adam tensed. "I didn't put her up to that."

Coach touched his elbow. "Of course you didn't. You know Renee — she always believes she knows best, and she was determined to help you however she could."

Adam had known his life changed forever because of Coach McKee — he could hardly be surprised that his grandma was behind it all. She could never do things up front to help him, knowing how his parents took it, but she was always there behind the scenes. She still was, he thought, swallowing to ease the tightness in his throat. She wanted him to come to Valentine Valley, and she'd found the perfect scheme to get him there. And he was glad for it.

"Thanks for telling me that, Coach." Adam set down his cup. "I know Grandma wasn't the only one supporting me in those days. I've never forgotten what you did for me. There aren't many who get a second chance."

Coach waved a hand, and said gruffly, "I just needed a team manager."

Adam grinned. "Now tell me where to start. I haven't done much home renovation, so I might need some instruction."

"No problem. We'll find plenty for you to do. How much can you work?"

"I never really know — depends on how the day goes at the ranch. I'm thinking a few times a week after work. Do you need to know in advance?"

"Nope, just wanted you to know that if you arrive here and we're gone, we could be working at one of the other houses. I'll write down the addresses for you. You're hired!"

They shook hands, and Adam felt good about being a part of an important cause. The Thalbergs could donate a house, a Desantis could donate labor. It all evened out in the end. But it was a reminder how different he and Brooke really were, their backgrounds, their families.

As Brooke waited for Steph to arrive for her barrel-racing lesson, she noticed that Adam's pickup was gone and wondered if he was visiting his grandma.

Or maybe he was going out with one of the women he'd met last night.

Stop it, she told herself. She admired the blue sky and reminded herself the weather was mild, and Steph would get a good workout. She didn't need to think about Adam. Or the fact that it had taken everything in her not to go to the bunkhouse last night when she saw his lights. It would seem . . . awkward, when they'd both spent time socializing with other people. But it had taken her a long time to sleep, with her body feeling achy and restless and not her own.

When Steph arrived without her horse trailer, Brooke frowned as the girl jumped out of her rusted old pickup.

"I thought we had a lesson," Brooke began.

"Oh, I'm sorry!" Steph said, her blond ponytail bobbing where it was threaded through the hole in the back of her baseball cap. "I needed to talk to you. Guess I didn't explain that . . ."

"It's okay. Give me a chance to let Sugar out with the other horses."

Steph accompanied her to the barn, saying little, her expression troubled. Brooke was concerned but could be patient, knowing it was best not to push a teenager in the middle of a crisis.

After putting away the tack, Brooke walked Sugar outside and sent her galloping into the horse pasture with a brisk pat to her haunches. Then she turned and studied Steph. "Is this a private talk? Maybe we want to avoid the house. My parents are home."

"Is that little cabin yours?"

Brooke didn't even have to look where the girl pointed. "That's the bunkhouse. Adam's living there right now."

"Oh. Must be easy for him to be right here."

Brooke barely caught herself before wincing. "It is, but that means we can't talk there. Come on into the tack room. My saddle can use some cleaning."

The room, situated in a corner of the barn, had two windows that let in lots of light. Halters and bridles hung from many hooks in the walls beneath long rows of shelves. Portable saddle racks were placed beneath each person's tack. Brooke pulled her saddle rack into the center of the room, gathered rags, leather cleaner, and oil, and sank onto a stool. Steph sighed and picked at a ragged fingernail. Brooke gave her time, focusing on rubbing the dirt out of her saddle with a rag.

Steph let out a deep breath. "I have a favor to ask. Tyler Brissette needs a place to do community service. I don't think he'd do well sweeping up someone's store, with everyone watching him. I just think he needs someone who's patient with him. Is there any chance he could work here for you after school on weekdays and Saturday mornings?"

Surprised, Brooke put down the rag and studied the girl. "This isn't a *little* favor, is it?"

"I wish I didn't have to ask. But did you ever feel with someone . . ." Her voice trailed off, and her blue eyes looked wistful. ". . . that maybe you were the only one who could help him? Me, I mean, not you. But you, too!" she added quickly.

Brooke chuckled. "I know what you mean. I guess I'd be willing to take a chance on him if you think we can help him."

Steph let her breath out in a rush. "Oh, thank you! I *know* we can help him. We just need time."

"What about his family? I know his brother just got out of jail."

She nodded. "I haven't seen his brother at all. I think my dad would be mad if I went near him. But . . . aren't we supposed to give people a second chance?" she asked plaintively. "His dad is gone, I guess, so it's just his mom working two jobs every day. His brother is trying to find a job, but since he's been in jail . . ." She trailed off.

"Fire is a terrible thing to ranchers and farmers," Brooke said. "People won't forget that for a long time."

"I know. But that was Cody, not Tyler. So can I give your name and number to his probation officer?"

"Sure. We'll give him so much to do he won't be able to do anything but sleep when he gets home."

Steph gave her a big hug, and Brooke gladly returned it.

"Thanks, Brooke. You're awesome."

It felt pretty good to be awesome, she thought, walking across the yard after Steph had gone. Then she straightened her spine and headed for the office. At the end of each day, her dad and brothers often gathered to talk over what needed to be done the next day.

They were all drinking coffee and eating cookies when she arrived.

Her dad put a finger to his lips. "Shh, we're spoiling our appetites on Gloria's cookies. Have some."

She pulled up a rolling office chair and grabbed a chocolate chip cookie. "Got some news. You know the Brissette kid who Joe Sweet caught joyriding on his land?"

Their nods were sober.

"He got community service for his first offense. Steph Sweet asked if he could serve it working for us after school, and I said yes. Is that okay with everyone?"

Her dad rubbed his chin. "Well, as long as you don't mind acceptin' the challenge of ropin' a teenager into line."

"I don't mind at all," Brooke said. "Figured I'd deal with him and not bother any of you."

"That's a nice thing you're doing, Brooke," Josh said, throwing his napkin in the garbage.

"Maybe naïve, too," Nate cautioned.

Brooke at last allowed herself a small smile. "I know. But if you'd seen the pleading look on Steph's face . . . how could I say no?"

At dinner, when she told her mom about Tyler's community service, Sandy smiled proudly. "Told you you'd make a good teacher."

Brooke blushed with pleasure even though she knew that her mom wasn't exactly objective. She was standing for minutes each day braced on a walker now, slowly regaining the strength in her legs. It took everything in Brooke not to stand beside her mom in case she weakened, but Sandy didn't want that.

As she set the table, Brooke said, "Mom, I'll be his boss, not his teacher."

"Bosses are teachers. I've seen you working with Adam."

Brooke paused at the silverware drawer, keeping her face neutral. "You have?"

"Well, I've mostly looked out the window, but your brother Josh has told me a thing or two. You're good at explaining yourself, and you have patience."

"Says my mom," Brooke said, surprised to feel embarrassed about the praise. "But thanks. Adam is a willing worker. Tyler's being forced. It probably won't be the same thing."

"No, but as I said, you have patience. You'll make it work."

The one person Brooke forgot to tell? Adam. When she went to his cabin after everyone had gone to bed, he swept her into his arms, kissing her greedily, pulling off her clothes, and then she was pulling off his. Everything else completely left her mind.

Two days later, the sky was blustery and overcast, with gusts of wind and occasional snow flurries, making every job on a ranch harder. Adam didn't much care. He was floating on a feeling of satisfaction, and not just from his erotic evening with Brooke. Though he'd been tired after work, renovating Scott Huang's future home had felt good. A house wasn't some kind of platitude, "Thanks for your service to your country, now pretend everything's the same." A house was a way without words to say "Thank you," and Adam was surprised to feel deeply grateful for the chance to say that to people who'd given up far more than he had. Every piece of trim he cut, every nail he hammered, he knew would be appreciated by Scott and his family.

As Adam came out of the barn after shoveling out the horse stalls, he saw a beat-up two-door car pull up in front of the ranch house, and a lanky young man wearing a ball cap emerged from the passenger side. He shut the door, and the car drove off. The kid put his hands in his pockets and hunched his shoulders against the wind. He was wearing a coat, but in the way of teenagers, it wasn't enough to keep him warm outside for any length of time.

As Adam strode across the yard, the kid looked up, and in that moment, recognition sparked between them. This was the kid who'd stolen the Thalbergs' ATV and gone for a ride, wrecking a fence post but luckily not damaging the machine. He had unruly black hair, sullen gray eyes in an angular face, and stubble on his chin as if he were trying to be older than he was. What was he — sixteen, seventeen?

The way he stood, hands in his pockets, hunched against the cold, went through Adam with a shock of sad memories. It was like seeing Paul Ivanick all over again, that first day at boot camp. Adam happened to be visiting Parris Island on another matter, and he'd seen the incoming recruits. Paul had been an inner-city kid, plopped into the middle of the swamps and marshes as if in another world, cut off from his old life. And all of the uncertainty and fear had been there on his face, poorly hidden beneath a sneer. By the time he landed in Adam's platoon, he'd become an eager, gung ho jarhead, confident in himself and his training, wanting to learn even more from Adam, barely recognizable from the kid he'd once been. And he'd served to the best of his abilities until friendly fire had wiped out his future.

Adam had given the ATV-riding kid a second chance — did that mean he'd come to apologize?

The kid stiffened and faced him as if they were about to shoot it out at high noon, and Adam tried not to smile.

"So you're back," Adam said mildly.

"I'm here to see Brooke."

"You mean Miss Thalberg?"

The kid opened his mouth, then slouched a bit, mumbling, "Miss Thalberg."

"So what are you here to see her about?"

The kid gave a sigh, and for just a moment, Adam glimpsed a lost boy rather than a defensive teenager. But it didn't last long.

"Who are *you*?" the kid demanded.

Adam strolled toward him and leaned a hand casually on the front railing. "Funny you should ask," he said, keeping his voice light. "I'm the guy who knows what you did on this ranch."

"You're going to turn me in, aren't you," the kid said bitterly.

"I didn't say that." Adam spoke quietly, and his tone alone seemed to get the kid's attention.

"Why not?" he demanded. "I bet you've been waiting to point me out."

"Actually, I haven't. I was hoping your close call straightened you out."

"Well, it didn't, so I guess I disappointed you, too. Welcome to a very big club."

Adam recognized the signs so well — arrogance, defensiveness, and a tough-guy exterior — to protect the kid from the world. More than just Paul, that was him twelve years ago.

"Why do you need to see Miss Thalberg?" Adam asked again.

"She told the courts I could do my community service with her. But go ahead, once you're done, I'm sure she'll kick me out. Why did I bother coming here?"

He turned away, hunched his shoulders, and started walking.

Adam raised his voice against the wind. "So that's it? You just quit."

The kid spun on his heels but continued to walk backward. "I'm not a quitter! I'll

321

find somewhere else to work."

"What happens if you don't? It can't be easy."

"Then they lock me up in Juvenile Hall. You don't need to care."

"You've obviously gotten yourself in more trouble since I last saw you, and rather than prove yourself a coward by walking away —"

"I'm not —"

"I suggest you go on into the office and talk to Miss Thalberg."

The kid came to a halt. "Are you playin' with me?"

"Nope."

"Well, you're just gonna tell her what I did. That'll be two strikes against me, and I'll go away for sure."

"What did you get caught doing?" Adam asked.

The kid scowled. "What do you think?"

"Joyriding an ATV. Was anyone hurt?"

"Naw, but I busted part of it. Sweet called the sheriff."

"I'm sure you meant to say 'Mr. Sweet.' Do you blame him?"

The kid didn't answer, only looked away and kicked at a rock framed in the packed snow.

"You know, I've already kept quiet about

you," Adam pointed out.

The kid narrowed his eyes. "What do you mean?"

"I didn't tell anyone what you did. I gave you a chance, but you're on a rocky ledge right now. We can try this again, and if you prove yourself worth my support, I'll continue to keep quiet."

The wind howled between them, and both squinted as snow danced against their faces.

"What are you saying?" the kid demanded at last, his disrespectful tone down a notch.

"You do your community service, and you do it well. And nobody needs to know it wasn't your first offense."

"That's like . . . blackmail or something."

"Really? If that bothers you, guess you can head back into town."

"Hey, Adam!"

He turned to see Brooke coming across the yard, her words almost garbled from the wind. She glanced the kid's way and came to a stop.

"You must be Tyler Brissette," she said, smiling even as she held out a gloved hand.

Tyler? That name was familiar to Adam.

Awkwardly, the kid put his bare hand in hers. "Afternoon, Miss Thalberg."

The kid had all kinds of manners when he desperately needed them, Adam thought

323

with amusement.

"Your mom couldn't stay to see you settled in?" Brooke asked.

The kid hunched his shoulders again. "Naw, she had to get to work."

"I see. Well, come on, we've got some paperwork, then I'll show you around. Did you meet Mr. Desantis?"

Tyler's gaze seemed to settle on Adam's chin. "No, ma'am."

"This is Adam Desantis, one of our hands. Adam, Tyler Brissette."

Adam put out a hand, and the kid finally took it. "Good to meet you, Tyler."

"Tyler will be here every day after school," Brooke said. "I'll be teaching him the ropes."

"I'll be glad to help," Adam offered.

She brightened. "Thank you! Come on, Tyler."

As Tyler turned to follow Brooke, he looked over his shoulder at Adam, his expression wary.

Someone came through the double doors of the barn behind Adam.

"Was that our new employee?" Josh called.

Adam turned and walked toward the barn. "You knew about him?" Stupid thing to say — Josh was family, and one of the bosses.

"After the fact," Josh said with amusement. "Brooke made this decision all on her own."

"Why am I not surprised," Adam murmured.

Josh glanced at him out of the corner of his eye, but only said, "Yeah, she keeps her soft heart pretty well buried most of the time. But she wants to work with this kid. Hope she doesn't regret it."

Me, too, Adam thought. He was uncomfortable with the position he'd put himself in, lying about Tyler to a family that had been good to him. But Tyler was right — if anyone knew, he could end up in jail, and Adam had to prevent that. Maybe hard work could straighten the kid out.

CHAPTER SEVENTEEN

At six that evening, Adam showed up at the kitchen door to wait for Brooke. He was driving her and Grandma Palmer to the town-council meeting early to save seats. The rest of the family and the other widows would be following. Sylvester Galimi had added an item to the agenda, a discussion of "new and inappropriate businesses," and townspeople on both sides were gathering.

Once they were in the pickup, Brooke dropped her head back and heaved a sigh.

"Did the kid give you too much trouble?" Adam asked with sympathy. "You know I'll be glad to help."

She reached across the seat and clasped his hand. "I know, thanks. Tyler has sixty hours of community service, two hours a day, six days a week. That's five weeks. I thought it seemed short — until today. I'm so sorry I forgot to warn you. I meant to the other night, but . . . things got out of hand."

Their eyes briefly met and held as they remembered intimate kisses, shuddering breaths, long, slow caresses. Adam gripped the steering wheel and forced himself to look at the road.

"I don't blame you," he said in a husky voice. "I wasn't thinking too clear either. And besides, I'm the hired hand, right? Who you hire is your business."

"Well, you have to work with him, too."

"Brooke, the whole reason we're a secret is because I'm your employee. Don't get me wrong — you can always talk to me. But I get where your allegiance lies. It's with your family."

She glanced away, her frown signaling her troubled thoughts. "Thanks for understanding," she murmured.

If honest words about their respective stations was a reality kick in the pants to her, it was best this way. Hearing that the Thalbergs had donated a house to veterans was just the reminder he needed of his place on the ranch. He might want more from her, a way into her life that was out in the open, with her family's blessing, but he had to accept that he couldn't *force* it to happen. But he sure could persuade . . .

327

"So how'd you get involved in community service?" he asked.

"Steph begged for my help."

He shot her a frown. "Steph? What does she have to do with —" And then it all came together and he gave a low whistle. "*Tyler.* Of course. I saw him at the Chess Club meeting, but his back was to me as he talked to her." Adam wasn't even sure what he would have done had he recognized Tyler that night as the ATV joyrider. Maybe he could have given him a warning; maybe the kid wouldn't have dared try that stunt at Sweet's.

But "maybes" were pretty useless now.

"The boy's had a tough time," Brooke continued, as they turned down the road that ran along Silver Creek to the Widows' Boardinghouse. "His dad ran out on them, his mom is working two jobs to afford their apartment, and his brother just got out of jail. I thought . . . well, you had Coach Mc-Kee's help. Maybe we can be the ones to give this kid a chance."

"He has to want the help, Brooke," he reminded her. "I talked to him before you got there. He's got a pretty big chip on his shoulder. And I never saw a kid move slower than when he was following us around on the tour."

328

She grinned. "I know. It was pretty funny. That heavy-duty coat I found him was too big, and he wasn't happy. He's never been around horses, so I was grateful to have you as my demonstrator while I talked about caring for horse and tack."

After he pulled around in back of the boardinghouse to park, he watched her practically bounce out of the cab, saw her excitement at this new challenge, and was impressed. Steph had put her in a tough spot with a personal plea. There weren't many who'd take it as well as Brooke.

Brooke's grandma was driving Mrs. Ludlow into town, and they followed Adam's truck to the town hall. Evergreens wound with Christmas lights grew three stories high on either side of the building. Town hall itself was a tall stone building with a clock tower, wreaths in each window, and spotlights brightening it for the season. Though you couldn't see it at night, he knew the Elk Mountains were the backdrop for town hall, and tourists always took lots of pictures.

He dropped off the women because there were dozens of cars lining every nearby street, and ended up parking at St. John's, three blocks away. Hearing a raised chorus of voices inside town hall, he had no problem finding the assembly room where the town council met. A Christmas tree presided in one corner, and fake boughs of greenery hung from the main table. Adam paused in the doorway when he saw his grandma walking briskly down the aisle, no limp in sight, back straight. She used her cane to point at people, asking whose side they were on and what she could do to convince the other side to change their minds. When she saw him, she leaned on her cane so fast it sent a ripple of chuckles through the audience. Adam pretended not to notice.

There were only a few seats left near the back out of about a hundred, and Brooke was gesturing to him from a few rows closer than that. She had coats thrown across a half dozen seats.

"It was all I could get," she muttered, shaking her head. "Sylvester has taken up more than half the room."

Adam glanced at the old man, dressed in a charcoal suit and bright red tie. "I didn't know there was a dress code."

"That Sylvester," Grandma Palmer said, tsking as she approached.

She did a slow slide into her seat, as if it were painful to bend over. It was hard for him to keep a straight face.

"Such a vain man," Grandma continued.

"Ignore him."

"Is Whitney here?" he asked.

"First row. I can't imagine what time the poor girl arrived. I made sure she knows we're here for her."

By the time the rest of the widows and Thalberg family took their places, the room was packed. The widows sat beside each other closest to the aisle, Adam sat beside his grandma, and Brooke was on his other side, near the rest of her family. Though Monica, Emily, and Nate arrived on time, they couldn't get through the crowd and had to stand near the door. The opposition was already displaying signs: "No Pornography!" "Protect Our Children!"

The town-council members filed in, five men and three women, and took their places at a long table in front. The mayor occupied the center, and that's when Adam remembered that she was Sylvester's sister. The expressions of each politician registered shock and speculation at the turnout, which Adam imagined might usually be a dozen people in this sleepy little town. After the call to order and the roll call, the restless spectators sat through the "student of the month" presentation, where the pimple-faced girl looked horrified to have to stand up before so many people; an update from the Economic Development Group; and a discussion of a restaurant's liquor-license renewal.

"I can't eat there without havin' my Manhattan," Grandma Palmer said loudly. "Give them their renewal and let's move on!"

The rumbling of discontented voices drowned out the laughter and got a little louder with each successive discussion, until at last Sylvester was called to speak on the item he'd added to the agenda.

"Ladies and gentlemen, Mayor Galimi," he intoned. "We have strict rules against pornography, and I am here to see that they're upheld."

The Honorable Mayor Galimi, a woman in her sixties with short hair she left its natural silver-white, peered over her glasses at her brother, looking like everyone's idea of a strict, spinster teacher. "Sylvester, what are you talking about?"

Adam and Brooke exchanged a surprised glance. He hadn't discussed it with his sister yet? Was that good or bad?

"A business called" — he hesitated, as if regretting having to speak the name — "Leather and Lace is trying to worm its way into our innocent, unaware community of Valentine Valley."

332

Whitney stood up on the opposite side of the room from Sylvester. She looked slender, unthreatening, but when she spoke, Adam thought her voice calm and rational.

"May I speak, Your Honor?"

"And you are?" Mayor Galimi asked.

"Whitney Winslow, owner of the Leather and Lace stores in San Francisco and Las Vegas. I am looking into purchasing a building off Main Street to open another branch of my store. I sell lingerie, ma'am, and I have a portfolio here with some of my work. Believe me, it is not pornography. Women can wear any type of undergarments they like. The whole point" — she gave Sylvester a frown — "is that they're worn *under* clothes."

Muted chuckles spread through their half of the room.

"Maybe we should have planned a fashion show," Mrs. Thalberg grumbled. "Or we could have worn our undergarments outside our clothing!"

Grandma Palmer slapped her knee. "Why didn't we think of that sooner?"

Before Adam could protest, Brooke leaned across the front of him, bracing herself with a hand on his thigh, to whisper at the widows. "Because it would be inappropriate and possibly damaging to Whitney's cause.

333

Now shh!"

Adam smiled at her, covering her hand with his until she quickly pulled hers away, wearing a blush. All this secrecy was such interesting foreplay.

"But such risqué lingerie will have to be displayed in the store, Your Honor," Sylvester was quick to point out, "without the benefit of being covered by clothing. I have been talking with my fellow townspeople, and most of us are appalled that —"

His sister interrupted him. "I'm not sure you even have half this room, Sylvester, so let's not make broad statements."

Adam and Brooke shared a relieved look. Sounded like the mayor could be impartial.

"You're welcome to see my catalogue online, Your Honor," Whitney pointed out. "I admit, some items are only for sale online because they would not be appropriate for a small-town store. My window displays will be tasteful, nothing that you wouldn't see in any department store."

"If it's for sale, it will find its way into her store," Sylvester insisted. "I have a petition signed by hundreds of people —"

"We do, too, Mayor Galimi," Grandma Palmer said, rising to her feet to be seen behind the half dozen rows in front of her. "Not everyone agrees with Sylvester."

As the petitions were passed forward, people started arguing with each other across the aisles. Mrs. Ludlow used her walker to block the way of someone collecting petitions for their opponents until Doug Thalberg pulled it back.

Grandma Palmer calmly waited her turn to continue. Adam realized she was dressed almost understated for her, in bright red that made her stand out but not in her usual wacky way.

"Mayor Galimi," Grandma Palmer said at last, "Miss Winslow approached the Valentine Valley Preservation Committee about grants to help her restore the old funeral home on Grace and Fourth. We've found nothin' objectionable, nothin' pornographic. I don't see how Sylvester can try to tell women what they can wear under their clothes!"

Over half the room roared with laughter, overwhelming the glowers of the rest.

Another woman stood up, and everyone else settled down when the mayor pounded her gavel.

"You have something to say, Debbie?"

The plump woman wore a sweatshirt with the logo of her B&B, an etching of an elegant woman with an Edwardian large-brimmed hat tilted over her face. "I'm the owner of The Adelaide, where Miss Winslow is staying. I'm planning to host a lingerie event so everyone can see how tasteful each garment is. If you remember, Mayor Galimi, many people resisted bed-and-breakfasts thirty years ago, claiming they'd bring tourists to ruin our wholesome family town. Well, tourists have saved us, and upscale lingerie in a town called Valentine can only help."

She sat down to cheering applause from half the room and boos from the other. People took their turns speaking about morality, and harming children, and anything they could think of. The elder Mrs. Thalberg talked about a woman's need to feel pretty for her man, and Adam noticed with interest that Brooke was blushing. Eventually, the mayor declared that the council would have to discuss this in executive session, promising a response at their next meeting, just before Christmas.

While the opposition went to the True Grits Diner to hash over everything, Emily opened up her bakery for Leather and Lace's supporters. A couple dozen people milled around, elbows brushing, and the widows helped her serve customers. Adam pretended he wasn't watching his grandma, but more than once, out of the corner of his eye, he saw her put the cane aside because it kept catching on Mrs. Ludlow's walker.

He tried to blend into the background, recognizing more than one face. He wanted Leather and Lace to be the focus, not him, but one by one, people came to greet him at his grandma's table and shake his hand, thanking him for his service to their country.

"I heard what you did," said Gloria, Nate's secretary. "You're a true American hero."

Much as he was resolved to accept his past and forgive himself, his heart was beating too fast, and he actually felt clammy.

"Adam?" Grandma Palmer touched his hand, her expression concerned.

Brooke was at their table, too, along with Coach McKee, and they were all looking at him.

"I might have told some people how proud I was that you saved all those men," Coach said. "I didn't think it would upset you."

Brooke said nothing, and Adam felt her watching him closely.

"I'm not upset," he assured the man. "I just . . . any one of those men would have done the same for me."

"Then if you're okay," Coach continued. "I need you two to leave Renee and me alone. We have some things to discuss for the preservation committee, and since you two aren't on it — scram."

Brooke had a hard time taking her eyes off Adam as they left the two old people in peace. He moved toward the back of the bakery, pretending to look at a cheesecake display in the glass cooler, but she knew he wasn't seeing it. He'd been wonderfully supportive of his grandma all evening even though he didn't seem at ease in big crowds. She imagined even if he knew the truth about his grandma's "condition," he wouldn't be all that upset. Sometimes it was hard to remember he was once that cocky boy from high school. When they were alone, he had humor and charm; more and more, he was his talkative self. But tonight, she was seeing a very different side of him.

Coach McKee had called him a hero — had told other people the same. And Adam's face had drained of color. What was that about? Coach had said Adam had saved men — *that,* she could believe. He was brave, and he cared about other people. In the Marines, surely his fellow soldiers were like brothers to him. But whenever she asked Adam for details, he would deflect and avoid, just as he'd been doing every time the subject of his military service came up. People were looking at him with speculation, since his back was to the room. And suddenly, she had to get him out of there.

"Hey, Adam, Emily needs us to get a heavy tray in back. Give me a hand."

He moved so swiftly to the swinging door, she felt the breeze of his passing. She followed him into the kitchen.

He looked around the deserted room. "Where's the tray?"

"I lied. Let's go outside."

Soon they stood out in the alley, beneath the light above the back door, hearing their own breathing and the distant sound of Christmas music coming from somewhere.

The question just spilled out of her. "So why don't you like being called a hero?"

"Because I'm not," he said tiredly.

"Maybe it would help to talk."

He stared down at her, then he reached up and very gently touched her cheek. She leaned her face into his palm and was surprised to feel the sting of tears.

"Oh, Adam," she whispered. "I wish . . . I wish things had been different for you."

Her heart broke with a sort of guilt at all the gifts she'd been given in her life: a good family, a career, friends. "Tell me what secret you carry inside you."

He hesitated, and she thought he'd refuse

once again.

"I'm part of the reason a dozen good men are dead," he said at last, his voice filled with quiet sadness.

She put her gloved hands on his waist, wishing she could see more than the shadows on his face beneath his Stetson. "Tell me. Please, tell me. I want to know everything."

"Why?" he asked, smiling down at her sadly. "You shouldn't have to live with this."

"I want to share everything with you." The moment she spoke the words, she regretted them. It was too soon. Or was it? Her heart felt oversized in her chest, full of sorrow and hurt over what he'd borne, and yet still he'd become this wonderful man. She almost held her breath, wondering if he'd push her away now, if he'd think she was getting too close.

"It was a routine mission until we started being shelled," he said in a hushed voice. "I called in the air strike on our position, knowing it was a Danger Close target. I might have saved some of the others after the bomb fell, but I'm no hero, Brooke."

She leaned into him, focused on his pain. "I know there's more. Tell me. Tell me what happened. Keeping it inside can only tear you apart."

He rested his hands on her shoulders and suddenly his breath seemed to catch, and a spasm of pain twisted his features. "They told me the wrong bomb size," he whispered. "I calculated the coordinates for a 250-pound bomb, but they dropped a 500. The blast radius —" And then he broke off with a choked gasp.

She pressed her lips together to keep from crying out, knowing it wasn't what he needed. He wouldn't want to hear her protests that it was an accident, that he wasn't the one who made the mistake. He knew all that, but the grief and the guilt still made him bleed inside.

"If I wouldn't have called in a strike, more of my men would be alive," he finished.

"You can't know that, Adam." She kept her voice calm and gentle. She wanted to insist, *You were under attack! Without the bomb, something else bad would have happened, maybe even your own death!* She felt a swirl of nausea in her stomach at the thought.

His hands gripped her shoulders almost painfully, but she knew he didn't realize what he was doing.

"I don't like being called a hero," he said, giving a sigh, even as his fingers relaxed. "And now you know why."

"But Adam, did you ever think Coach already knows the facts and thinks you're a hero anyway? Can't you search for this kind of stuff online?"

Then he stared down at her, and the light above them caught his square jaw, the way his Adam's apple moved as he swallowed. "Maybe."

And then he buried his face in her neck, and she clutched him, trying to share all her strength.

She kissed the side of his head, his neck, whatever she could reach.

"I don't want you to worry about me," he said, his voice muffled. "I know I have to forgive myself, that I can't let guilt and regret rule me. I'm working on it."

They held each other, and she thought of all the terrible things that had happened to him. He didn't have any kind of life in Valentine Valley — only dreadful memories of parents who treated him like unwanted garbage, and a grandma who couldn't save him. Had he been too young to understand why not? Had he lain awake wondering why no one wanted him?

She wanted to protest that he had *her,* but maybe he didn't want to hear that. Maybe he never wanted to hear that. She gave a little shiver, and he suddenly straightened from their embrace. She saw a flash of his tired smile in the darkness.

He had so much courage, she realized in wonder. He'd left their small town and braved war and danger, and now he was trying to summon up a new courage, to go on when it seemed the worst had happened. Somehow, she had to follow his example, to find whatever she needed in her life and make it happen.

"It's cold out here," he said, rubbing his hands up and down her arms. "We should get you back inside."

She nodded, preceding him into the little hall with its two doors.

"Where's that one go?" he asked.

"Emily's old apartment. It's pretty cute. Right in the heart of town."

"You sound . . . wistful. Do you wish you lived in town?"

"Oh, no, of course not. I have my family."

"That was a very quick denial." One side of his mouth turned up. "We wouldn't have to sneak around anymore. There'd be no one to care that I spent the night in your bed." Then he put his arms around her in that little hallway.

"Well, making you happy is all that matters," she answered.

She got a chuckle out of him and was so

relieved. For just a moment, she rested her head against his strong shoulder and closed her eyes.

"Someone could see us," she murmured, not moving. He smelled good — she felt so good.

His hands moved up and down her back, and even through her jacket, she absorbed the strength of them, the steadiness. She remembered every moan those hands had elicited from her. He kissed the side of her head, and she snuggled beneath his chin. When he looked down at her, she couldn't resist, but kissed him slowly, gently, searching for something, but she didn't know what. His tongue parted her lips, and she let it happen, knew if anyone came looking for them, they'd see —

She tilted her head back. "Okay, okay, we can have kisses another time."

"When we're alone and hidden," he whispered, kissing her forehead, her nose, her chin.

"But that's how we want it."

Why wasn't he agreeing? She was the one who risked the most — her family's respect, her ability to do her job. Yet she was teetering here, finding it so difficult not to touch him in public.

She stepped back, and his arms fell to his

sides, and he looked almost resolute as he stared at the door to the Sugar and Spice kitchen. But he didn't hesitate to go back inside.

CHAPTER EIGHTEEN

"Lunch at Monica's Flowers and Gifts," Emily said with a sigh. "It's been a while."

They sat behind the showroom counter, crowded together shoulder to shoulder. Monica needed to be available to her customers, and Brooke and Emily were used to the interruptions.

Brooke smiled at her friend — her future sister-in-law. "Well, we've been in the midst of the holidays for over a month, now, and it's almost Christmas. I'm amazed either one of you has time for me what with the tourists breaking down your doors." She took a big bite of her chicken drumstick.

Emily exchanged a grin with Monica, and said, "It *has* been a good Christmas season. I've been open less than three months, and I already have more business than I can handle. I'll hire some more seasonal help, but in the meantime, I'll be looking for another full-time employee to go along with the part-time widows."

"Good for you!" Monica cried. "I might have to hire another part-timer, too. Josh's work is so popular, I'm getting worried he won't be able to keep up."

"I think he solved that," Brooke said. "This morning he discussed hiring Adam to help him prepare the leather. There's a lot of work, but you don't have to be an artist to do some of it."

The bell above the front door rang. "I'll be back." Monica went to deal with a customer.

"That's nice of Adam to help Josh," Emily said, between bites of salad, "considering you guys must be keeping him busy at the ranch. Do you enjoy working with him?"

"We get along okay," Brooke said, opening a container of her mom's coleslaw.

"You two seemed pretty . . . friendly last night."

"We're friends," Brooke said, then filled her mouth with a forkful of coleslaw. When she still couldn't meet Emily's eyes, she knew her friend was watching her.

Monica came to sit back down, picked up her sandwich, then looked from Emily to Brooke with suspicion. "What did I miss?"

"She stopped looking at me after I asked about her and Adam," Emily said slowly.

"There's more going on, isn't there?" Monica demanded.

Brooke swallowed. So now she was supposed to lie to her best friends? With a groan, she briefly covered her face. "I can't talk about it."

"You're sleeping with him!" Monica hissed in a low voice.

Brooke winced.

Monica gasped. "You can't even deny it!"

"Okay, okay, keep your voices down," she whispered, glancing over her shoulder at the empty showroom. Someone walked by the front windows and paused to look at the display before moving on.

"It's true?" Emily cried. "Nate never said anything —"

"He doesn't know! And you can't say a word, neither of you."

"You're not dating him, but you're sleeping with him," Monica said, sitting back in disbelief. "I don't know what to think of this modern, twenty-first-century woman."

"We just couldn't keep our hands off each other — that's all it is," Brooke admitted at last.

Monica closed her eyes. "Oh, God, that sounds so sexy."

"Why haven't you said anything?" Emily asked in bewilderment. "Why the secret?"

"Because I'm his boss! Do you know how that would look to my family? The first guy we hire that's my age, and I jump him?"

"Did you?" Monica asked with a giggle.

"No!" She hesitated, then smiled. "Not exactly."

"But Brooke," Emily continued, "people have office romances all the time."

"Their offices aren't their family business. How would sleeping with an employee look to my dad, my brothers? And besides . . . I've really enjoyed having this — relationship, or whatever you want to call it — all to myself, you know? It's like my private little thrill."

"So you like being with him?" Monica asked softly.

"I do. Even when we're working together. He's funny, and we never run out of things to talk about."

"Sounds like it's more than physical," Monica pointed out.

"Because it is — it's friendship. And it feels good."

"As long as you're happy," Emily said, regarding her with worry.

Brooke grinned and touched both their arms. "I'm *happy,*" she insisted. "He makes me feel incredibly sexy and beautiful."

When a customer entered and approached

the counter, Monica got up to help. Soon she was opening coolers, displaying various bouquets that the rushed man could choose from. After ringing up the purchase, she sat back down and toyed with her celery sticks. "So I guess you didn't appreciate the date with LeVar?"

"It wasn't a date, and you know it," Brooke said, wearing a mock frown. "You ambushed, then deserted me."

"Well, I didn't know you already had a guy in your bed," Monica pointed out.

"And then Adam showed up at the pool tournament," Brooke confessed. "It was pretty awkward."

"Sounds like it would have been fun to watch," Monica told Emily. "Guess I left too early. Did they fight over you?"

Brooke just blinked at her, then they all burst into laughter.

Monica saw to a couple more customers, and when she returned, Brooke started packing up. "I can't stay much longer. Tyler will be coming after school."

Emily sighed. "Okay, I'll admit it, I feel bad Steph didn't come to me for help with Tyler's community service." She lifted a hand. "And yes, I know, he probably wouldn't have enjoyed working in a bakery."

"No, he wouldn't have," Brooke insisted

gently. "She really wants to help this kid, and I can't help admiring her. I think she's gaining a lot of maturity from this, maybe seeing how good she's got it with a loving family."

"True," Emily admitted. "How's Tyler doing?"

"It's only been one day. I'm just teaching him about horses for now. But he's been sort of respectful, and that's a good thing. It probably helped that Adam worked with us, too."

"Not one of your brothers?" Monica asked curiously.

"Nope. I admit, I was surprised. I didn't think Adam would want to be involved with a punk kid, but he's incredibly patient, yet firm."

"He was a sergeant in the Marines," Emily pointed out. "He's used to dealing with new recruits."

Brooke had a fleeting thought about Adam's military past. After everything he'd told her, she thought he might have stayed as far away from Tyler as possible, but he hadn't. Surely that was a good sign. But she couldn't discuss his confidences, so it was time to change the subject. "Speaking of my brothers . . . Nate is insufferably happy."

Emily grinned.

"He's left the ranch at almost a decent hour instead of lingering too long these last couple days. He's actually *delegating,* which is something that idiot brother of mine needed to do more of. You're good for him. How are you enjoying setting up house?"

Emily blushed. "It's wonderful being together. I keep hoping you two will find someone, fall in love, and be just as happy." She hesitated. "Or maybe find someone who can make you happy in *every* way."

"I don't know if I'm ready for that, Em," Brooke said. "I don't know about her," she added, pointing with her thumb at Monica.

"It's Christmas — I'm too busy," Monica insisted. "I never put any more pressure on myself during the holidays than I have to. And then I'm taking an online class in January for the flower side of my business."

"Wow, that's a lot of denial," Emily said. "Maybe a nice guy will rent my apartment, and you'll hit it off."

"So you're advertising it already?" Brooke asked.

Some of her disappointment must have leaked through because both women turned to stare at her.

"Why? Are you interested?" Emily leaned forward with eagerness.

Brooke sighed. "I . . . maybe. Interested,

anyway. But it's just not easy to leave my mom. She's getting back on her feet, but . . . a relapse could happen anytime."

"You work there all day, every day," Monica pointed out. "You see her more than most of us ever see our moms."

"And you'll only live a couple miles away," Emily added. "Oh, say you'll rent it. I was really worried about a stranger being right above my bakery."

"I don't know." Brooke felt unable to explain away her unease. On the one hand, she longed to have a place of her own, where she could be independent. She was twenty-eight years old! But on the other hand, there was her family, and all their expectations.

"I'll tell you what," Emily said. "I won't advertise it until the new year. That'll give you a few weeks to make a decision."

Brooke smiled her relief. "Thanks."

"She wants a love nest," Monica said casually.

Both Brooke and Emily groaned.

The bell jingled again, and Brooke glanced over her shoulder — and did a double take. Whitney Winslow had stepped inside, looking over the flower arrangements and hometown crafts with interest.

Brooke stood up. "Hi, Whitney."

She glanced behind the counter, then her

face broke into a wide smile. "Hello, ladies! I saw the display but didn't connect your name, Monica."

"Can't blame you," Monica said, going past the counter into the showroom. "We only met a couple times."

"I really like your merchandise." Whitney strolled through the side of the showroom devoted to unusual gifts. "These are all locally made?"

"I sell them on consignment," Monica said, following her. "The wedding quilts are a big seller, along with the knitted and crocheted layettes."

"I'm interested in the leather," Whitney mused.

Brooke gave a snort of laughter, then realized she might be offending the woman.

Whitney met her eyes and grinned. "Oh, sorry, guess that could be taken many ways. But the tooling on these purses is just so . . . exquisite. Who's the artist?"

Before anyone could answer, a young couple came through the door. Whitney went back to browsing, and Brooke and Emily exchanged a glance. The two customers were holding hands, barely able to keep their eyes off each other. They were newly engaged, they explained, and wanted to make an appointment to discuss flower arrangements for their wedding.

When at last they left, Whitney came back to the women and gave a happy sigh. "Romance! That's what Valentine Valley is all about, right? How can Mr. Galimi and his friends not see that my store could be a part of that?"

Brooke shrugged. "Maybe his wife makes him have sex with the lights off, and he's never seen her nightgowns."

They all laughed.

Whitney's gaze strayed back to Josh's purses. "I have to know who the artist is. Maybe I can give him some sales, and he can help be a bridge between the townspeople and me."

"He's my brother, Josh," Brooke said.

"How perfect." Whitney opened her purse and pulled out a gold business card case. "Can you give him my card? I'd love to talk to him."

"Actually, you met him that night at the diner," Brooke reminded her. "He helped me get you out of there."

"Ooh." Whitney's eyes widened. "I had wondered who he was. He seemed to disappear like Superman reverting to Clark Kent."

"Superman?" Brooke echoed with a grimace. "Let's not say that to his face, okay?"

Whitney laughed. "Deal, as long as you give him my card."

Brooke agreed, but after Whitney had left, she turned to her friends, and said, "Can you see my brother making naughty S&M leather? I don't think so."

"Now who's the one judging?" Emily said, hands on her hips. "You don't have any idea what she might want from him."

They all looked at each other — and grinned.

The following Monday, Brooke's dad was running an errand to a motor-supply store in Carbondale, so Brooke drove her mom to an appointment with Doc Ericson in Valentine. As they arrived back home, they could see Josh walking across the yard, Tyler trailing behind him at a sloooow pace. Brooke drove around to the ramp built to bypass the kitchen stairs, parking and helping her mom use her walker to get inside.

"You're not going to work with Tyler?" Sandy asked.

"Josh and Adam can deal with him today. I thought we were starting on the cookie dough we mean to freeze before Christmas."

Sandy eyed her. "Hiding from the boy already?"

Brooke grinned. "Not at all. He's good at

356

letting you know he's only here because he has to be, but he's more interested than he lets on. Smart, too. I just thought Josh should take a turn, so I could hear all about it."

"So you think our stint as a community-service ranch is going well?"

"I do." Brooke sat on a stool at the breakfast counter and considered her mother. "It just feels good to make a difference in someone's life, you know? I mean, look at Adam." She hesitated, realizing it might be a bad idea to discuss him, but it was too late now. "He was in even more trouble than Tyler, but Coach McKee took a risk and ended up making a man out of him. Adam says Coach changed his life. I wish more kids could have that opportunity. Tyler's not bad, but his mom can't be around much, and it's too easy for him to hang with guys who are only interested in having a good time. Who knows if his brother is getting sucked back into the wrong crowd, too? That's got to be bad for Tyler to see."

"That's two students you've taken on," Sandy pointed out, seating herself with a sigh beside her daughter. "You just . . . glow when you talk about your work with them. What about taking on more students?"

Brooke chuckled, linking her arm with her

mom's. "You think Dad would approve of turning our ranch into a probation-department resource?"

Sandy laughed, too. "No, we're too small an operation, spread too thin, to do much of that. You've taught Steph to barrel race because she asked, but what if you advertise yourself as a riding instructor? You've been teaching Tyler to ride already. You could take on other students."

Brooke stared at her mother in surprise, feeling the revelation wash over her.

Sandy continued, "Yes, part of the year the weather will inhibit you, but you'll manage."

"Mom, Josh and I are the ranch foremen. I think it might take too much away from my job."

"Josh has something he loves, sweetie. So does Nate. Do you begrudge them that?"

"No, of course not!"

"Why would they begrudge you? I think you can all work it out together. It wouldn't be full-time, after all. And maybe Adam wants to stay on. That would really help."

"I don't know about that," Brooke warned her. "When his grandma is better, he'll probably leave. I don't think he feels like he fits in here anymore." She forced herself to act casually as she stood up to reach the recipe box.

"Do you think there's something troubling him?" Sandy asked.

Brooke hesitated even as she sat back down, looking into her mom's concerned face. "You should have seen how he reacted when people called him a hero the other night. He told me a few things about what happened to him in Afghanistan. It was . . . pretty terrible, and he blames himself when he shouldn't."

"They say time heals — and they wouldn't say it so much if it wasn't true. He seems like a strong man who'll be able to figure things out. I don't think you need to worry."

But I do worry, Brooke thought bleakly, knowing she probably worried too much. She was getting more and more involved with Adam, and not just in bed.

"As for you," Sandy continued, "give the idea of becoming an instructor some thought. It will be a challenge — but you're good at challenges."

Brooke leaned over and kissed her cheek. "Thanks, Mom."

They were elbow deep in flour, making chocolate-chip-cookie batter and sugar-cookie dough, when Josh came in.

"I'm calling a family meeting," he said.

As Doug and Nate strolled in after him,

Brooke asked sharply, "There wasn't a problem with Tyler, was there?"

"Nope, nothing to do with him," Josh said. "Although if I say so myself, he took to my riding instruction well."

Brooke rolled her eyes, then tapped Nate's hand as he tried to take a fingerful of dough. "Get a spoon! And Josh, I taught that kid everything he knows, and don't forget it."

While Brooke and Sandy worked on the cookie dough, and Doug prepared a salad to start off dinner, Josh took a seat at the breakfast counter and gave them all a serious look.

Nate, who'd grabbed his ringing cell phone, sent it to voice mail. "What's up?"

"You know this Aspen boutique who wants to buy some of my work?" Josh began.

Everyone nodded, and Doug added, "That's impressive, son."

Josh gave a half smile. "Thanks. Well, it's getting even bigger than that. Whitney, the owner of Leather and Lace, contacted me through Brooke, and she's interested, too — in my work."

Nate chuckled.

"It's not like that," Josh said, shaking his head. "I haven't met with her yet, and don't know if I'd do it — I'd have to feel comfortable, after all — but, this is just getting too big for me to make decisions on my own, a bigger time commitment than I ever thought I'd make to something that was always a hobby for me."

"You're training Adam to prepare the leather, right?" Brooke asked, licking her finger. "That'll help."

"Get a spoon!" Nate commanded.

She stuck out her tongue.

"But that's not the point." Josh sighed. "We're a small ranch, and we all have to work. I don't want to make any of you work harder because I'm off doing something that will only benefit me."

"Nobody ever said you had to devote every wakin' moment to this ranch," Doug said as he dumped sliced carrots into the main salad bowl. "We've got Adam now — and if we have to hire someone else, I think we can, right, Nate?"

Nate nodded. "We've really diversified the last couple years. We're okay. I wouldn't ever want you to feel like you owed us, Josh. Just like you showed me I could pursue my favorite part of this job, you can do the same."

Brooke scraped her dough into a plastic container and labeled it for the freezer. She was afraid to look up, afraid to show any disappointment. Now wasn't the time for

361

her to bring up her own idea that would take her away from the ranch part-time. No way would she let her dad think they were all deserting their parents. Maybe she should just forget it.

Sandy cleared her throat and looked pointedly at Brooke, who shook her head quickly.

"What is it?" Doug asked.

Everyone was staring at her, and for once, words failed her. She gave her mom a pleading look, but Sandy just waited patiently for her to speak.

"Mom and I were just talking about an idea when Josh called this meeting. What a coincidence," Brooke added with an awkward attempt at cheerfulness, looking at her hands as she washed them at the sink rather than at her family. Her nervousness showed her how much the idea of teaching kids and adults to ride already meant to her. "I've been enjoying working with Steph and Tyler, and thought maybe I could be a part-time riding instructor here at the ranch."

For a moment, there was complete silence. Gritting her teeth, she made herself look at everyone, saw her mother's encouraging smile, Josh's grin, Nate's eyes wide with surprise — but she couldn't read her father's impassivity.

"We already give sleigh rides in the winter," Josh said. "Riding instruction would be another way to generate some tourist money and help the town out, too. We don't have anything like that right in Valentine Valley."

She'd known Josh would support her. She looked at Nate.

He shrugged. "I have nothing against it. If we're already talking about keeping Adam on, if he wants it, or hiring someone else, that should cover it. Dad?"

Doug sighed. "It's strange to know that if I'm callin' myself 'almost retired,' I shouldn't have a say in this."

"Of course you have a say, Dad," Brooke said earnestly. "I would never do anything you didn't think would benefit the ranch."

"If you three think you can make all these part-time jobs work, then it's fine by me."

Sandy looked relieved, but Brooke wasn't. She didn't feel like her dad had actually approved, but he hadn't said no, either. Her excitement took a little hit, but she was determined to make it work.

"No point in worrying about this now," she said briskly. "It's almost Christmas, and we have enough to do. We'll talk about it after the holidays."

CHAPTER NINETEEN

That night, Adam cradled a naked Brooke in his arms, satisfied and sleepy and so comfortable in his bed. He could hear the crackling of the fire in the living room and the quietness of her breathing.

He still couldn't believe he'd shared the truth of his past with her but had been so surprised at how right it felt. The weight seemed off his chest, as if he could inhale deeply again. His dreams weren't full of death and dying, but occasionally the bittersweet memory of the good times he and his friends had shared.

He'd shared something he hadn't discussed with another soul — did that mean he was falling in love with Brooke? It was such a surprise to even think about, and he knew better than to mention it aloud. He wasn't even certain himself and knew she wasn't ready to hear it, regardless. He could be patient and wait until the moment was right.

"Is that Ranger snoring?" Brooke asked in the middle of a yawn.

"Guess I'm used to it. And I was just about to say how quiet you were tonight." He gently threaded his fingers through her hair, sweeping it back from her face, so he could see her expression. "Is something wrong?"

"Not with you," she murmured, then came up on her elbow and looked down at him with wicked intent in her slumberous gaze. "That was . . . incredible."

He smiled. "You're trying to distract me."

She leaned down to kiss him, and her hair slid along his shoulders and about his face, like a waterfall hiding their kiss from the outside world.

Heaving a sigh, she laid her head back on his shoulder. "I have a lot of crazy thoughts going on in my head."

"About Tyler? He's taken up a lot of your valuable time."

She grinned. "My valuable time? What about yours? I thought you'd do my work for me while I dealt with him."

"You didn't order me to," he pointed out.

"True. But I admit, I like watching you

work with him. I think you're a good influence."

He winced. "Unfair. Next you'll expect me to be a saint."

She tweaked his navel. "Never." Then she sighed. "He's not totally enthusiastic. Maybe his buddies have been giving him a hard time. It can't be easy trying to change your life."

"It's not, but then, you know that."

She looked up at him with a frown. "Me? I don't know anything about that. I've always been this way, with ranching as my goal. I'm pretty boring."

"Really?" He studied her. "I think people can have more than one goal, and maybe you're figuring that out."

Her smile was slow in coming. "What are you, a mind reader?"

"I just know you."

"Okay, maybe you're right."

Adam listened as she told him about her enjoyment working with teenagers, and her mom's suggestion that she might like to become a part-time riding instructor.

"So what's the problem?" he asked. "Seems to me you've been handling your work duties and Tyler. How would teaching be any different?"

"Because Josh is going to expand his work,

366

too," Brooke explained. "I just don't know if we can all pull back like this."

"So Nate and Josh get to do what they want, but not you?"

Her gaze on him softened, and when she caressed his cheek, he turned to kiss her fingers.

"My champion," she murmured.

"I'm being serious," he countered.

"I know you are. I guess I just have to . . . see how it goes. But I came up with a way to test myself where kids are concerned."

"Should I even ask?"

She grinned. "I'd like to volunteer to host an outing for the Chess Club. I could get the greenhorns on a horse, maybe lead some of the more experienced ones on a trail ride up into the mountains. But I'd need help. You up for it?"

"Wow, give a woman great sex, and she expects a favor in return."

"Excuse me, but I think *I* gave *you* great sex, so I'm asking a favor in return."

"You're my boss. I think I have to do everything you say."

Laughing, she leaned to kiss him, and the kisses turned passionate.

"Whoa!" she said at last, gasping. "We can't do this again. I have to sneak back to my own bed."

He groaned and rolled away. "This sucks."

"So . . . what would you think if I moved into the apartment over the bakery?"

He lifted his head and stared at her. "You're considering that?"

"Just considering because I have to also consider my mom's health. But I think it would be pretty good to fall asleep with you sometimes," she added, wearing a sexy smile.

He sat up. "I think you'd be shocked at how male and gross I am in the morning in my skivvies."

"I'll take my chances."

Tuesday morning, Brooke texted her invitation to the Chess Club for a Friday afternoon riding instruction, a sleigh ride, followed by a bonfire. By Wednesday, Steph excitedly responded back that everyone was in.

Brooke was just telling Adam about it when Tyler's mom, Wendy, drove up to drop off her son. Instead of racing away when the teenager hopped out, she leaned toward the open door and peered out.

Her smile was tired but genuine. "Hey, Brooke, I can't thank you enough for asking Tyler to work here. He's having a good time and learning so much."

"Glad to help, Wendy." She glanced over her shoulder and saw that Tyler was already walking toward the barn. "How's Cody?"

That was a mistake. Wendy's gaze dropped, and she turned to grip the steering wheel. "I don't know. Sometimes I think he's learned a lesson, other times . . . that he's given up. I guess I can only wait."

She drove away, and Brooke stood there wincing at her own stupidity. If she were in Wendy's place, she wouldn't want people ignoring the existence of her older son, who'd made a mistake, paid the price, and was starting over. But Wendy had *two* sons in trouble, even as she was struggling to support them without their dad's help.

With a sigh, Brooke turned around, wrapped her scarf tighter around her neck, and saw Adam and Tyler together, leaning on the corral fence looking at the horses, talking. She liked looking at them together, and it made her think of Adam as a dad. The sweet tenderness of it shocked her, and she knew she had to put it out of her mind, before she started angsting over him leaving town.

As Brooke moved closer, Adam glanced over his shoulder at her. "Tyler here has volunteered to be your assistant Friday night. I told him it would be okay to enjoy his time with his friends, but he disagrees."

Tyler scowled. "Look, they all know I'm here for community service. I'm not hidin' anything. And they're not really my friends." He stalked into the barn.

Brooke raised an eyebrow at Adam, who only said, "He's embarrassed. That's a good sign."

"If you say so."

Friday was a half day for school, and after lunch a caravan of cars and pickups started dropping off teenagers, a dozen in all. A couple of parents stayed to help chaperone and prepare hot dogs and s'mores for the bonfire later. A few unloaded their kids' horses from trailers.

As Steph was helping call in horses from the pasture, Brooke found her.

"Before you can say anything," Steph began, "this kind of exploded. I thought maybe five kids would come, but they told their friends and . . . I hope you don't mind. I'll help teach, too."

Brooke slung an arm around her shoulder and squeezed. "I don't mind at all. I prayed for good weather all week, and here we are, in the forties and sunny. The more the merrier!" Then she lowered her voice. "How's Tyler?"

Steph grimaced. "You see him more than

I do. I can't because of my dad, you know. And Tyler doesn't talk to me much at school. I think he doesn't want to get me involved with the guys he used to hang out with."

"Used to?"

"He's trying to stay away. They're still around, but he's grounded and can't go out at night. This is his first party since he got arrested. I was worried his mom wasn't going to let him come."

"He volunteered to be my assistant today. Maybe it's easier for him to keep busy."

"I hope so," Steph murmured.

Another car drove up, and Emily emerged, waving happily.

Brooke eyed Steph, who shrugged. "I asked if she wanted to chaperone."

"That was nice of you."

"Maybe not," Steph said ruefully. "This is kind of a wild crowd."

And it was, but Brooke had the best time. Between her, Adam, Steph, Tyler, and some of the more experienced kids in the crowd, they got everybody comfortable on horses. There were a few old mares and geldings who would follow the other horses with no guidance, and those were given to the greenhorns. The dogs raced around wildly while the chaperones smiled and called out pointers. Soon they were riding through the scenic beauty of her ranch, and Brooke felt so proud and humble at what her ancestors had created in this mountain valley. Water tumbled through ice down Silver Creek, glistening in the sun. Slow-moving herds of cattle lowed and raised their heads from behind fences as the battalion of riders went by. The riders were able to climb a bit into the foothills on a gently sloping path, and Valentine Valley spread out before them, the spires of the churches and town hall pointing into the blue sky.

Adam was surprised how much he enjoyed the afternoon with the kids. They were eager to learn, even if a few of them tended to talk when they were supposed to be listening. He felt . . . peaceful, bringing up the tail end of the line, Ranger trotting at his side.

After oating the horses and turning them loose in the pasture, the kids gathered to start on the bonfire. Adam drove the sleigh, taking groups of two or three kids out at a time, while the others roasted hot dogs and gulped hot chocolate. Tyler asked to ride alongside him to learn about driving the sleigh. Adam suspected it was to avoid some of the other kids, but he wouldn't force Tyler to participate.

Once they were gliding through the countryside, they couldn't quite hear the chattering of the three girls behind them, as the wind scattered their words. Instead, the bells chimed softly along the sleigh, and the snow and ice crunched and crackled beneath them.

Due to the secret that hung between them, Tyler's joyriding with the Thalberg ATV, the kid was usually defensive and close to crossing the line into insolence. Adam knew he himself had probably behaved the same way with Coach McKee at the beginning. It was hard to believe he ever resented Coach, for they got along great now. Adam had been lucky enough to work beside him several times at the Huang house.

"So what was it like being a soldier?" Tyler suddenly asked.

Adam raised an eyebrow at the kid.

"If you don't mind me askin'," he shot back, frowning.

"I don't mind." And surprisingly, he didn't. "I hated it for a while in boot camp, but when I made it through that, I was proud of myself and the skills the Marines had taught me. I felt like a warrior, the first line of defense for my country. Marines are often the first called in when there's a problem."

"I bet you were happy when you killed the bad guys."

"A Marine celebrates surviving, not the killing," Adam said quietly. "It's not like a video game — you know for every person lost, there's someone grieving."

"But when they're trying to kill you —"

"You do what you have to. But you don't enjoy it."

Tyler said nothing for a few minutes, watching Adam's hands on the reins. "Did you get hurt?" he finally asked.

"I did. But some of my friends died, so my injury is just a scar that reminds me to be glad I'm alive."

And he *was* glad to be alive, he thought. Not just glad to have survived, but to be alive, to experience life — to be with Brooke.

"It doesn't sound like it's good to be a soldier," the kid said dubiously.

"I'm honored to have served my country, Tyler, to have made a difference. There's always a risk, of course, but if a guy wants every day to be challenging, to experience incredible pride in what he's accomplished, then he becomes a Marine." Now he sounded like a recruiting officer, but he didn't want to give the kid only one side about life in the military.

Tyler gave him a considering glance, then nodded and looked ahead to the mountains.

When they returned to the house, Adam couldn't help but notice how Tyler kept himself on the outside of this group of kids. Since he was doing his community service, the club chaperones had agreed to give him one more chance, but Adam well remembered how Tyler must be feeling — caught between two groups of kids, trying to leave the one behind but not feeling like he fit in with the new crowd, who didn't trust him.

Steph tried to include him whenever she could. She insisted he eat hot dogs sitting on a log beside her, not realizing that another young man glowered at the two as they laughed over something. Tyler might have competition for her attention.

As the teenagers were picked up one by one, and the sun was setting, Adam ended up sorting through tack with Tyler in the barn, the double doors behind them wide open.

"Did Steph leave?" Adam asked.

Tyler just gestured with his head behind them. Adam turned and saw Steph talking to the boy who'd been glowering at her earlier.

"Did you get a chance to say good-bye?" Adam asked.

"She's busy. It's not like we're together or anything."

Adam caught the other boy giving Tyler a victorious look before he sauntered away to his own car. Adam hoped Tyler missed it.

The two of them straightened the tack room in silence for a while, then Adam considered that since Tyler had asked him personal questions, he could do the same.

"This might be none of my business," Adam said, "but I was wondering how your brother's doing."

Tyler shot him a scowl. "What do you know about my brother?"

"Only what Brooke told me, that he served his time and was out."

Tyler took down rope and re-coiled it, though Adam thought it was just busywork to keep from talking.

"My dad was in jail a couple times when I was a kid," Adam said. "Then he had a hard time getting another job."

Tyler's shoulders briefly sagged before he stiffened. "He'll find a job. I know he's trying. He doesn't ever want to go back to jail."

And there was the crux of the boy's worry, that his brother wouldn't find a job and end up hanging with a bad crowd again, leading to worse things.

"You're straightening out your problems,"

Adam said. "He will, too. I had to confront the same thing in myself."

"Yeah, yeah, your dad went to jail."

"No, I spent two nights there."

Tyler stilled, then turned to face him, his expression one of wary disbelief. "What you'd do, get drunk?"

"No, that was my old man's problem. I stupidly stole a car to joyride."

Before Tyler could catch himself, his mouth sagged open. "What — *you*? Sergeant Perfect Marine?"

Adam chuckled. "Now that's a nickname. Never knew I was perfect. Don't tell Miss Thalberg that, or she'll find plenty more for me to do around here."

"But . . . what happened?"

Adam leaned back against a beam that rose up through the ceiling. He had Tyler's full attention — the boy didn't even try to pretend to work.

"My parents didn't give a crap about what I did growing up," Adam began slowly. "But, of course, when I screwed up, they had to notice. My screwups just kept getting bigger, until I landed with a bad group in high school. I had to prove I was big and cool enough to be in charge, you know?"

Tyler nodded silently, his eyes focused on Adam.

"So I stole a car — and it happened to be the football coach's. My parents were going to let me rot in jail, but Coach McKee stood up for me, just like your mom stood up for you."

"How'd you know that?" Tyler demanded.

"It's a small town, isn't it?"

"What did the old guy do to you?"

"Let me serve my community service with him as a manager on the football team. I found better kids to hang out with, and Coach — he didn't preach to me, just showed me how to take responsibility. It felt good. And since Coach impressed me, I decided to do what he'd done, and enter the service. But whatever you choose to do is up to you. As long as you go forward, not back, you'll find the next stage of your life."

Tyler let out a heavy sigh, his expression bleak. "It's hard to get away from those guys, you know?"

"I know. But you have to do what's best for you and your family. Your mom is dealing with a lot, right?"

Tyler nodded. "She cries at night. She's worried I'm going to do something stupid like Cody. Cody's worried about that, too."

"It's good that they both care. That must help."

Tyler pushed away from the rail and

headed toward the open door. He paused, and said over his shoulder, "Thanks."

Adam followed him a minute later, to find Brooke just closing a stall door nearby. She gave him a searching look.

"You overheard," he said.

She glanced toward the barn doors, and although they were open, he could see no one in the yard beyond. She came to him, put her arms around his waist, and gave him a gentle kiss.

"You're good with him."

He shrugged. "Not much to figure out. I've been there. At least his mom cares. Mine didn't even want to be a mom. Condom broke."

She winced. "And she actually told you that."

"Oh yeah, every time she was furious I didn't get her a beer or, later on, cook them some food. I'm glad Tyler's got a better mom. Makes me think he'll be all right."

She kissed him again, slowly, sweetly, and he found himself so hungry for the taste of her, the scent of lemons and coconut in her hair. He almost pulled it out of its braid before he remembered himself.

They heard a casual whistle from the yard and just broke apart in time.

Josh came strolling in. "So how'd it go?"

Brooke grinned. "It was so fun, Josh! You could have joined in, you know."

He raised both hands. "Just like you, I've got to prove I can do two jobs. Lots of purses to make — which sounds a little strange coming from a cowboy."

Adam grinned. "You said it first." He glanced at Brooke. "Good night, boss — bosses," he added for Josh's benefit.

Brooke gave a wave, and Josh glanced over his shoulder as if making sure Adam had gone.

Brooke's relief was quickly replaced by tension. "Something wrong?"

Josh eyed her. "You seem to think so, by the way you're hiding what you're doing with Adam."

Brooke tried one more bluff. "What are you talking about?"

"I saw you kissing. I backed out and gave a whistle because I didn't want to embarrass you."

Brooke winced. "I'm sorry."

"Why?" Josh asked, surprised. "Why would I care if you're dating him? Why the secret?"

She lowered her voice. "So if Nate had some hot new secretary, and you decided to go after her, you don't think Dad would have a problem with that?"

He hesitated. "I don't know. So you're going after Adam?"

"No, not like that."

Josh's brows came together. "So he went after you?"

"Of course not. We both felt it, and we both resisted, then we caved. But it's temporary. I don't want anyone else to find out. Can you keep this between us? Please?"

He sighed. "Of course. As long as you don't frighten the horses, guess I shouldn't care what you do. You kept enough of my secrets."

"You bet I did. I remember Jill."

"Oh, come on, we were seventeen!"

"And you kept sneaking out of the house at night and riding off to meet up with her. I never told a soul."

"And I'll never tell your secret. But Brooke, how do you know it's temporary?"

"I just know," she said, feeling bleak at just the thought, and that scared her. "He'll be leaving when he thinks his grandma no longer needs him." And if he found out she was faking her decline — he might leave even sooner. She didn't want to feel anything more for Adam, knew it wasn't a good idea. But more and more, she couldn't imagine her life without him.

CHAPTER TWENTY

The sun was already below the mountains, the sky an ominous gray after such a gorgeous day. Brooke finished closing up the barn for the night after calling in the couple riding horses that spent nights indoors. She petted horse noses and dog noses, then headed toward the house. She'd already checked the weather for the night — more snow. Great for the ski slopes as the tourism season truly began to kick in, but not so good for barrel-racing lessons. She'd already canceled her morning lesson with Steph, and it made her feel discouraged. Much as she wanted to teach, it would be difficult through the winter.

She caught another glimpse of the ruined barn, black beams sticking up through the snow like an animal carcass.

And then she came to a stop and just stared at the piece of land that was waiting for a new purpose. They'd been having nightly conversations about what to do when they could clear the wreckage come spring. It had been all about building another barn closer to the house, or adding on to the one they already had.

That still left this land. Everyone had been behind her idea of giving riding lessons — what if they took the insurance money and built an indoor riding arena? She got a shiver of excitement that she quickly suppressed. She'd seen lots of different arenas, of course, from a covered pavilion to a fully enclosed building. She'd have to do her research before she even presented such an idea to the family. But the thought of being able to instruct students year-round, and even rent it out to other groups . . .

"Brooke?"

She gave a little jump of surprise and turned to find her dad coming toward her.

"You have snow buildin' up on your hat," he said, smiling as he shook his head. "Been woolgatherin' out here a long time?"

She smiled, then decided she needed facts and figures before presenting her plan to her family, so she put her idea aside.

"Guess I'm just reliving the day," she answered. "The teen outing went well, Dad. I really enjoyed myself, and I'm looking forward to working with kids more."

He nodded but said nothing.

"I still feel strange that I sprung my riding instructor idea on you without warning," she continued. "Each one of us kids has been coming up with new life goals that aren't just about ranching. Are you sure you don't mind?"

"I already told you what I think," he said, his expression confused. Then he glanced at the ruined barn and gave a wince, as if it still startled him.

"I've been feeling that something in my life needed to change," she said, her voice husky. "There's a part of me that's looking for some independence. I've even been thinking of moving into town. Would that bother you?"

"Cookie, I never thought you'd live at home forever. If I ever gave you that impression —"

"No, Dad, you didn't."

"— it only seems that way because I've been consumed with my worries about your mom. I know how well you two always get along, and if I showed any doubts about things you were sayin', it's because I've been worried about your mom's reaction and how she depends on you."

She took Doug's gloved hands in her own. "I'll be here all the time, Dad. Regardless of where I live, I'll see Mom every single day and spend lots of time with her. She's the one who's been encouraging me to spread my wings a bit. Heck, she saw how I loved to work with kids before I did."

He gave a heavy sigh and squeezed her hands firmly. "I sometimes forget how strong her mind and will are when I'm so worried about her health."

"She wouldn't want us to be that way. But it's hard, I know. I won't say anything about moving until I think the time is right. I haven't even made up my mind yet. Em gave me until January to decide before she puts the apartment up for rent."

He nodded. "It sounds like the perfect place for you."

She slid her arms around his waist and hugged him tight. "It's so difficult to make these decisions, Dad. You know how much I'll miss being home in the evenings with you both."

He lifted his head, then cupped her face. "But I'm the lucky parent, Cookie. I'll get to see you every day."

He kissed her cheek, and she pressed her face into his shoulder so he wouldn't see her tears.

Saturday evening, Brooke walked toward

her Jeep after a Christmas concert at the Royal Theater, the widows having gone home in their own car. She was parked a couple blocks away and passed a poster from Sylvester Galimi in a store window, asking townspeople to write their councilmen and -women, to take a stand against immorality and Leather and Lace. Every time she expressed anger at his ignorance, one of the widows assured her they had a plan for the next phase, and they'd let her in when it was time.

To her surprise, the lights were still on at Sugar and Spice, splashing a welcome beam out across the snowy sidewalk and street.

Brooke felt a hint of cheer and hurried to open the door, only to find the place deserted. "Hello?"

Emily rushed out of the kitchen, wiping her hands on a towel, wearing a flour-stained Christmas apron. "I forgot to lock the door. But you're a good surprise."

Brooke sat down in a chair and stretched her long legs out.

"Want a cookie before you spill your problems?" Emily offered.

"No, I need the hard stuff. Cheesecake. With as much chocolate or caramel as you've got."

"Turtle cheesecake."

Brooke gave her an appreciative nod. When she ate her first bite, she sighed. "That almost makes me feel better."

Emily's smile faded. "Maybe you feel bad because you're keeping Adam a secret."

"So I'm dishonorable," she said, then helped herself to a big forkful of the cheesecake.

"You're not dishonorable — you're just confused."

"I'm very confused. Maybe if I move upstairs, I can get some distance from Adam instead of seeing his cabin right out my window every night."

"Maybe. If you can't see the forbidden fruit . . ."

"Then I'll just think about him all the time."

"Do you?" Emily asked in a quiet voice.

Brooke nodded. "This isn't good for me. It's going to end. Maybe *I* need to end it."

"Do you want to?"

She shook her head and met Emily's gaze earnestly. "I told myself this was a temporary fling. My emotions weren't supposed to get involved. But Emily, I really like him."

The door banged open, its bell jingling wildly. Both women turned with a start to find Steph running across the room and throwing herself to her knees to hug Emily.

Emily closed her arms around her sister, but gaped over her head at Brooke. "Steph, honey, what is it? What's wrong?"

"Tyler got into a fight at the Chess Club, and he got kicked out." Her voice came out in a shuddery sob. "I — I was so mad that I — I quit, too!"

Several strands of Steph's blond hair were stuck to the tears on her face, and Emily smoothed them out of the way. "If he was fighting —"

"But it was all Matthew's fault! He's just jealous that I'm interested in Tyler, so he told everyone that Tyler sets fires like his brother does, that Tyler burned down the barn at the Silver Creek Ranch." Steph turned her blotched, wet face toward Brooke. "You know it isn't true!"

"Of course not, it's been officially declared an accident," Brooke agreed.

"I told Tyler to ignore it, but — but, he's so sensitive about his brother, and Matthew just kept on . . . kept on . . . . Oh, it's all my fault!" she added in a wail, burying her face against Emily's shoulder again. "How could I stay there after that? I used to date Matthew, but I never thought he could . . . could be so cruel!"

"Has Matthew been kicked out, too?" Emily asked.

"No, he claimed he was only defending himself after Tyler threw the first punch." Steph sagged back on her heels. "And that's true. Oh, this is going to be the worst Christmas ever!"

When she wiped her face with her forearm, Brooke handed her a napkin. "Where's Tyler now?"

"I don't know. He ran out. I was supposed to give him a ride home tonight, so I drove around, but I couldn't find him. And then I saw your lights, Em." She blew her nose hard, still trembling.

"He doesn't live far," Emily said in a soothing voice. "He'll get home all right."

"What if I talk to your chaperones?" Brooke asked.

"They won't care." Steph sniffed. "The rule is one fight, and you're out. And they've already given him a second chance, after the ATV thing with my dad. I tried so hard to help him, and I made everything worse."

"Tyler'll be back to work Monday," Brooke said. "Maybe Adam can reach him."

By Monday, Adam had heard about Tyler's fight from Brooke, but the kid still showed up for his community service. He was surly and uncommunicative, doing as he was told without any enthusiasm.

389

When Brooke got a phone call on her cell, Adam eyed the kid as they stood just inside the barn, out of the wind.

"So this is how it's going to be?" Adam asked dryly. "You make a mistake, and you sulk?"

Tyler turned blazing eyes on him. "What do you know about my problems?"

Adam arched a brow. "Did you forget where you live? This is Valentine Valley — everyone knows everything. And they talk. Why don't you tell me what happened."

"You already know, don't you? That's enough. I don't need Chess Club."

"Apparently neither does Steph, because she quit, too."

He stiffened, then watched Adam warily. "She did?"

"Didn't you know?"

He hung his head. "I've been ignoring her calls. She trusted me, and I screwed it all up."

"It was a mistake — now you know there are always going to be people out there who push your buttons."

Tyler didn't say anything, just gripped the shovel hard between his hands like he'd snap the handle.

"So now you've got time on your hands, right?" Adam continued.

Tyler snorted and waved a hand around. "Oh yeah, I'm just lazin' around."

"It's almost Christmas break. If you get bored, you can always put your hands to work for a good cause. I'm working on the project renovating houses for veterans, right now at the Huang house on First Street this side of town hall. You'll see lots of trucks there every day."

Tyler frowned. "I don't know how to do anything like that."

"You can swing a hammer. We can teach you the rest. You can clean, too — I've seen you do that," he teased.

Tyler looked past him. "Miss Thalberg, he's trying to recruit me for even more work."

Adam turned and realized that Brooke had ended her call and was looking at him all soft-eyed, like his girlfriend rather than his boss.

"I already got enough to do," Tyler said, stalking outside with his shovel.

"So that's where you've been going," Brooke said in a quiet voice.

"Sorry I've been gone when you had an itch," he murmured.

"Stop being a wise-ass." But she wore a sweet smile.

"It's not a big deal, Brooke. I'll never be

able to repay soldiers everything they did for me." He cleared his throat. "Now what do you need done?"

"There's an escaped cow on the road down by Cooper's Mine."

"I'm on it." He went to call for Dusty in the horse pasture, leaving Brooke behind.

Late that afternoon, Adam went to the Huang house, knowing Tyler wouldn't come, but hoping. Coach was there, and they worked side by side, sealing the walls of the basement.

"I'm surprised I don't see you much in town," was the first thing Coach said that had nothing to do with painting.

Adam shrugged. "I'm busy working, busy doing this."

"You've only been out of the Marines how long?"

"Six months."

"Not long at all. I bet you're feeling like it's hard to have fun when some of your friends have died."

Adam used the roller carefully, then glanced at the other man. "I had some problems, yeah."

Coach's sympathetic eyes watched him. "You can't feel guilty you're alive, and they're not, son. That's an easy path to follow, and one that'll only give you pain."

Quietly, Adam said, "I used to feel like the guilt was eating away at me. But . . . it's been better lately. I talked to someone about it, and that's helped."

"Your grandma?"

"No, not yet. I think there's still a part of me that never wants to disappoint her."

"You wouldn't be doing that, son. She'd appreciate your honesty."

Adam nodded, then decided to change the subject. "I have another question for you. You hear anything about Tyler Brissette?"

Coach frowned. "I used to know all the boys when I was still with the school district. But nope."

Adam explained Tyler's past, his work at the ranch, his recent fight. "I'm worried he's giving up, Coach. Maybe you can tell me what to say to him since you did such a great job helping me."

Coach put the roller in the long pan of paint and shook his head with regret. "There aren't magic words, son. I can't even tell you what I said to you. I just expected your best work, and your respect. And I was there if you needed to talk. If I remember correctly, you didn't want any lectures from me."

Adam reluctantly smiled. "What a surprise."

"Sounds like the young man knows he's made mistakes and regrets them. That's a good start. Just be there for him."

CHAPTER TWENTY-ONE

The sun was already behind the mountains when Brooke saw Adam's truck come slowly down the road toward the ranch. She leaned on the handle of her snow shovel and watched him until he disappeared around the far side of his cabin. Snow was softly falling, making it seem lighter outside in the growing dark. She wanted to go to him, to ask if Tyler had come to the Huang house so she could reassure Emily and Steph.

But she let it go and turned back to keep shoveling.

A few minutes later, he called out, "Are you standing on the pond?"

She turned her head, pulling her cap back over her ears against the wind. "Yep." His winter coat gave his shoulders even more breadth, made his hips look lean in his faded jeans. Her heart gave a dangerous tug just looking at him, and she forced herself to turn away.

"And you're shoveling the pond?" he asked in a tone of disbelief.

"I need to see how bumpy it is. If it's smooth, the kids can use it to skate, like I used to."

"You mean the Chess Club Steph and Tyler no longer belong to?"

She listened to his boots crunch through the snow as he approached. "They can bring their friends. It doesn't have to be formal. And I'm almost done."

The patch of ice glittered beneath the rising moon. The world was painted in shades of gray, the moon reflecting off the snow.

"I can remember coming here once with my dad," he said, "and I saw you skating."

She looked at him again, wondering if those memories with his dad were always bad ones, but his expression wasn't mournful.

"I took some skating lessons when I was a kid," she admitted. "Then I realized I was never going to be graceful enough."

"I've seen you on a horse. You're pretty graceful." He dropped his voice. "And you move —" He caught himself and glanced over his shoulder toward the house.

"We're far enough away," she said, smiling, the heat he invoked with his words warming her.

"So how's the ice?" he asked.

"Pretty good."

"Do you still have skates?"

"I do, but you can't tell me you want to skate."

"I don't, but I'd like to watch you. I'll finish shoveling while you go get what you need."

He approached her and took the shovel, and they stared at each other, the white puffs of their breath mingling.

"Is this a date?" she asked, disbelieving. "Because you know, I'm not dating anyone at the moment, so my social calendar is free."

"What happened to the 'babe' guy?"

She grinned. "I had to turn him down. I can't juggle two men."

"Did you want to date him or other guys?" he asked.

She leaned into him and put her arms around his waist. "No."

He cupped her face in his gloved hands. "Good."

She swallowed, afraid to say she was feeling more for him than simple lust. "If I can't date other people, you can't either," she finally teased. "When I saw you with those women at Tony's Tavern, I almost started pulling hair."

He laughed. "That would have been something to see. Now go get your skates."

Her skates were in the mudroom behind the kitchen, and she ran there and back, feeling giddy. The men were gone, and her mom was supposed to be taking a nap until Brooke came in to help make dinner, so she had a little time to spend with Adam. She kept cautioning herself that nothing had changed between them except exclusivity, but wasn't that a good sign?

He'd finished shoveling the snow off the ice, and except for a weed or two frozen upright, the surface of the pond was pretty clear. He'd even found a blanket and set it on a log so she could sit down. She slipped on her skates and started lacing them up.

"Isn't hot chocolate the usual skating refreshment?" he asked, stamping his feet against the cold.

"Did you want me to risk waking my mom?"

"No."

"Maybe I should have found a short skating skirt while I was at it."

"Believe me, your jeans hug you in all the right places."

His voice had that husky quality she associated with his lovemaking, and it made her shiver with pleasure to hear it now. With intent focus, he watched her take her first long glide across the ice. It was a little bumpy, but manageable, and she made a tight turn at the end to face him again.

"Impressive."

He studied her from beneath the brim of his cowboy hat, his face conflicting shadows in the moonlight. She could see the cut of his square jaw, the darkness that was the cleft in the center of his chin, the blade of his nose, just the glitter of his eyes.

She felt — so different from herself, foolish and feminine and even giddy with the way he focused on her, the way he wanted her. Their affair had flamed and lasted, and if anything, had burned even hotter the longer they were together. She wanted him more now than she had that first night, and it suddenly scared her. What if she was falling in love with him?

And then he was coming toward her, sliding carefully along the ice in his boots, and she laughed and eluded him. He didn't fall, just changed direction, then pushed himself into a long slide.

"Not bad, eh?" he said, tilting his head so she could see the white teeth of his grin.

It felt so wonderful to be here with him, out in the open, flirting, teasing. Did he *want* her to fall for him? She couldn't believe that. He wanted to leave this place and never come back, and soon he'd have to find out about his grandma's exaggeration that had brought him to Valentine. But . . . not now.

"Did your brothers skate with you?" he asked, coming alongside her.

She darted away before he could catch her arm. "Yep. We did most things together, especially Josh and me, since we're closer in age. You didn't have a brother or sister, so who did you play with?"

"The kids in the trailer park. I played a lot of football there, in the open lots. It came in handy by high school."

She did a little one-foot spin, calling, "Ta da!" when she struck a pose afterward.

He laughed. "I had my dad's horse, too, don't forget. I was the one who took care of old Star."

Brooke did a hockey stop near him. "I remember Star! We bought him when your dad had to sell. Sorry to say, he only lived about five years after that."

"But they were good years, here with you," Adam said, relief evident in his voice. "I always worried what had happened to him since he was too old to be of much use."

They fell silent. She continued to skate, and he slid at her side. He caught her hand

and held it, and she thought it was the most romantic thing to be with him under the moon — even if the temperature was dipping into the twenties.

"I'm surprised you're not worried someone will see us," Adam said at last.

"I could say the same thing about you." She hesitated. "You should know that people have begun to guess the truth about us."

He slid to a stop. "I hope I haven't made things hard for you."

"No, no, nothing like that." She couldn't be surprised he was more concerned about how it affected her, than himself. He was far too honorable for all this sneaking around. "Josh overheard us that day we kissed in the barn a couple days ago. He didn't give me a hard time or anything. He'll be quiet. Monica and Emily guessed, too. We're not as good at hiding as we thought."

She skated around him once, then came to a stop before him. "Adam? Shouldn't you say something?"

"I've put you in the position of lying to your family," he said soberly.

"I'm an adult. It's nobody's business but ours, and we agreed on that."

They looked at each other, and in that

moment, she panicked at the thought of losing him. Oh God, it was too late — she'd already fallen in love with him, a man who didn't want a relationship, maybe didn't want love. He wanted to be free to nurse his wounds and move on.

And then he took her hand. "If you're sure," he said slowly.

"I'm sure." Relief swept through her, and she pretended to lose her balance rather than show him how dizzy the thought of losing him made her feel.

And then she knew what she had to do — find a way to win him over, to prove that they belonged together, out in the open. She no longer cared that he worked for her, was done worrying how appearances affected her relationship to her family. *Adam* mattered — Adam and her. Josh understood — she could make the rest of them understand. But not until Adam wanted that, too.

When Brooke dropped her skates and coat off in the mudroom, she had every intention of plopping her freezing butt in front of the fireplace until she felt singed.

But she found her mom in the kitchen, using her walker to move between the stove and the refrigerator.

"Mom, I said I'd cook dinner," Brooke

said, guiltily checking the clock on the wall. She was a little later than she had meant to be . . .

"No, you deserve to have fun, too," Sandy said, giving her a smile. "I saw you skating on the pond."

Brooke turned her head away to wince. *Damn.*

"You haven't done that in a couple years," her mom continued.

"I was clearing the pond for Steph and her friends, then Adam challenged me to prove I could still skate." It wasn't like she could hide his presence now.

"I always said it's like riding a bike," her mom agreed.

She said nothing else about Adam, and they worked companionably, preparing a shrimp salad for just the two of them.

Brooke thought about what her dad had said, that he worried about how everything affected her mom. But Sandy had been the one who helped Brooke figure out her passion for teaching — Sandy would never want Brooke to stay a little girl at home forever. Brooke had to take the chance that she was strong enough to hear the truth — some of it.

"Mom," she began slowly, "you've been such a help to me as I figured out some

403

things. It's like I'm finding myself at last, you know?"

"I do know," her mom said, touching her hand. "In some ways, when I met your father, it was like I saw a whole new side of myself — but then, I know this isn't about a man."

Brooke swallowed. One stressful thing at a time. "No, it's about being my own person, being independent. I've been thinking about moving into town. Emily's apartment is for rent, so I could have a place if I wanted it. A place of my own." And then she risked a glance at her mother.

Sandy was smiling, her eyes crinkling in the corners and full of warm understanding. "I've been wondering when you were going to say something at last. I knew something was up with you. Of course you should have your own place. It will be such an exciting new time for you. You'll be in town and be with more young people."

Brooke flung her arms around her mom and hugged her tight, feeling love like a warm blanket that would always protect her. "Oh, thank you!"

Sandy at last took her daughter's upper arms in her hands and gave her a disbelieving look. "Did you think I'd object?"

Brooke hesitated.

"Why would you think — oh, tell me you didn't assume my MS would play any part in this."

"But I want to do whatever helps you, Mom," Brooke said quietly.

Sandy kissed her cheek. "Sweetie, you are a good daughter — no matter where you live. So, will you need some help packing?"

"Now?"

"Don't you want to decorate your own place for Christmas?"

The thought seemed suddenly magical, and she grinned. She had so many new plans for her life: research to explain the appeal of an indoor riding arena to her family, the business plan to begin her own riding school — and somehow making Adam Desantis see that he could take a chance on loving her.

"Hey, Mom, let me tell you about my idea for an indoor riding arena."

The next afternoon, Adam was breaking up the ice in the water tanks in the nearest cattle pasture when Tyler came striding toward him, hands deep in his pocket. The snow whipped all around them, forcing them to narrow their eyes as they regarded each other.

"Bad weather," Adam said, hoisting the

pickax over his shoulder. "Thought your mom wouldn't be able to drive you out."

Tyler shrugged. "She was on her way to work."

Adam nodded. "Give me a hand breaking up the ice, then we'll go see if there's anything to be done in the truck shed — out of this near blizzard."

"A lot different from Louisiana," Tyler said. "You going back there?"

"No. I need to be here."

"For your grandma?"

"And other reasons."

Once they were in the truck shed, and sorting the burn barrels from the scrap-metal barrels, Adam found a football lost behind them. He held it up and gestured for Tyler to go long.

Tyler blinked for a moment, grinned, then ran past the trucks to the far end of the building. They tossed the ball for a while with silent camaraderie.

When the passes were short, with only a couple ATVs between them, Tyler spoke. "You said I could come to the house renovation for that soldier."

Surprised, Adam tossed the ball back. "Invitation's still there." He had a sudden inspiration. "Maybe you could bring your brother, too."

Defensive and wary, Tyler demanded, "What made you think of my brother?"

"Because *you* think of him, Tyler. And it's hurting you."

"It's just . . . no one will hire him, and he's going out every night. I'm worried he'll do something stupid."

His words all came out in a rush, and he seemed to deliberately drop the ball so he had to go find it beneath a tool bench. When he straightened, Adam thought his eyes were shiny with tears.

"I hope you can persuade Cody to come. I'd like to meet him."

Tyler's shoulders slumped, and he suddenly slammed the ball down hard on the seat of an ATV without letting it go. "Miss Thalberg trusted me, and now maybe she thinks I tried to burn down her barn because of what Matthew said."

"She doesn't think that, Tyler," Adam said, coming to stand on the opposite side of the machine from the boy.

"Matthew just wanted to screw me over. And if my brother had been out of jail at the time, he wouldn't have burned the barn either," Tyler insisted.

"I know." It was as if the weight of the world — of his family — was on the kid's shoulders. "Bring him to the housing-renovation project tomorrow. Maybe someone will see he's a hard worker and offer him a job."

That evening, Brooke happily accepted her brothers' teasing as they helped her load her boxes into her Jeep and their pickups.

"She's trying not to be an old maid," Nate told Josh.

She elbowed him in the side so that he let out a "woof" of air.

"She's sick of fighting me for the cookies," Josh answered.

"No," Brooke said to Josh, "I just don't want to be the last little kid at home."

"I think that's you," Nate said to their brother. "The baby of the family."

Josh shrugged good-naturedly. "Both my jobs are here. My new apartment is almost done. I'm happy."

Both of her jobs were here, too, Brooke thought — and then she saw Adam walking toward them from the bunkhouse, his shadow long and lean in the fading light. Even her lover was here — but she thought of him spending the night in her arms, and couldn't wait to be in town. She gave him a friendly wave and trudged back toward the house with her brothers.

Adam caught up. "Need help?"

Between the four of them, they quickly filled up the vehicles and headed into town. Adam offered to come along, too, and her brothers seemed grateful for anything that made the unloading go quicker. Brooke kept waiting for Josh to make some kind of accidental comment about Adam's participation, but he'd always been good about keeping her secrets.

Emily came up from the bakery with a platter of cookies, and Monica brought a big poinsettia for the coffee table. Brooke knew she was grinning stupidly. Emily had left all the furniture since Nate's cabin was already furnished, as well as the Christmas candles in the window, and the big Christmas tree. Brooke couldn't help but stand still and admire it, so thankful that she was making her dreams come true — some of her dreams, she thought, glancing surreptitiously at Adam.

When the last of the boxes were piled along the hallway wall and in the spare bedroom, they all stood around and munched cookies.

Josh swallowed his, and said, "Did I tell you guys that Whitney Winslow from Leather and Lace tracked me down at the ranch to see my workshop?"

"Are you going to make stuff for her?"

Monica asked.

Josh hesitated. "Not the stuff that you already sell. You don't have to worry about that."

"Oh, I'm not worried," she insisted. "There's plenty of your talent to go around."

"I still feel kinda weird about this," Josh said. "I asked to see her catalogue before I agreed to anything."

"I happened to see the two of you talking," Adam suddenly interrupted.

Everybody turned to look at him in surprise, and Brooke knew it was because he was usually so quiet around everyone but her.

Adam smiled at Josh. "She invited him back to her B&B to see her . . . laptop."

To Brooke's delighted surprise, Josh actually blushed. "Did you and she . . . ?" Brooke trailed off.

"None of your business," Josh said. "But I might be making some leather uh, necklaces."

"Don't you mean collars?" Nate asked. He pulled Emily against his side. "Don't give me any honeymoon presents, okay?"

"It's for a good cause," Josh insisted innocently. "With a local craftsman on board, maybe more people will let up on the town council. And all of the lingerie is really beautiful."

"He's so altruistic," Brooke said to Adam.

For the next few minutes, they ate cookies and made lewd fun of Josh. Then, one by one, they all took their leave until Brooke was alone in her new apartment. She stood in the picture window and looked out on the beauty of Main Street only a few days before Christmas. Snow was still falling, and shoppers hurried from store to store. Across the street, every window in the Hotel Colorado was lit from within, as tourists and extended families took every available room.

It seemed so exciting to Brooke, who was used to the quiet views of the ranch — and the bunkhouse that had once held no interest for her.

She heard the chime of the back doorbell, and ran down the stairs, wondering who forgot what. Once she entered the little hall shared with the bakery, she could see Adam through the door window that faced the alley.

Smiling, she opened the door and leaned against the frame. "Well, well, are you my first visitor?"

And then he pushed her back up against the wall and kissed her, slow and deep.

When he moved to her throat, she bent

her head for him, hearing his hat fall off onto the stairs, feeling the softness of his wavy hair.

She whispered, "You know the bakery is still open. Either of our grandmas might be working tonight."

Then she muffled a cry as he tossed her over his shoulder and carried her up the stairs. The impact took her breath away, but she didn't care. They threw a sheet on the bare mattress, rolling around on it in wild abandon as they made love.

When at last they were breathing hard and exhausted, Adam pulled a blanket over them, and they settled into each other's arms.

"Now this is the way to celebrate a new apartment," Brooke murmured, kissing the side of his neck, caressing his warm, damp chest. "I even have wine. Do you want some?"

Soon they were sitting up against the headboard, still naked except for the sheets and blankets gathered across their laps.

As they sipped their wine, Brooke hesitated, and said, "This is off topic, but did Tyler ever show up to Scott Huang's house to work with you?"

"Not yet, but he asked me today if he

could still come, and I invited his brother, too."

"Really? That seems like a good sign."

"I think so, too." Adam stared into his glass of wine for a minute, looking unusually serious. "Coach McKee told me your family donated a house to the renovation project. That's generous."

"Now let's be correct here. We bought it for them at a really reduced price since it needs a ton of work. I never mentioned it to you?"

He shook his head, still pensive, and she felt their mood begin to shift.

"You never want to talk about the military," she said, "so I didn't think you'd be interested. We were inspired by Challenge Aspen, a group that works with people with disabilities, running various events through the year. They host a big ski week with the Wounded Warrior Project." She paused. "Why did you bring this up?"

"It's stupid, but I think it made me remember darker times in my childhood."

"Now I'm really confused."

A rueful smile touched his mouth. "My father . . . much as he needed the work your dad offered him, he complained about it a lot."

She put down her glass on the bed table,

then took his hand. "We never did offer him full-time work, I think."

"He wasn't capable of it. I'm not talking about that. He always wanted me to believe your family considered themselves better than us."

Brooke's throat grew tight at the thought of a father making his son feel that way. "That's terrible, Adam. I'm so sorry."

"I think the donated house made me remember that because there was a part of me last month that thought you offered me a job out of pity, remember?"

"And I told you that wasn't true."

"I know at the worst it was a favor to my grandma, and it's obvious you really did need a ranch hand. I've felt useful, even valuable, and it's been a while since I felt that way. I'm letting go of the past."

"I'm glad. So . . ." she began, trying to lighten the serious discussion, "now that we've broken in the bed, do you want to stay the night?"

He shook his head. "I still have nightmares, and I don't want to wake you up. Or maybe I'd hurt you thrashing about."

Her heart ached for all he'd suffered, still so much in silence. She leaned forward and kissed him. "Can I take my chances?"

They stared into each other's eyes, and

for a moment, she realized that only weeks ago, he would have refused.

But a smile played around his mouth, and his gaze dropped to her naked breasts. "I would, but you don't think the first night you're here, your family might wonder why I never came home?"

"Damn," she whispered, briefly closing her eyes. "I leave home to find some independence, but you still live there!"

"You have no idea how much I regret it at this moment," he said with mock solemnity.

"Then don't go yet." She took his glass away, set it beside her own, then pushed him back into the pillows.

CHAPTER TWENTY-TWO

To Adam's surprise, a lot of people showed up to work on the house being renovated for Scott Huang and his family. Brooke brought his grandma, who'd made pans of ziti to serve everyone dinner. In her wig she wore barrettes made of Italian flags for the Italian dinner. Adam liked his grandma's eccentricities — she was never boring.

He watched her as she leaned on her cane and looked over everything for the meal to be served later. He kissed her brow when she finally stood still long enough.

Grandma Palmer arched a surprised look at him. "What was that for?"

He shrugged, and she smiled.

Tyler and Steph arrived next, and Steph ended up being the most proficient with tools, after spending much of her life helping her dad at both the ranch and the Sweetheart Inn. She and Tyler went into the basement to help build storage shelves.

Tyler stuck his head past the basement door and said to Adam, "When my brother gets here, could you send him down?"

When a half hour went by, Adam came out of the master bedroom closet to find Tyler standing in the window, looking out at the storm.

"He didn't come yet?" Tyler asked, eyes narrowed, mouth pursed.

Adam shook his head. "Maybe he got held up by the weather."

Tyler arched a brow, and said with sarcasm, "You may have been gone for ten years, but the rest of us are pretty good drivers in the snow."

"And you with all your experience," Adam said with a straight face.

But Tyler didn't crack a smile.

"Give him some time." Adam put a hand on Tyler's bony shoulder.

The kid nodded.

An hour and a half later, everyone gathered in the kitchen to get in line for some of Grandma Palmer's legendary ziti. Adam smiled at the jostling people, feeling far more comfortable than he had just weeks ago. And then he spotted Brooke in the living room staring out the window just as Tyler had.

Adam frowned. "Have you seen Tyler?"

Brooke shook her head. "He and Steph are gone."

He tensed, looking back outside, where he couldn't even see the other side of the street. "Are you certain?"

"Coach saw him leave, and didn't think anything about it. Steph was driving. Do you think . . . ?"

"He went to find his brother," Adam said with certainty. His stomach gave a twist. "It was my idea for him to bring Cody here, and Cody let him down."

"Cody lets him down all the time, Adam," Brooke said. "This isn't anything new."

He shook his head. "Something was different this time. Tyler seemed determined to help, or to stop Cody from ruining his life for good. And now he's done something reckless — going out in this mess," he said, pointing toward the window.

"Steph's a good driver, with a solid pickup. But I'll try her cell, just in case."

Adam was standing close enough to Brooke that he could hear as it went to voice mail. He swore softly.

"They might have bad reception," she said. "It happens all the time."

They both knew the reception would be fine if the teenagers had stayed in Valentine. They were either deliberately not answering

— or they'd left town in search of Cody.

"Adam?" Grandma Palmer called, limping into the living room. "You two should get in line before it's all gone."

"I'm going to find Tyler, Grandma," he said, rooting through the coats tossed on an empty box until he found his. "I'll be back soon."

"I'm coming, too," Brooke said.

"I already found your coat."

Driving had gotten far worse in the last two hours, so he went as slow as he could, heading toward the Sweetheart Inn first, to look for Steph's truck.

"You have a death grip on the wheel," Brooke said. "Cut yourself some slack. You aren't responsible for all the things that have happened to Tyler."

"I wanted to give him the help I got," Adam said between gritted teeth. "But maybe I made a mistake." He told her about seeing Tyler joyriding one of the Thalbergs' ATVs.

She barely reacted. "So? You offered him a second chance, and we were able to be of some help. He told you things he never told anyone else, right?"

He nodded, but it didn't make him feel better. Tyler was out there somewhere, trying to stop his brother from doing — something. Cody's posse had to be far worse than Tyler's high-school friends.

When they didn't find Steph's truck at the inn, Brooke called the ranch, using a barrel-racing lesson as an excuse. They didn't want to worry anyone just yet. But Steph's mom said she was at the renovation project.

"Do you know where Tyler lives?" Adam asked Brooke.

She nodded.

"Guide me there."

Steph's pickup wasn't in the parking lot of the apartment complex either.

He could have banged his head against the steering wheel in frustration. "Any idea where the bad kids hang out now?"

"Oh, hell, the town isn't very big," she said. "Let's drive up and down the streets and look for her pickup."

But it was as if Tyler and Steph had simply disappeared. There were few cars on the road with the snow so bad.

"They aren't here," Adam admitted at last, pulling over to the side of the road near the only McDonald's in town.

"They wouldn't have been so foolish as to go out on the highway in this storm," Brooke said, pointing to Highway 82 just ahead.

"There was an intensity about him tonight," he insisted. "He's not letting this go. So if he was following his brother out of town, where would he go?"

"I can't believe he'd go to Aspen. What would be there for Cody? It's not like he's a thief looking for rich fools to fleece."

"Then we go the other way, to Basalt. I just can't sit and wait."

Leaving the shelter of the town buildings and entering the full force of the storm only made him even more aware of the danger Tyler and Steph could be in. They crept along the road well below the speed limit, flashers on, the window defrost blasting them in the face with heat. But that was the only way to keep the windshield from icing over. Snow blew directly into the headlights, distorting their perception like some kind of video game.

Neither of them spoke, as he needed all his concentration to stay on the slippery road. Occasionally they passed a car creeping along even slower than they were, but it was never Steph's pickup.

"What's that?" Brooke demanded, pointing ahead.

Through the snow, he could see the red flash of a flare on the far side of the highway.

"I think it's an accident," she said quietly.

Adam gripped the wheel even tighter. As

they got closer, they could see a car's hazard lights tilted at an awkward angle, and eventually he realized the vehicle had slid off into a ditch. A pickup. They couldn't see inside the fogged cab, and soon had to keep driving past.

"Was that Steph's?" he demanded.

Brooke twisted in her seat to look behind them. "It might be!"

He had to wait for the next light to make a safe U-turn without heading into a ditch themselves. It seemed to take forever to get back to the pickup, and all he could imagine was finding the kids hurt or bleeding, or —

And then the bright light of the flare finally appeared out of the swirling snow. He pulled in behind the pickup, flashing his high beams. For a moment, nothing happened, then the passenger door opened and a figure half fell, half jumped out of the tilted vehicle.

After trudging up the knee-high snow in the ditch, the person waved his arms. By their headlights, Adam could see the grinning face of Tyler.

"He looks pleased to see us," she said dryly.

"Way too pleased."

Adam and Brooke jumped out of their own pickup. Snow stung his face and tugged at his wool cap. He was tempted to yell out every worry, every fear, but he knew he'd only make things worse.

"Wow, are we glad you found us!" Tyler called, rubbing his arms.

Of course, his jacket couldn't even be called a winter coat.

"Steph's okay?" Brooke asked, speaking louder as the wind roared across the highway.

"She's in the pickup. It's tilted at such an angle it's hard to get out, and it's wet at the bottom of the ditch." He pointed to the water that drenched him to his knees. "No point in both of us getting soaked."

"You'll catch pneumonia like that!" Brooke said.

"It's warm in the cab," Tyler insisted. "Do you have chains to pull us out?"

"What the hell happened?" Adam demanded. "Why did you drive out into this?" He flung both hands wide.

Tyler didn't even bother to look remorseful. "I had to find my brother, to stop him doing something crazy. I mean, he disappeared every night, and wouldn't tell me where he was going or what he was doing."

"And did you find him?" Brooke said with exasperation, stamping her boots in the cold.

Wearing the most lighthearted grin, Tyler nodded as if he no longer had a care in the world. "He has a job! He's been going every night, but after all his talk about making something of himself, he didn't want me to know he was working at a fast-food place in Basalt. He was embarrassed! What an idiot!"

Adam glanced at Brooke, whose lips quivered as she strove to control a smile. "And you thought it was necessary to risk your lives to discover this *tonight* of all nights?" he demanded.

Tyler finally had the grace to wince and look around. "Yeah, I can see it looks pretty stupid now. And Cody *meant* to come to the house renovation, but he got called in to work at the last minute. I told Steph if there was any damage to the truck, I'd pay for it, though it might take me a while. I have to wait until my community service is over to get a job."

"I'm not sure that'll satisfy her father."

The last of Tyler's smile faded. "He already doesn't like me, and he doesn't even know Steph and I've been hanging together."

"We can't deal with that now," Adam said. "Let's get the chains out and see what we can do."

It took some effort, but at last he was able

to pull Steph's pickup back onto the road. The snow had died down somewhat, but not the wind. Brooke drove the teenagers in the pickup, and Adam followed behind, alone and thinking too many crazy thoughts about everything that could have gone wrong and thanking God for seeing the kids safe.

By the time they dropped Tyler off at his mom's, the snow had almost stopped, and Steph drove herself home, cheerfully waving good-bye to them as she passed. Adam returned the salute, shaking his head.

When he dropped Brooke off at her apartment, she gave him a quick kiss.

"Go take care of your grandma," she murmured. "I'll see you at work tomorrow."

Adam drove the couple blocks back to the Huang house in a thoughtful mood. Many of the cars and pickups were gone, but Coach was still there, keeping Grandma Palmer company in the kitchen over coffee.

Coach stood up when Adam walked in, and Grandma gave him an expectant look.

"Everything okay?" Coach asked.

Adam nodded and explained what had happened.

Coach shook his head. "Fool kids. You think they'd know better, being born and raised here."

"Teenagers don't think things through," Adam countered. "I know I didn't." He turned to his grandma. "Ready to go?"

He helped her load her ziti pans and equipment on the back bench of the truck, and once at the boardinghouse, she made him come inside to eat his missed meal. They sat together in the cheerful kitchen, listening to the wind howl.

Grandma seemed to be patiently waiting for him to speak, and though he resisted, it was like words were drawn out of him.

"My parents were only a year older than Tyler when they had me," he said at last, using his fork to push ziti around on his plate. "There's no maturity, no common sense at that age — and I should know."

She sighed, cradling her mug of coffee. "Adam, you got a taste tonight of what it's like bein' a helpless parent. You lecture or you lead by example, you pray, you even beg, but in some ways, there's little you can do to make certain a teenager makes the right choices. And that I understand too well. Your mother always saw me as the enemy, and that hurt more than I can say."

She gave another sigh that ripped at his stomach.

"I know you don't remember your grandpa, but he was good with your mom, who was twelve when he died. Nothin' seemed right after that."

"I'm sure the drugs didn't help," Adam said dryly. "Or even my birth."

"I think there was more goin' on," she answered after a long pause, "maybe some kind of mental illness."

He frowned. "I've never heard that before."

"She was always unstable, but she got worse the last few years of her life, and I began to realize that maybe drugs had masked her condition. But that's no excuse for my ignorance. She was my baby. I should have seen. Instead, I couldn't help her, and she died too young."

He reached across the kitchen table and squeezed her hand. "You shouldn't carry so much guilt. She was an adult and made her own choices."

"I could say the same to you," she said quietly, her expression full of compassion. "And I'm not talkin' about Tyler. I know what happened in Afghanistan."

She brought her other hand up to encompass his. Her warmth flowed into him.

"I knew somethin' was wrong from your first letter after the accident happened," she continued. "When you were injured and so very silent, I wrote letters, I called, and

Rosemary even found clues on the computer from newspaper articles. Yes, you were a hero to many men in the end, Adam, but the cost must have been so very difficult to bear. You don't have to speak of it — I know you blame yourself for the terrible accident, but you gotta know that others don't."

"I'm trying to believe that. And I'm better, I promise."

"I'm glad to hear that. Does Brooke know?"

"Brooke?" he asked nonchalantly.

"I may be old, but I'm not blind."

"Apparently you're not the only one," he said, shaking his head with amusement. "Our secret relationship is getting not so secret."

"That's your business, of course. But does she know about your past?"

"I told her, yeah. But we're not like that, Grandma. It's . . . casual."

She pressed her lips together, obviously hiding a smile, saying, "Uh-huh," as if she thought him silly. "So you won't be spendin' your first Christmas together?"

"I — first Christmas?" he echoed.

"It's in a few days, you know," she said, speaking as slowly as if he were a kindergartener.

"She'll be with her family, and I'll be with you."

"Well, I appreciate that, of course, but you can invite her over."

"We haven't talked about it yet." He wanted to see her Christmas Day, to share the holiday. *Patience,* he told himself again, although right now he felt anything but.

"So what are you buyin' her?"

"A sweater or something."

"I see." She raised both hands. "Far be it from me to tell you what to do, Adam Desantis. Now just sit there and let me fetch you some pie for dessert."

"I can get it myself." He stood up, then bent to kiss her soft cheek. "Thanks for worrying about me. I've caused you a lot of that over the years."

She smiled up at him gently. "Without family to worry about, life would be empty, Adam. You remember that. I won't be here forever, and I want to know you have a family of your own. Just be open to the possibilities."

Brooke appeared in his mind, a flash of different images — balancing on hay bales at his side, her grin full of knowledge and certainty; riding her horse at full speed around the barrels; the way her face lit with excitement when she worked with the kids;

and lastly, when she lay beneath him in bed, soft and womanly and vulnerable.

He'd wondered if he was falling in love with her, but there was no lying to himself anymore. He did love her. Now to find the best way to tell her.

CHAPTER TWENTY-THREE

Brooke attended the preservation-fund-committee meeting held at the Sugar and Spice the next night. The widows had come up with a wacky idea of a protest for the town-council meeting two days before Christmas, and delegated her the job of keeping Adam away. Mrs. Palmer didn't want her grandson knowing she was more fit than she pretended. Brooke felt guilty admitting to herself that even she didn't want Adam to know the truth. She wanted to have him all to herself for a little longer.

She sat alone that night with the lights off except for the Christmas tree, and the lights of the candles in her window. She heard carolers singing their way down Main Street, and she watched the happiness of the holiday season below her window as people came out to enjoy the music.

She hummed a Christmas song, trying to cheer herself up, remembering that she and

Adam were exclusive now, and maybe they could be more. But alone in the dark, her doubts suddenly swelled. How had her secret wild fling turned into a love that might not end as happily as she wanted?

Two days before Christmas, Adam still couldn't believe how cheerful Tyler was. Now that the kid knew his brother was trying to straighten out his life, the surliness and anger had loosened their hold on him. Tyler actually hummed while he worked, not a complaint in sight. He even confided in Adam that he hoped the Thalbergs would offer him a part-time job when his community service was done.

Adam did his Christmas shopping although it had been harder to buy for Brooke than he'd imagined. Nothing seemed right — clothes were too casual, and jewelry seemed too presumptuous. But he got her a little of each, feeling dissatisfied. He'd stared too long at engagement rings but figured Brooke didn't like surprises.

She had an errand in town, and had left him with a list of chores that had taken him well into the dinner hour. He was just closing up the barn when Mr. Thalberg came down from the house.

"You still workin', Adam?" he asked.

"Just finished up, sir."

"Brooke or Josh around?"

"No, sir."

Mr. Thalberg shook his head and rocked back on his heels. "All these 'sirs' are hard to take. You can just call me Doug."

"Thank you, sir — Doug."

He chuckled. "It's a start. So my kids are gone, and I seem to have lost my wife. I think she might have gone to the town-council meetin'. You want to go into town with me and look for everyone? We could get a bite to eat."

"Sounds good. Give me a minute to change."

On the drive into town, Doug asked him, "So are you stayin' in Valentine after the holidays? You just got out — I know it takes time to make plans and decisions. I just wanted you to know you've got a job with us as long as you want."

Adam glanced at him in surprise. "Thanks. I appreciate it." But would Brooke want him to stay when he told her he was in love with her?

As they crossed the bridge over Silver Creek, Adam could see the lit-up town hall pointing toward the sky, with the immense Christmas trees like sentinels on each side. "The town-council meeting must be another big one. There are lots of cars parked on the streets. I'm surprised Brooke didn't mention it," he mused, remembering the meeting he'd attended a couple weeks before.

"Is that a crowd out front?" Doug asked. "I'm going to pull over here."

The sidewalks were pretty clear of snow as they walked the final block past the Huang house and others. The crowd was getting thicker; Adam heard laughter and cheering, and when that briefly faded, the sound of raised voices in protest.

He and Doug exchanged concerned frowns.

They passed the local-history museum, and someone had a cart out front selling hot chocolate and giant pretzels.

"It's almost like a street fair in the dead of winter," Adam said.

They pushed past a few loosely gathered clumps of people, all of whom were laughing and pointing. Then Doug and Adam came to a stop. Dozens of people were marching in a long circle in front of town hall. They were holding signs that read, "Don't Discriminate Against Women," and "Women Need Pretty Panties."

Adam could see everyone he knew, from the widows to Brooke and her best friends, even the Chess Club and its outcasts, Tyler and Steph. He realized they were marching around an aspen tree — with bras hanging from it.

Doug started to laugh.

"What the hell — ?" Adam began.

"It's a bra tree," Doug said. "Do you ski?"

Bewildered, Adam shook his head.

"Skiers pick a tree beneath a chairlift and people drop things on it through the season, like long beads — and bras. It's a holdover from the sixties. I'm thinkin' these bras are for Leather and Lace."

As Adam watched, openmouthed, Monica used her red lace bra like a slingshot, and it wrapped around a branch with unerring accuracy. The crowd cheered. Then Tyler scrambled up into the tree, pulling a string of lights behind him.

Adam knew the moment Brooke saw him because her sign faltered, and she looked sheepish. Then, with a mutinous pout, she tossed her sign, pulled her arms inside her own coat, and with a wiggle that had the crowd laughing, she pulled out her polka-dotted bra and tossed it up into the tree.

Adam realized there was more than one sturdy old-lady bra up there, too. He saw his grandma next, holding up a sign with ease, no cane in sight. When their gazes met, she looked a bit guilty, but she only held her "I Wear Leather and Lace" sign higher and kept marching.

And then Adam started to laugh, so hard that tears eventually ran down his face. He saw Sandy Thalberg, holding a cane with one hand, and tossing a bra with the other. Mayor Galimi, arms folded across her chest where she stood at the top of the town-hall steps, was obviously trying not to laugh herself, even as her brother droned into her ear, gesturing at the demonstration wildly.

Brooke walked toward Doug and Adam, wearing a grin. "Hi, Dad!"

"Your mother should have told me the demonstration would be so exciting," Doug said dryly. "I might have changed my mind about comin'." He walked past them toward Sandy.

Brooke smiled up at Adam. "My part in this plot failed."

He wiped tears from his eyes, still chuckling. "I don't know — your bra landed the highest."

"No, I was supposed to assign you enough work to keep you away, on orders from your grandma."

"Why?" he asked in disbelief.

She silently pointed. Grandma Palmer was practically doing a two-step in line, smiling and waving as people took pictures. Her coat sagged open, a bold red poinsettia pattern on her vivid green dress.

"So you knew about her robust health, too?" he asked, shaking his head.

She gaped at him. "You *knew*? I suspected almost from the beginning. I was afraid to tell you, afraid you'd leave if you knew she didn't need you. She *does* need you — you know that, right?"

He focused on her lovely face, the tension she didn't hide. The cheering crowd seemed to fade away until there was only the two of them. "What makes you think I'm leaving?" he asked softly.

"You came because you thought she was ill," she said, her expression confused and wary. "Now that you know the truth —"

"I've been staying for you, too."

He saw the way her eyes softened and shone with tears that glittered under Christmas lights. She caught her lip between her teeth.

"Really?" she whispered.

"I'm gonna kiss you right now." They stepped toward each other, then he grimaced. "Let's go find your parents first."

"But —"

He caught her hand and tugged her with him until they found Doug and Sandy

437

standing together. Sandy leaned against her husband like he was all the support she'd ever need.

"Mr. Thalberg — I mean Doug," Adam began. "I'd like to date your daughter."

He heard Brooke gasp, but he didn't let go of her hand.

"If you want me to get another job," Adam continued, "I'd understand, her being my boss and all."

"Don't worry about it." Doug gave a loud sigh even as his wife laughed.

"I win!" she told her husband. "Now pay up."

Brooke gaped at her parents. "You were betting on whether we were dating?"

"Hell no, we already guessed that," Doug said in a grumpy voice, pulling out his wallet. "We were bettin' on when you'd finally admit it."

"I guessed you'd tell the truth before Christmas," Sandy said smugly. "I didn't think you'd be able to wait, what with all the gift-buying."

Adam and Brooke stared at each other, and his relief changed over to a kind of excitement he hadn't felt in a long time, the excitement of new beginnings and hope — and even the spirit of family at Christmas.

Adam pulled Brooke into his arms and

kissed her, right in front of everyone. He imagined the cheering might even be for them.

Everyone converged on the Widows' Boardinghouse after the protest, and Brooke was grinning so much she felt like her cheeks would soon break. The town council had ruled that Leather and Lace wasn't pornography and could apply for a permit to do business.

In the living room, Grandma Palmer was already hard at work on her tablet computer coordinating the next phase of their attack.

"Nice iPad," Adam said dryly.

Grandma Palmer gave him a saucy grin. "I hid it because I wanted you to think I was behind the times, as well as feeble."

He rolled his eyes.

Brooke kept her hand in his, even as she asked his grandma, "So what's the preservation committee's plan?"

Grandma Thalberg and Mrs. Ludlow clinked beer mugs over the head of their roommate, who laughed.

Grandma Palmer said, "I think we'll be orderin' some Christmas gifts from Leather and Lace for the women on the town council, as well as the wives of the councilmen. They all deserve a nice thank-you."

Josh raised a beer. "Here, here! The store better get its permit because I'm already working on orders for it."

"Tell me details!" Brooke demanded.

Whitney Winslow appeared out of the crowd and tugged Josh away by the elbow. "That's proprietary information," she called over her shoulder. "You'll just have to wait and see."

Brooke winced. "Do I even want to know?"

"Of course you do," Adam said, laughing. "But you're sneaking around on your own."

Brooke pulled him closer and pointed. "Look, there's Steph — with Emily! Have you ever seen such an animated conversation? My brother is doing his best not to look bored, so it must be wedding details."

"It's about time," Adam said. "All this fuss because of a teenager."

"I can't believe *you* have the nerve to say that! And I'd rather see Nate bored than giving us dirty looks, now that we're out in the open."

Adam shrugged. "It wasn't too bad. He gave me the big-brother speech, but his handshake was firm enough, and I thought he was hiding a smile."

"That's good," Brooke said with relief.

Tyler appeared through the crowd. "Hey,

440

Adam, I didn't get a chance to thank you for standing up for me with the Chess Club. They let me back in on probation. Maybe you can talk to Mr. Sweet about Steph . . . ?"

"Forget it," Adam countered. "Only you can prove yourself to a woman's father."

Tyler grumbled halfheartedly as he walked away.

Brooke felt all mushy inside as she smiled up at Adam. "You're pretty good with kids."

He tugged her toward the front hall, where they had a little privacy. "So are you."

"I know. I even talked to my dad about building an indoor riding arena," she admitted. "I never thought I could be this happy, finding something for me and starting over."

He smiled down at her, his eyes laughing in a way they never had before.

"You seem at peace with yourself," Adam said. "No more uncertainty or doubts."

"I could say the same about you."

He shrugged and leaned against the wall in the front hall. "I won't forget the hurt because it will always be with me, but . . . I'm alive. How can I not do justice to that? I want to start over, to live life looking forward, not back." And then his gaze searched her face. "I want that life to be with you."

"You do?" she whispered breathlessly.

"I fell in love with you, Brooke. I think you worked some kind of magic on me."

She laughed, even as she quickly wiped her eyes. "I love you, too, Adam."

They looked at each other for a moment, full of wonder. She could sense a world of possibilities opening up before them.

"You felt you'd never have a real family," she said. "But Christmas is almost here. Let me share my family with you."

And there was even more to share, a tender kiss of promise. Brooke couldn't help overhearing her dad say, "They don't look like they're just startin' to date."

Her mom shushed him.